IN FIELDS OF GOLD AND RED

Christopher B Legg

ISBN 13: 978-1-9997491-0-1

ISBN 10: 1-9997491-0-3

Copyright © Christopher B Legg 2017

All rights reserved. No part of this publication may be reproduced, stored in a retrieval system, or transmitted, in any form, or by any means (electronic, mechanical, photocopying, recording or otherwise) without the prior permission of the publisher.

This book is sold subject to the condition that it shall not, by way of trade or otherwise, be lent, hired out, or otherwise circulated without consent in any form of binding or cover other than that in which it is published and without a similar condition including this condition being imposed on the subsequent purchaser.

Acknowledgements

I would like to thank my parents, who have had enormous patience in letting me take over their conservatory to write this novel. To Maggie who got my plot back on track and saved me from floundering in the void. Thank you to Penny, who without I wouldn't have got the semi-colons, full stops or grammar in any clear order to make a readable book and finally, a big thank you to Henry who designed the book cover and got exactly the look and feel I wanted without any delay.

About the author

Christopher is forty-six and lives in Bridport, Dorset. He grew up in village not far from the market town and has a deep love of the countryside. In Fields of Gold and Red is his first novel and at the time of publishing he is busy working on a sequel.

To my parents who have given me more patience than I could have ever expected.

1

5th August 1914

Redver Kingson pulled the dark grey blanket back. He put one aching foot down on the naked floorboard. He was careful to miss the nail which stood proud. His lower back, his shoulders and his knees all screamed. Nineteen; nineteen, and he felt like this. How old must that make his father? By his reckoning he must be at least fifty; fifty-one more likely. How must he feel?

There was no light. Red splashed his face from the bowl on the large oak dresser. The water was warm. Red was glad it was summer. By instinct, he picked his work clothes from the floor. He put on his white striped round-necked button shirt. He stepped into his green fustian trousers and pulled them up over his underdrawers. He tightened the brown braces over his shoulders. He didn't need his black waistcoat today, not out in the field under the summer sun. Red picked up the old leather belts and pulled tight, one under each knee.

He pulled back the makeshift sackcloth covering the window and looked out; there was a clear sky brightened by the crisp white moon. He saw the silhouette of the barns across the lane. It would be another hour before the sun rose. The soft sound of the morning song thrush, accompanied by gentle mooing from the pasture, passed in through the window. He breathed in deeply; he could smell the heat in the air.

He crept down the stairs, careful not to wake his sister; the less reason he gave Edna to moan at him the better. In the kitchen, the brown wooden half-crescent clock on the mantel showed ten to four. The only heirloom passed down from Granfer. He was first down. He topped up the range with coal from the scuttle and opened the vents. He filled the black cast iron kettle from the tap and placed it on the range. The water was fresh, pumped from the well from under the brow of Ashcombe Beacon. They were lucky to have running water; many in the village hadn't been connected, but Admiral had insisted when the cottages were built. He sat down on one of the wooden chairs by the table.

He heard his father and mother shuffle to get ready in the bedroom above. His father coughed and mother nagged him to stop. Red chuckled to himself; he hoped he would marry one day and have his wife nag him. He knew who he wanted. His trouble was, what did he have to offer? Him just a lowly farm labourer with little or no prospects. His older brother George had managed it. He'd found Dorothy and settled down and he seemed happy with his family.

Did he want to stay on the farm all his life like his father? Every day milking, feeding and bedding, every day of the year. He loved the animals and the farm and he loved the village. But how could a man only do that until he died, all for only twelve shillings a week, and a tied cottage? He wanted more. He wasn't educated; been yanked from school at thirteen, to work on the farm. Him and Jimmy: needed to replace poor old Freddy Hansford, who'd been severed in two by the steam plough.

Mother came down into the kitchen and they said morning, her dark brown hair brushed back from her face. She fussed with the teapot and cut thick slices of bread, placing them on the table. She sighed. She filled a pan with water. Mother was a Dorset woman through and through, stout and hardy. Her round shoulders falling forward, bent near double by the strain of hard work. Her thighs, thick like oak trunks; and a forehead criss-crossed with wide tracks.

Mother rubbed her shoulder and scratched her nose and said: 'Red, fetch in more eggs, would 'e.'

He remembered how he and Connie had gone to fetch eggs all those years ago. She still lived next door with her father, Stephen the shepherd. He hoped he would see her later. He moved to the back door, opened it and sat on the threshold to tie his hobnailed boots. Behind him, he heard his father falter down the stairs, regain his balance then enter the kitchen.

'Hey up, boy, you're keen this morning, ain't 'e.' Red stood up and looked back. His father hunched over, limping with arthritis; he stopped and held the back of the chair for support. His father cleared his throat. Red looked at him. They shared the same face: deep hazel eyes, skin tanned by the long-drawn-out days. Short brown tousled hair. Father would have been taller when he stood straight, six foot or an inch over. Red himself five foot ten. His father less muscled now but in his day, muscular arms, and large tree trunk legs, bred for hard work. Redver's brow and forehead clear and tight, his father's brow rutted, deep and ingrained with dirt.

Red went past the outside loo to the henhouse. A rickety old affair made by Granfer when he was still alive, shod together from scraps of wood and old nails. The chickens happily chattered as he let them out. He collected a half dozen eggs and returned to the kitchen and sat down.

Mother boiled the eggs and then placed them on a plate next to the teapot and jug of milk. She poured three mugs of tea; there was no point pouring for Edna. She would be in bed to the last possible minute. Her job in Gundry's net factory started at eight.

He missed having George there. The squire, Admiral Fox, had made sure George got his own cottage when he married Dot. Admiral was good like that; he wanted to keep his workforce. In the last twenty years many men had moved their families to town. Looking to improve their pay, their hours and their homes.

He hadn't known his younger siblings, John and Ellen; they died of scarlet fever when he was three. He supposed he was lucky to be alive. It had spread through the village, very fast, claiming ten of the class of twenty children. It hadn't returned in the last fifteen years. He could remember being sick with chicken pox. In bed with his mother looking down at him, telling him not to scratch. She'd worried he would die too, so his brother had told him.

He helped himself to one of the thick slices of bread and smothered it in butter; he then cut it in half, then each half into strips. He wasn't too old for that. Red took an egg, cracked the top with the back of his knife, sliced off the top, then dipped in his neat soldiers. The golden yolk mixed with bread and butter tasted of heaven. He finished off the egg with his teaspoon and had a second; he washed it down with the milky tea.

'Come on, son,' Father said to Red as he staggered up from the chair and limped his way to the back door to find his boots. 'We better get started.'

'Thanks, Mother,' Father and Red said in unison.

'Hamilton, you make sure you don't get running after them cows. You need to look after them dodgy knees of 'ees,' she said to her husband.

'Ay, I'll try me best, Martha,' he answered as he did up his bootlaces.

They left Mother in the kitchen. They walked around the back of the cottage up the garden path and across the lane into the farmyard. There was a faint damp mist hanging in the air. Father stopped to pick his wide-brimmed felt hat, once green, from the rusty nail. It was crusty with mud. Mother wouldn't let the dirty, smelly hat anywhere near indoors. She said it stank. It smelled of Father's sweat, mixed with the odour of cows and horses.

They found the clean pails where they had put them yesterday and walked the short distance down the lane. He could smell wild parsley, blown by the breeze from their white crowns. The sun creeping from behind Ashcombe Beacon glowed on the red shorthorn cows. With its steep cliff sides facing the village, the large flat plateau surrounded by embankments, ditches and runs, Ashcombe Beacon dominated the landscape.

'Oh, shittle bum hurdle,' Red said. He looked around the dark green grassed pasture.

'Wass up, boy?' Father asked. He limped from right leg to left.

'I don't see Bumble; I bet 'e's gone and got out,' Red said, scratching his ear. 'Bloody hell, tha's two days in a row.'

'That bleedin' little calf is a right nuisance. You go find 'im and I'll make a start on the milking,' Father said with an annoyed look.

Red had named him Bumble because when he was born he'd slept in his own yellow poo.

Bumble: always boisterous, only a week old. He must have leapt the hurdle that filled the gap in the hedge. Red knew they should've put two hurdles there to stop him after he escaped yesterday. Ragamuffin, the female calf with her big pink nose, slept up close to her mother.

Red ran back up to the yard, checking to see if Bumble was there. He wasn't. He knew his father would be angry if he didn't find him soon and get back to help him. He ran to the lane; no sign there, either. Oh, today of all days, they couldn't be late – not with them having to start cutting the wheat. He could do without wasting this time searching for Bumble. Red made his way back to the yard and checked each of the barns. Nothing. He took the rope hung over the nail. He could hear the shire horses moving, restless for their breakfast.

After searching all the barns, the big shed, the stables and the workshop, Red raced back to the lane. Out of the corner of his eye, he noticed movement in the golden coloured wheat field. Was that Bumble in there? There were ripples and large waves; yes, it was. Red stood stock still. He couldn't believe what he was seeing. Bumble was running, leaping and kicking up his hoofs as he chased a fawn. The fawn would turn around and then chase Bumble before they licked each other's noses. The mother deer looked on, supervising.

'Come on then, come on then, come on, Bumble!' Red called out.

Bumble pricked his ears and seemed to recognise Red's call.

'Shittle bum hurdle, come on Bumble.' The fawn and the mother deer ran away. Bumble was distracted by a ladybird on his nose and didn't notice his new friend leaving, giving Red the chance to slip the rope over his neck. He was able to coax and pull Bumble back to the pasture.

'What kept you?' Father said; he'd milked half the cows.

Red slipped the rope from Bumble who, smelling his mother, ran to her. He went and suckled, hungry for his breakfast.

Red picked Old Eileen; she was old and needed getting

up.

'Come on, old girl; come on then; get up,' Red said, keen to get the old cow moving.

Eileen, riddled with arthritis, lurched forward on her knees before she tottered up. Red picked her because she was unlikely to try and kick him when he started squeezing and pulling on her udders. It didn't take long for him to milk her as she had little to give.

Red made sure to get another hazel hurdle to fill in the gap in the hedge. He tied the hurdles together with some old twine from his pocket, hoping Bumble would not escape tomorrow. He watched as his father went to the far end of the pasture and back.

'Look at this, son; I've two good'ens here. Mother will be happy, I reckon,' he said as he showed Red two dead rabbits, fresh from his snares. 'Hmm, Mother will make a good stew with one, and rabbit pie.'

The sun was burning down through the hazy mist. They poured the milk into the large churns and put them up on the platform. Mr Grey would take them down to the station later.

The milking finished, they went over to the stables. The twelve shire-horses were loud, neighing, snorting and stamping. Captain was shaking his head in impatience. Red could smell their sweat; they wanted their breakfast and they wanted to get to work. Father fed them their oat and chaff mix while Red forked out the dirty dung. He threw down fresh clean straw. He loved the smell. Once they had been fed and watered with bedding done, Father took his favourite three, Captain, Tully and Trudy, and put on their black leather harnesses. He then tied them to the reaper. Captain stood at seventeen hands tall. He was strong-shouldered, with a long brown mane that flowed over his black body, and white tufts of hair on his fetlocks. He dwarfed Red and Father; he was strong and his stamina was huge. Tully and Trudy were sisters, smaller at fifteen and a half hands. They could keep pace with Captain even if they didn't have his strength. Red heard the blast from the harvest horn, carried on the summer breeze from atop Snowdrop Hill. It would be Mr Grey, the farm manager, calling the villagers to the field. Red thought it outdated; everyone knew where to be; but he supposed it was the custom.

Red walked, leading the horses as Father drove the reaper to the wheat field. They drove up the lane; villagers pushed against the hedgerow to let them past. Red greeted each by name. Seeing the smithy's three boys, Thomas, David, and Ken, he shouted out. The youngest, Thomas, was fifteen but tall and thin; nothing like their father, Robert, who was as wide as he was tall. David and Ken took after their father, both broad, eighteen and twenty-one. All had girlfriends. Robert must have spared them from the forge for the week.

In the rippling field of wheat, Red could see that Mr Grey was overseeing the harvest. Made to look tall by his slender black hat, the estate manager wore his black jacket and waistcoat in all weathers. His pocket watch on a chain, always close at hand in his top waistcoat pocket. His grey and white flecked beard was kept neatly trimmed. He put the calling horn away in his jacket pocket.

Red's uncles, Charlie and George, along with his brother George and best friend James (Jimmy) Crabb, scythed the headland. They moved as one, in time, in rhythm in staggered formation. The scythes swinging methodically, sharp, cutting the golden yellow stalks with each sweep.

The women and children followed behind, stooping to pick the cut wheat, then tying up into sheaves; Mother was out telling the younger ones what to do. Where were Connie and Violet? They should be out too. Things would go quicker once Father set the horses to work. First, he needed the channel around the edge.

Red picked up his scythe from the parked-up wagon and joined the line behind James. Jimmy was shorter in height, dressed in white shirt and green cord trousers and slim as a straight hazel pole. His hair short and black, his face dark as wheat, covered in flecks of earth, seed and the odd fly. His eyes clear blue ponds. His shirt was open at the neck, his sleeves rolled to his elbows. His arms flexed, his hands large on the wooden handle.

'What, you been havin' a lie-in? I don't know, reckon you been skiving at the back of the cowshed,' James said. He continued to sweep with the scythe, moving in rhythm with Charlie and George senior and George up ahead. 'Have 'e a woman back there?'

'Ha, I wish. If I did I wouldn't be here!' Red couldn't help but think of Connie.

He looked down at the tall slender stalks with their drooping ears. He breathed in the aroma of perfect ripe corn as dust blew up in his face.

Red watched his father position Captain, Tully and Trudy in line to make the first run. His father sat up in the middle on the high seat. The reaper six foot wide, with rotating reel in front, made of thin wooden bars; the reel rotating as the contraption was pulled by the power of the three horses; it looked like a small paddle steamer on land. The reel pushed the yellow stalked wheat down on the knife and sickle. The knife, moving in rhythm to the pace of the horses, cut the stalks which fell on the canvas before being tied and neatly deposited. Father kept an eye out for large stones and stumps, the reaper needing more attention than the horses, who were glad of the exercise in the morning sun. They sailed up and down the ocean of gold leaving a wake of sheaves. The labourers flocked like seagulls to stack them in avenues of stooks.

2

The light filtered through the window panes and onto the kitchen table. Constance Stevens could hear tree sparrows, blackbirds and song thrushes singing from the garden. It was going to be another sweltering hot day, and she would have to do her share as the shepherd's daughter. It wasn't like there would be any children to teach; they would all be in the field. The truth was she didn't much like the work; it was boring and made her feet ache. She'd much rather spend her time reading, learning, or writing; or even better, helping the younger children with their reading.

The door opened and Violet May bustled in.

'Where've you been?' Connie said, as she bent over to find her boots. 'Mr Grey sounded the horn ages ago. You know how he looks at us when we're late.'

'Don't worry, Connie, I'm sure Jimmy and Red have covered for us,' Violet replied. Her dark brown hair was tied up under her bonnet, an old hessian sack was tied around her broad waist and an expansive bosom was restricted under her shirt. Connie always felt Violet had such a pretty and friendly face, with her slim nose and an infectious wide smile which reflected her personality.

Connie picked up an old apron and tied it around her thin waist over her yellow dress. The dress was faded and worn; it would do for farm work, but still she didn't want it to get dirty.

'Have we got time for tea?' Violet asked, as she made her way to sit down on the chair. 'I'm worn out from that walk up from the station.'

'No, Vi, we don't. You know we've got to get a move on.' Connie walked to the door and put on the old boots, Martha's hand-me-downs. She had on two pairs of her father's socks to make them comfortable. Martha was kind like that, seeing to it she was well prepared. She was like her adopted mother. What would her own have been like, if she'd survived? Father did tell her, but it wasn't the same. Not knowing your own mother: that hurt. What had her voice sounded like? She'd never heard; she didn't even have a picture to see what she looked like. She'd died nine days after giving birth. Her father told her she'd fought and fought but in the end she succumbed.

'Oh well, I suppose we better get on with it,' Violet said as she went out of the door. They walked together and into the lane. There were no other villagers walking to the top of Snowdrop Hill; they were all working in the wheat field.

The hedgerow was full of life. Tree sparrows chirped as they searched for food. Bees flew, gathering nectar from honeysuckle. The yellow dandelion heads bobbed in the breeze. The sky was clear except for three fluffy white clouds creeping over Snowdrop Hill, blown from Bridport Harbour. The smell of natural garlic, parsley and honeysuckle floated on the air. The blackberry bushes bloomed, the berries not yet ripe.

It reminded Connie of years ago, when they had all played together: Violet, Red, James and Sampson. Playing in their gang, making camps, building dams in the river, running from farm to farm. Running from the older gang and Sampson's brother. Playing after school and working in the fields under the hot summer sun. She was glad for Violet, her first friend, made on her first day at Moreton School.

'So how are you and Jimmy? Has he proposed to you yet?' Connie asked, feeling the sun warming her back.

'Not yet. I've given him enough hints; I don't think it will be long,' Violet replied. She noticed a small red raspberry in the hedge; she picked it and ate it. 'Mmm, these taste wonderful; try one.' She picked another and handed it to Connie.

Connie took the raspberry and popped it in her mouth and said: 'Oh yes, tastes so lovely.' It was the perfect taste of light sweetness.

'I don't think Father can wait to get me married off; then he's rid of me and his job is done.' Violet smiled at Connie.

'Haha! I'm sure he doesn't think like that.' Connie felt warm under her bonnet.

'Well, I can only see him agreeing. He can't wait to get me out of the house.' Violet looked for more wild raspberries in the hedge and she walked even slower. 'And the best thing is you know, there is a cottage free in Ashcombe. Right in the centre of the village; you know, it's still empty after old man Whittle died.'

'Yes. He was creepy, wasn't he? Did he ever have a wife? I never saw her or knew her, did you?' Connie began to relax; Mr Grey wouldn't notice they were late.

'Well, I know we were frightened of him as children, his long white beard, him hunched over. He would swear at us kids to get away. His garden is massive, and there is a small orchard back behind the cottage. I mean, I'm sure Admiral would let us live there. I want a lot of children; me and Jimmy have already been talking. I want four or five.' Violet looked for more raspberries, careful not to scratch herself on the brambles.

'He wants the same, does he?'

'Yes, we both love children.' Violet adjusted her bonnet which was falling into her face. 'What about you, Connie? It's about time you got yourself a boyfriend. How about you and Red? You know he has a soft spot for you. Or what about Sampson? Bloody hell, he would be a catch! The squire's son! Bloody hell, one day you could be living in the manor house; think of that!'

'Violet, shut up! I'm too young; I'm only seventeen, for heaven's sake.' Connie blushed. 'And me and Red, we've been friends and neighbours for our whole lives. He's been like a brother. Crikey, we spent so much time together growing up. I don't think we ever could. And going out with Sampson? You're being silly. Think about all the beautiful sophisticated women he's met at university. He isn't going to look at the likes of me, a plain schoolteacher from Dorset.' She felt her cheeks burning.

'Oh, Connie, don't put yourself down! You were always the smartest in class; and my god, if I had your figure and looks! You can pick any man you want, I'm sure of that.' Violet blew out her cheeks, hot from walking.

'Anyway, before I think about me, I want my father to find someone; you know, someone he likes, someone who cares for him. I don't know if I want to get married and have lots of children like you. You know I'd like to be a good teacher and do more; who knows, if I keep doing well? But I can't be a wife and teach and I love doing it. I really do, so it's no good for you to keep on. Look at the headmistress, Miss Appleworth; I mean, she can't marry because of the law.'

'Yes, but come on, Connie! You mean to say if your prince came along you wouldn't marry him and give up teaching? I don't believe it! And not having children? I couldn't think of a life without. That's not right; you don't want to be an old lonely spinster, do you?'

'Well, no, but Miss Appleworth isn't lonely, is she? She's the most intelligent woman I know, and she's lots of friends and interests that keep her busy.' Connie looked over at her friend and looked her in the eye. 'And look, I'm sure you will need plenty of help with your brood. I've the children at school, so it's not like I won't have children and all the fun, laughter and happiness in my life. I won't have the downside of being up in the middle of the night, or having to clean up after them, will I.' She touched her bonnet, making sure it didn't become undone.

'I guess not, but it's not the same, is it, as having your own.' Violet coughed and cleared her throat as she looked back at Connie. They came to the gateway of Langdon Top and Connie could hear voices and shouting. She looked in and saw the field full of villagers and farm labourers. It would soon be time to put the nets out for the rabbits.

Connie and Violet walked in the field and made themselves busy stacking sheaves, as Hamilton continued with the reaper binder. Red and Jimmy looked over from the corner and waved.

'Look, don't they look so handsome, with their sleeves rolled up working hard and their brown muscly arms!' Violet said.

'Violet, shush and stop daydreaming. Mr Grey's got his watch out over there watching us.'

'Don't you get feelings? You know. Me and Jimmy, we've kissed. We haven't made love or anything like that; but... well, when we've kissed it's so passionate.' Violet wiped her brow with the back of her hand.

'Violet, you can't, not before you're married!' Connie stacked another sheaf in the stook and they moved on together, waving and greeting the other women. Martha, Red's mother, came over and said morning, then went off to start churning butter. 'Anyway, what would I do if I didn't teach? I want to do something. I don't want to just be a housewife and I don't want to go into the net factory in Bridport and I don't want to work on the farm. It's not like I've a huge choice.'

'You could come and work with me in the station café. We get busy and I could do with the help. Mother can't do as much as she used to; and think of all the fun we could have and all the men we could eye up! 'Course, I would only be looking for you, because I would be happy with my Jimmy. And 'course you would have to run it when I'm having my babes.' Violet sighed heavily with the exertion.

'Oh, Violet, you make me laugh! I can see it now: you will be out the back popping out babies and I'll be running the café, day and night. Sorry, but I don't think it's for me.' Connie grinned.

'Well, the rope works and net factory: it's good money and you can work your way up.' Violet bent down, picking up more sheaves.

'Oh, I don't know. I love teaching. I don't know.' She bent down, feeling her back.

'Anyway, let's talk about something else. If the situation gets any worse, things might be a lot different.'

'Well, Father was reading the *Daily Express* this morning. And he said that Mr Asquith has declared war. Germany didn't pull out of Belgium and the country expects every man to do his duty.' Violet stopped to take a breath and looked over at Connie. 'You don't think Jimmy will have to go, do you?'

'I don't know; who does? I mean, we are going to need food and they're needed here. I'm sure Jimmy will be fine.' Connie said it but didn't believe it. She had no idea what would happen or how many men would have to go.

'Father said that the railways will be coming under control of the government. So they can control them to move the soldiers.' Violet seemed calmer. 'Think, all those troops, coming through Moreton station! You can grab yourself an officer!'

'Violet, will you stop!' Connie looked at Violet, at her wide smile.

'Anyway, it's Moreton Fair Sunday; you better make sure your frock is washed and ready.'

'I don't think I'll go, not with your carrying on,' she bluffed. She knew how much she looked forward to it. 'Are you hoping Jimmy wins the hundred yard dash again?' She smiled.

'I don't think there's anyone quicker. Them Smyth boys can't keep up; and unless someone ties up one of Jimmy's legs, I don't think there's a chance of him being beat!'

3

Red walked down the garden path. He noticed the white daisies and yellow dandelions growing up through the grass, their pollen ripe for the dumbledores. He reached the front porch; the aroma of honeysuckle was abundant. He looked back and saw Father loping and weary. He was very tired from the long day of harvesting behind the reaper. He seemed to tire easily these days; he didn't have the energy he once did. The arthritis was deep in his bones. He hunched over, wrecked by years of lifting, hauling and lugging of corn sacks, churns and pails of milk. Red waited for Father to catch him up.

'You all right, old man?' he said.

'Less of that, young 'en! I can give 'e a run for your money. Where's that ball of 'ees? Let's have a kick,' Father said.

'You get on with you, after the day we've 'ad.' Red knew it was bluster; even so, it impressed him. His old man wouldn't give in to it. 'Ay, why not? Think the ball is around here, back here.' Red looked in his old favourite hiding spot behind the oak tree. There it was, worse for wear. He picked it up and drop-kicked it over to his dad, who trapped it between his foot and the ground. Dry dust flew up.

Red could smell baking pastry drifting from the kitchen door and his mouth watered.

'What are you silly gallybaggers up to?' Mother shouted from the kitchen window.

'Aye, Mother.' they both called back.

'Here, Father; bet you can't score.' Red stood in the pretend goal between the oak tree and the corner of the hencoop.

'Hey, I can shoot straight; you 'ave no worries about that, son! Anyway, we need the practice if we are going to beat Moreton on Boxing Day!' Father said as he stretched out.

Red stood firm and watched the ball. He knew how hard Father could kick it. Father took a run up to the ball and hammered it with his right foot. It flew past Red before he could blink. It hit the hedge behind, burying itself deep. Tree sparrows chirped in surprise and scattered, flying out one after the other.

'One goal to yer old man and time for supper,' his father said, stooping down to rub his knee.

'Good idea.' Red watched his father limping to the back door, where he took off his boots and went into the house.

Red went over the stile in the wall to fetch the chickens in. He walked through the tall gold barley. The ground smelt of baking dust. It was warm and humid and he felt so tired. The sun would fall in an hour. He was looking forward to the rabbit pie, a cup of tea and his bed. He rounded up the chickens and shut them in the henhouse.

Connie walked out of her back door. Her blonde hair flowed to her shoulders. She smiled, with her lips creasing her whole face. Red looked at her tall slender figure and perfectly tapered hips which led to her fine waist; he couldn't help but smile back. She walked barefoot across the grass to him. Her yellow frock flowed to her ankles.

'Hey, Connie, what a day, eh?' he said, and he felt his throat tighten. He looked into her deep green eyes, which sparkled back at him.

'Hi, Red; it's so hot.' They sat on the wall; Red took his boots and socks off and dropped them in the garden. They faced the field of barley, their feet bathing in the corn tops, the ears tickling their soles.

'I'm glad that's done for the day,' Red said. He could smell fresh lavender on Connie; he looked at her face, full of colour, bright, her small nose and sleek cheekbones. 'How's Violet? What's the gossip?'

'Oh, you know: same as always. She wants me to ask you to find out when Jimmy is going to get around to proposing.' She smiled at Red as she rubbed her arm.

'Haha! I can't possibly say! Who knows? I can't think it will be long now. God, they've known each other long enough, haven't they? Bit like me and you; we've seemed to have known each other forever.' He laughed and stretched out his legs, tickling his soles with the top of the barley. The sun began its descent back behind the far woodland. The few clouds that were in the sky made a ribbon of red and the temperature cooled. A family of six swallows flew in, diving, catching and eating insects.

'Look at them; they're so majestic, royal and gracious, aren't they?' She smiled and looked over at Red.

'They are; so quick too; they know how to catch their supper.' His heart skipped and he smiled back. 'So are you going to the fair on Sunday?'

'Oh, yes; Violet was on about that all day. I kept teasing her that I wouldn't go, that I had something better to do! Yes, I will be.'

'Yes, me too. Jimmy can't wait to win another bloody prize. 'Bout time somebody beat him; trouble is, I can't catch him.' Red scratched his head and let out a deep breath, feeling more relaxed. 'Nobody can, he's like his father. That bloody Crabb family! Don't know what's in their blood but they can't half run, can 'em.'

'Haha! Violet wants her proposal; then she will be happy.'

'So how about we have a ride in the swing boats?' he asked.

'Of course; wouldn't miss it!' Red looked at her and saw her raise her hand to push a stray hair from her face.

'Come yerr, you two; supper's ready!' Mother called from the back door. He felt like he was twelve again. He picked up his boots and followed Connie; he watched her silhouetted outline pass over the threshold. He felt hairs stand to attention on the back of his neck.

He left the back door open to let the breeze in. Unfortunately, the flies would follow.

'Leave that door open; we need the air,' Mother shouted from the range as she filled the teapot. Edna and Father were seated at the table, both with plates full of rabbit pie and boiled potatoes. Red looked at the large pie in the middle of the table and the aroma of baked pastry made his mouth tingle in anticipation. He pulled the chair out for Connie, walked round her back and sat down. His sister Edna was sitting opposite, with Father at the head and his mother's chair next to him. The kitchen was sparse: a door to the larder, the sink under the window, which looked over the garden towards the henhouse. The floor made from square flagstones; an old wooden sideboard; and the door leading to the front room. Red felt the heat from the range, welcome in winter but stifling in summer. A small breeze circulated from the open window to the door; the sound of birds preparing to roost carried in.

Edna greeted Connie and Red with a grunted word. She scooped up pie and potato on her fork and shovelled it into her mouth. Edna's hair was dark brown and black, limp and oily, her nose stubby like a gnarled oak knot. Connie served Father, Mother and then Red before her own plate.

Edna, twenty-three, worked net braiding in Bridport. She had her claws dug into Sydney Palmer, her foreman. She always had plenty of money for herself, but she didn't share it. What poor Sydney saw in her Red couldn't work out. Red thought she was very lucky, especially with that big old conker of a nose. Red chuckled to himself. Sydney five years older, his frame thin and wispy; he must be thinking he should marry soon. If only he would get on with it then Edna would be out of the house and out of his life. 'Red, you smell of horse shit! Couldn't you go and wash before you come in 'ere, eating your tea?' Edna exclaimed. Why did she have to say something so embarrassing in front of Connie?

'We all smell bad; we've had a long day out in the field after all,' Connie replied. Connie didn't have any time for Edna, not since back when they were children, with Edna in Theodore Fox's gang.

Mother came and sat down in the spare chair next to Father; she coughed to clear her throat, then louder. Red thought her cough was bothering her more and more, and Father's was as bad. It seemed constant since winter, persisting through spring. They should have shaken it off in this heat.

Stephen, Connie's father, came in and joined them with Jess, his sheepdog. She sprawled out in front of the fire. Stephen, with kind hazel eyes and a thick grey and black flecked beard, took his worn waistcoat off and put it over the back of the chair.

They all ate supper in silence. Edna washed up and Connie wiped the plates dry. Mother made a second pot of tea, which they mixed in their mugs with fresh milk from the afternoon's milking. Red liked the cream from the top in his. He shared it into Connie's mug.

Father picked up the *Express* brought home by Edna from the sideboard and leafed through the pages.

'This ain't going to go well, is it, this business,' Father said. 'What do you reckon, Stephen?' He sighed.

'No, it ain't. Mind you, we're too old to do owt about it.' Stephen sipped his tea and scratched his beard.

'Ay, we are that.' Father looked over at Red as he lowered the paper. 'I don't want you going and getting any ideas about joining up, lad. We need you to stay here and help on the farm. We still need men, even with them bloody great steam engines.'

'In the factory, they're all talking about joining up. Sydney says it's the right thing to do, you know, for men of his age and younger. You know, if they're single and all,' Edna said as she looked at Red.

'It's such a waste! Why the hell are we fighting anyway?' Mother asked.

'Says 'ere that Germany didn't respect Belgium's neutrality or summink.' Father slurped his tea. 'Says, Prime Minister Mr Asquith announced in the Commons Germany hadn't answered the ulti… ulti-summink.'

'-matum. Ultimatum, Hamilton,' Mother said.

'I don't know what that means, an ultimatum,' Red said.

'It only means that they haven't done what we've asked them to,' Connie answered.

'Bloody hell, look at this!' Father said. He put the paper down in the centre of the table. Red pushed his chair back; they all got up and leaned over. Red read the large advertisement positioned in the centre of the page in bold thick type.

"YOUR KING AND COUNTRY NEED YOU."

'Bloody hell!' Red and Stephen said together. Red looked down below the headlines at the smaller print.

In Fields of Gold and Red

'Connie, you read it out loud, will you, love?' Stephen asked.

'"In this crisis, your country calls on all her unmarried men to rally round the flag and enlist in the ranks of the army."' She took a deep breath and continued. '"If you're unmarried and between 18 and 30 years old..."' She hesitated.

'Go on, Connie, finish reading it out,' Edna said.

'"Will you answer your country's call? Go to the nearest recruiter whose address you can get at any post office."' She stopped. Red looked down and saw the large type underneath: "JOIN THE ARMY TO-DAY".

'Don't you dare think about that, Redver Kingson! I can still put you over my knee if I 'ave to,' Mother said as she looked him right in the eyes. 'I didn't raise you to go off doing any daft fighting.' Red could see her cheeks flushed and blowed out. 'I've had enough heartache for my lifetime, raising the three of you. I ain't havin' you off over there in this bloody waste of time.'

'Oh, Mother, don't worry! Sydney says it won't last long at all, 'cos we will go over and give them a real beating. It won't last very long at all!' Edna said.

'I don't know about that; these things have a habit of lasting longer than anyone thought,' Stephen said, as his hand stroked the side of his face. They all sat back down on their wooden chairs except for Mother who went and lit two candles on the sideboard.

'They've been panic-buying food up in the large shops in London, scared they ain't going to get enough.' Father carried on: 'Don't s'pose we will be too bad hit, not all down here, long as them rabbits keep breeding!'

Red looked over at his Mother. He didn't want to defy her; but shouldn't he do his duty? Wouldn't it be right for him to join up? He should go to Moreton Post Office and see about where his nearest recruiter was.

4

9th August 1914

Connie and Violet walked down Farm Lane, past the ten-acre field, its wheat uncut. They could smell the honeysuckle, cow parsley and hedge garlic. The dock leaves, nettles and brambles were fighting for space; bushes of redcurrant and dog rose, too. Like steps walking tall, the hazel, oak and ash lined the lane, casting their welcome shadows overhead.

Two blackbirds rustled busy in the hedge, arguing over territory, and sang out, *tek-tek-tek*. Connie was wearing her long, light green and white dress and white bonnet, her Sunday best worn to church that morning. The heat of the summer continued; it seemed to Connie it would never end. They walked past the Farmer's Arms, where men stood outside drinking and having a good old yarn; she thought men could gossip as well as the women. The talk was of fighting and war and the news from Belgium. It was all the village had talked about over the last few days. The vicar, Reverend Thomas Wrixon, was preaching in his sermon for men to go and fight.

The sky was clear light blue. Violet looked over at Connie and said: 'I can tell you, Connie, Jimmy I think will propose.

For god's sake don't tell anyone; we want it to be a surprise.' Violet touched Connie on the arm. 'And Father will give his blessing. He's so bothered by the bloody Ministry; as stationmaster he just wants to be left to get on. He hates the civil servants meddling with his station.'

'Violet, I don't think it's going to surprise anyone, is it! You two have been talking about it so much for so long. It's about time!' Connie looked over. Violet was in her blue striped dress down to her ankles; it was a bit too long and touched the ground as she walked.

'I shouldn't tell you this either. Last night, it was so romantic out under the stars; this owl hooted and I jumped out of my skin. Well, Jimmy, he put his arms around me, kissed me and whispered in my ear. It was so lovely; and – well, one thing led to another.' They walked round the bend and started down Palmers Hill, joining the busy throng of villagers. Connie was happy for her.

'You didn't, did you, Vi? You know you shouldn't! Not before you're married.'

They came to the crossroads and turned right on Moreton Lane. After fifty yards they came to the small bridge on their right and crossed to the meadow. Already in the early afternoon it was full of villagers exploring the stalls. They saw Jimmy and Red waiting for them by the riverbank, Red carrying a crimson blanket rolled under his arm, sure to be filled with a picnic.

All Ashcombe and Moreton seemed crammed into the flood meadow. That summer the grass had grown tall and luscious; cut and dried, the hay had been taken away, so they walked on short brown and tan stalks. The smell of sweet hay rippled over them.

The stalls either side made a straight avenue. To the left the ground rose up the valley side and over to the right the river meandered through bends. The stalls of coconut shy, toffee apples, horseshoe toss and candy floss, the owners eager to take the crowd's pennies.

Connie watched as Jimmy strolled over and gave Violet a big hug, lifting her feet off the ground. She hesitated as Red came close and hugged her. Connie thought Vi and Jimmy made such a good couple. She smiled, thinking how happy they would make each other. Jimmy, shorter than Red, was only an inch or two taller than Violet; his eyes were sharp blue, his waist was thin, the opposite of Vi's; and he was full of life.

The swing-boat owners were two thickset men from Cornwall, late of tin mining. They looked like they were hewn from cliffs, tall and craggy, with long beards. They shouted 'Penny a ride!' as they tossed their top hats to one another. 'Penny a ride!' enjoying putting on a show. Connie thought them intimidating; they didn't look so trustworthy.

'Come on, let's all go on! Me and Vi against Red and Connie,' Jimmy said with his arm around Violet's shoulder.

'Can we, Red?' Connie said smiling.

'Course we can,' Red said as he paid his penny to the thickset Cornish brother. He held Connie's hand as he helped her into the swing-boat. She pulled down on the rope in turn with Red. As they reached higher she felt her tummy somersault, dipping down and up. Her smile wide, she looked at Red as they held tightly onto the ropes; he smiled back. She looked out over the fair, and saw the one hundred yard track running the entire length of the field through the avenue of stalls. She yelled with laughter and heard Violet shrieking for Jimmy to slow down. When their time was up they got off; Jimmy and Red joshed whose boat got the highest. They called it a tie.

The fair was buzzing; Jimmy and Violet arm-in-arm. Connie walked close to Red, but it wouldn't be right for her to hold Red's hand. They walked around the different stalls, past the toffee apples and roasted chestnuts and on by the horseshoe toss. They stopped and chatted with George Kingson, Redver's older brother. He was trying to keep control of his seven-year-old son Charles, who was pulling on George's arm; he wanted to play a game of football. Dorothy was holding Mary, their daughter, in her arms. Dorothy, Connie thought, looked pretty in her light green frock and white bonnet; she smiled as the men talked about the fighting. She hadn't seen men be so animated since the end of the football season in May. George was taller than his brother, wide-shouldered; his hair wasn't thick like Red's but was thinning from his creased forehead. George and Dorothy seemed so much older. People said Connie was mature for her age, but she couldn't see herself having children for years. Dorothy could only be twenty-four, but the gap seemed much wider. Dorothy was petite with a delicate face and long brown hair to her shoulder; a wide smile. She worked at the manor as a maid.

After a couple of minutes Jimmy grew impatient and dragged the four of them to the coconut shy.

'Come on, Red, let's have a go then,' Jimmy said.

Connie and Violet stood back as the young men pulled their shirtsleeves up to their elbows, revealing dark-tanned, thick, muscled arms.

'I'll show you, Jimmy,' Red said. Connie saw a look of determination spread across his face.

'Want a bet on it?' Jimmy said, laughing.

'Go on, then; I'll do the milking for a week for you if you knock down more than me; and if I win you can muck out the horses!' Red said.

'It's on.'

Connie and Violet giggled and held each other's arms as they stood back. Jimmy went first and missed with all three throws.

'Your aim was never that good!' Red said as he missed with two throws. His third strike cannoned into the coconut full on and knocked it flying into the grass.

'Oh, bloody hell, you lucky noggerhead! You were always good at throwing! Why did I bet?' Jimmy shouted as he came back and pecked Violet on the cheek.

'Tough luck, Jimmy! Make sure you clean out Captain's stable good and clean; he doesn't like a mess. Give him plenty of oats for his breakfast!' He punched Jimmy on the arm.

'Here you are, Connie.' Red passed the prize coconut to her.

'What the bloody hell am I meant to do with this hairy thing?' Connie said, laughing. 'Thank you anyway, Red.' She hesitated before she gave him a small kiss on his cheek.

'Why don't we leave them to it, Connie? We can walk up to the old castle and have a picnic,' Red said. She'd wondered what he had rolled up in his blanket.

'Why not? It's such a lovely day,' Connie replied. She thought it best to leave Violet and Jimmy; anyway, they would be too preoccupied with each other to notice them leaving.

She looked at Red as they walked together. He was smiling; he always smiled broadly around her. He seemed taller, his arms thick. His hair was dark brown and fell away from his face, his eyes hazel, sharp as the summer sky; and his wide smile curved like a new moon. He looked smart in his white shirt and Sunday trousers, his shirt sleeves rolled up revealing his dark brown skin. She allowed herself to think him handsome. Her stomach flipped, her mouth curved into a smile. There was only a year or so between them. Has he kissed a girl? He must have. She thought, who?

They walked away, leaving the noise of the fair behind.

The meadow narrowed as beech trees encroached forming a passage. The field ended and they climbed over the stile into the narrow path where hazel and hawthorn grew up and over. They went up through the tunnel, Red leading the way, turning right into the open field, finding the green carpet of pasture dotted with yellow buttercups. Connie felt the long grass tickle her ankles. They came to the grassed-over banks, ditches and ramparts of the old castle. Red laid out the faded maroon blanket. She looked up at the view of Ashcombe Beacon, standing tall in the landscape.

'We should have asked Jimmy and Violet. It's such a lovely spot; it's a shame for them to miss out,' Connie said as she sat down cross-legged, careful to make sure her dress didn't ride up. She untied her bonnet and took it off, shaking her head to loosen her hair. She pushed a stray straggle behind her ear.

'I'm sure they're having their own fun,' Red said. Connie smoothed down her hair.

'I guess. Red, do you know when Jimmy will propose?' Connie said as she picked up a piece of bread.

'No, I don't; I can't tell you that.' Red wiped his hand on his trousers.

'Oh, go on! She's so excited; is he going to do it today, tonight?' Connie looked at him, watching his face.

'I can't possibly say.' Red was blushing; she could tell he knew. His eyes moved to avoid hers.

'He is, isn't he? Oh, Violet's going to be so happy! She really loves him. He won't ever hurt her, will he? Else he will have me to answer to!' She pinched him on the arm.

''Course not! He loves her, don't 'e. He'll do anything for her; you know he would never hurt her,' Red said as he propped himself on his arm and looked over at her.

'Connie, you look prettier than a butterfly, and more beautiful than this 'ere buttercup,' he said as he picked the buttercup and held it under her chin. His hazel eyes shone.

'Thank you, Red, that is really nice; you don't have to say it.' She blushed and her heart quickened; her stomach flipped as if on the swing-boat.

'I do; it's true,' Red said as he took her hand in his. His hands felt warm and she felt the roughness of his skin. Blood ran to her face and she hoped Red didn't notice. She touched him softly on the shoulder and saw him blush. Why were they like this when they were friends?

'Do you remember when we first met?' Red said.

* * *

He leapt to the lowest branch and clung on with all his strength. His small arms working hard he pulled his body up, contorting his legs to get his feet over. Not content, he looked for the next higher branch; he climbed up one, two, and three. He was at his favourite place; he could see the fields of dark velvet green speckled with grazing flecks of white, alternating with golden patches of wheat, barley and oats stood tall, rippling like the sea, baking in the July sun. The breeze rustled the thick green leaves, releasing their musky odour. Looking out to his left between the gaps he could see Ashcombe Beacon, the highest point for miles. To his right Snowdrop Hill, not any higher than him; in front, the buildings of Kingcombe Farm.

Looking out, away from Snowdrop Hill and down the narrow lane, Red heard the chug-chug-chug of the steam engine as it was heading towards Bridport, smoke from the engine's chimney blowing out behind in a long ribbon of grey.

He knew it wouldn't take long for the walk up from the station. His heart was beginning to beat faster: the excitement of having a new friend next door. After all, Granfer said he was coming with his young 'en.

He took the penknife and broke off a smallish twig and

began to whittle away like Granfer had showed him. When he next looked up he saw the man coming through the garden gate, a bearded man, with a child in tow who in turn was holding a dog by a piece of string. Mother and Father were already out giving them a friendly welcome and Edna was watching from the edge of the path.

Red climbed down to the lowest branch. He jumped into the long grass; he landed. He made a roll before getting up and running to meet his new neighbours. Mother would tell him off for getting grass stains on his Sunday shorts. He didn't care. He ran along the narrow path which lined the vegetable patch, the ground broken by huge cracks caused by the baking heat. He couldn't remember the day that it last rained. He flew around the corner of the cottage; he couldn't believe what he saw.

'You're a girl!' Red shouted, showing his annoyance as he raced up to everybody on the path.

'Yes, I am, and my name is Constance, but you can call me Connie; and this is our dog, Jess; she's the same age as me,' the girl replied, with confidence beyond her five years. The sheepdog sniffed Redver and licked his hand.

'Son, that's no way to greet Stephen and his young 'en, is it?' Father said.

'Yes, Red, remember to say good afternoon. Good manners cost nothing,' Mother said. Red could see Edna was giggling behind her hand.

'Sorry. I'm pleased to meet you both, I mean sir, and you, Connie, and you too, Jess,' Redver replied as he stroked Jess.

'I might be a girl but I bet I can beat you in a race to that old tree.' And before she finished talking she was running as fast as she could towards the tree, with Jess following at her heels. She ploughed through the centre of the standing adults.

Red, caught by surprise, was not slow in taking up the

challenge; he raced through the middle of the three adults as they were trying to regain their balance. He made sure to brush his shoulder against Edna.

Connie was still in front as she ran down the narrow path towards Joe's old oak; she was running as fast as she could, Jess the sheepdog keeping pace. Red was closing fast; the path became narrow, patchy, and angled into the vegetables. Connie misplaced her foot; she went sprawling. Following close behind, Red couldn't react and tripped over her flailing legs. They both landed in the leafy green potatoes. Red got a mouthful of dirt. Jess was soon on them, thinking it was a big game, barking, spinning around, and licking both of them as they floundered.

'You silly gallybagger, you,' Red said, spitting the dirt from his mouth.

'You're a noggerhead,' Connie said. Red and Connie laughed as Jess tickled them with long licks of her tongue. 'I was as fast as the boys back home.'

'I was going to catch you anyway; I've decided you can be my new best friend, as long as you don't try and kiss me like the girls at school playing kiss chase!' Red said.

'I promise, Red. Yes, let's be best friends,' Connie said, giggling.

* * *

'Haha! What's reminded you of that?'

'The summer, the heat... That summer when you arrived we had such a good time, running and playing.' His eyes looked at her, sharp and full.

'Yes, I remember, and you were so disappointed I was just a girl. You wanted a boy to live next door so you could play football all day!' Connie said as she put her hand to her hair and lightly curled it around her ear. 'And you said, "You're only a girl."'

'Did I? I didn't, did I?' he said, trying to keep his face

straight. 'I was only seven; you can't blame me for wanting to play chase and football.'

'Haha, yes! You were a typical boy! I kept up with you. In fact, I think I beat you then and I can beat you now to that oak tree!' She got up, hitched her dress and dashed for the oak tree at the corner of the field.

Connie felt free and happy. The warm sun on her skin, she ran through the long grass. She looked around and saw Red running fast; he was gaining on her. She could see his smile beaming on his face. She ran as fast as she could, but Red was catching her; she could hear his feet in the grass. Her breathing was fast. She was close to the oak tree; Red was alongside her. They reached the shadow of the tree and touched the trunk together. Before she knew it, Red was holding her, kissing her on her lips. Her heart quickened, in rhythm, like the reaping reel beating down on wheat. They lay down together under the shade of the tree in the long grass. She stopped kissing; it wouldn't be right.

* * *

Red and Connie walked back to the fair. The crowd were gathered around the one hundred yard track. Connie could see that Brigadier Appleworth, the headmistress's father, was busy with Mr Martin, tying the string across the finish line. The Brigadier stood six feet tall, with a full handlebar moustache. His back straight, not like the older workers. His old army uniform was pressed clean, his medals pinned on his chest. He would marshal the entrants and start them by firing his Webley Mark IV army revolver. Mr Martin, the schoolteacher, would judge the finish. He was shorter, meek and mild-mannered, thin and pale. There was no prize money, only a trophy: a small model deer on a wooden plinth, it got awarded every year.

Connie and Violet watched from the finish line. They could see at the far end the racers lining up: Jimmy, George

In Fields of Gold and Red

Kingson, Redver, Thomas, David and Ken Smyth, the Hansford boys: John, Richard and Edward.

Connie could tell the Brigadier loved this, organising the runners as if they were his soldiers, barking orders for them to get behind the line. He kept them back. He fired his black Webley in the air. Jimmy, first to react, got a lead that was never beaten, even by a late surge by Ken, the youngest Smyth. Connie watched as Red made third. Red and George grabbed hold of Jimmy and raised him up on their shoulders; his face was beaming and he punched the air. They lowered him to the ground, where Violet planted a large kiss on his cheek.

The vicar, keen to have the ear of the crowd, got up on an upturned crate. He stood straight, his shoulders back. His thin hair blew up in the breeze. He looked down over his glasses which were perched on the end of his nose. He wore his dog collar and large black cassock, which swept to his ankles. The crowd hushed, used to being quiet for his sermon. He had everyone's attention as they held their breath to hear him. Connie could see sweat on his forehead.

'We are celebrating here today, and that is right.' He looked at the faces in the crowd. He wiped his brow with his hanky. Connie hoped he wouldn't look to Red and Jimmy. He dominated his audience. Most eyes looked at their feet, only glancing up to see the vicar in full flow. Reverend Wrixon continued: 'The good Lord looks down on us and blesses us with this good weather. It is only a few miles across the sea. We face a great evil. Many of our men, our fathers, husbands and our brothers, are giving their lives so that we can be free. So we can have our freedom. I know we have God on our side. We are just in our cause to repel evil. Those evil devils from Germany. It is the right action to take, to fight for your God, for your King, and for yourself and your family, for your children and for your children's children. Think this: as we speak, poor Belgian families are losing their homes and are forced to flee. It could be us next if we don't stand up and fight!'

Connie couldn't help but feel intimidated; she felt that if she was a man she wouldn't be able to ignore his sermon.

The Brigadier clapped and led the cheering, his peaked hat under his arm. The vicar then made the presentation of the trophy to Jimmy. Jimmy handed it to Violet. Connie had her coconut and Violet her trophy. Connie remembered her kiss with Red; she touched her lip with her finger. The kiss had felt so light and tender. How could something so small feel so intense, so full with energy?

5

10th August 1914

Red leaned over the stable door as Jimmy mucked out Captain's cubicle. Red loved the musky odour of horses. He didn't even mind the smell of manure.

'You enjoying that, mate?' Red said, laughing, with a piece of hay in the corner of his mouth.

'Shut it, I'll have 'e back, don't 'e worry,' Jimmy said. He didn't like breaking his back with the pitchfork, and he didn't like the horses, not like Red. 'See anyway, I was saying: after the race and everyone went on back home, me and Violet we went and sat down in that old bend by the river. You know the one that's all cut away after them winter floods covered the meadow. I don't mind saying my heart was beating so fast, so bloody fast I didn't think I would get the words out.' Jimmy gulped.

'It ain't like you, being short of words and all,' Red said, chewing on the end of the piece of hay.

'We were sat there, our feet dangling over the edge not reaching the clear water. You could see the gravel, and minnows were floating there, eating insects. We sat and watched as two kingfishers came to hunt; their bright orange bellies glowed in the evening sun. It was so perfect; the kingfishers sat there as we did. They perched on the old willow branch and me and Vi on the bank. So I felt for the ring in my pocket. Thought I'd bloody lost it for a minute; I couldn't feel it at first, then there it was deep in my pocket. It's a wonder I never dropped it in the bottom of the river. Anyway, she's said bloody yes! Her father's given permission. You're to be best man and Connie is to be bridesmaid. We've the vicar to see; Vi says we're to see him straightaway.' He leaned on the pitchfork, gasping for breath.

'I... well, I didn't think there was any chance she'd say no. God, I hope she knows how bad your farts smell,' Red said. He chucked a ball of mud at Jimmy, who ducked. Jimmy picked up a clod of dung and threw it back, missing. They heard the bugle horn, faintly coming from Langdon Bottom.

'Your aim's still shit. You should get practising before next year and I beat you again,' Red said as the two of them laughed. 'We better get a move on, else father and Mr Grey will be having words.'

'Ay, they will that. But we've to finish 'ere first.' Jimmy worked hard to finish laying out the bedding. 'Did you see them three Smyth boys? They went straight to Brigadier, to see about signing up.'

'Did they? What do you think? Jimmy, it's different for 'e, now you're getting married and all. But I was thinking, should I go and sign up?' Red said, removing the stalk from his mouth and throwing it to the ground. Jimmy came out of the stables and put the pitchfork up against the wall.

'Nah, we're needed 'ere, ain't we. Someone's got to cultivate the land and bring in the harvest. Father was saying there could be food shortages and all sorts 'cos so much food comes in from America. The Germans are knocking out ships, you know. We might not be fighting but we're as important in a way, he says. I suppose he's right.' They walked out of the farmyard and into the lane.

'Yes, but don't you want to see what France is like? What we might learn? You know, see something different.' Red looked at Jimmy.

'I've got my Violet. And what's more beautiful than this Dorset countryside? Why'd I want to leave and go over there putting my life at stake? If I don't have to.' The sound of the hobnailed boots on the lane scared the tree sparrows and blue tits from the hedge.

'Yes; it's different for you, I guess. It's that when I see those Smyth boys going, and you hear the vicar, the Brigadier; and then I see that advertisement in all the papers saying it's my duty; well, it just makes me think and all.'

'You think too much, Red. You should get on and do, like me.' Jimmy took off, running towards the field. Red shook his head and chased after his mate.

When they got to the field, Mr Grey walked over to them. He was wearing his tall black hat, his waistcoat and black jacket. He was tall and upright, unlike the older labourers who were all hunched over. He was the only estate manager Red had known. He took out his silver pocket watch and said: 'Ay, you two; have 'e finished up in the yard?'

'Yes, sir, horses all cleaned out,' Jimmy replied. Red looked at him and tried to suppress his grin.

'Good lads. Red, can you take over on the reaper? Your father's not feeling so well. Think he's had too much of this sun. 'Tis been so hot, this past week, I'm sending him home to rest. He ain't happy 'bout it but I think it's best he gets hisself to his bed before he makes himself worse.'

'Yes, Mr Grey.'

Red headed to his father who was sitting atop the reaper in the middle of the field. Jimmy went off to grab his scythe and join with the gang cutting the perimeter. Father drew Captain, Trudy and Tully to a stop and clambered down from his seat.

When Red got to his father, he could his eyes seemed cloudy and dull, his movements slow and deliberate: his father usually upbeat and the last to finish. Red couldn't ever remember him going home sick; other workers, maybe. His uncle Charlie, for instance, always seemed to be off-colour, especially after he'd drunk too much cider; but never his father. He kept going and going even in the hardest of conditions: wind, rain, hail, snow, thunder and lightning, year after year, day after day. His father being foreman and carter, he was proud of his position. He was up there with Stephen: carter and shepherd, the two lead men.

'Here, son, I've to lie down for a bit. I shouldn't be long. A bit of a lie-down, get me head right, I'll be back out in no time,' Father said as he left Red. Red heard him coughing, trying to clear his throat as he stumbled across the stubble.

Red got up on the wooden seat. Father had shown him how to operate the reaper on many occasions, letting him share or take a turn when his father had elevenses or lunch. He loved being up running the machine, behind the horses. He got Captain to trot on; Trudy and Tully snorted and followed the large black shire. They were immensely powerful, and Red could sense through the reins their impatience to move on.

Red relaxed into the rhythm, sailing on through the wheat, the field a busy hive as Jimmy, his brother and his uncles scythed. He saw his mother go to his father and support him; a look of worry spread across her face. Connie and Violet were out instructing the young children on picking the sheaves. He waved across. Had he really done that yesterday, kissing Connie? He didn't believe it possible! How perfect; he'd tasted her lip, and felt her want more. She'd said they shouldn't but he knew she wanted to, as much as him. It felt so right; should he ask her to walk out?

In Fields of Gold and Red

Red watched the knives and sickle, checking in front like his father taught him, making sure no large stones got in the cutter. If they did he would have to stop as quickly as possible to clear them before the knife or sickle got damaged. The field was surrounded by hedges on three sides, with the copse to the ridge above and to the left. He continued up and down the field, happy with the thought of going out with Connie; a smile formed on his face. He turned at the headland, Captain easy to control as he knew what to do.

One day, he could be carter. He knew father got a couple extra shillings. If he did marry in the future he would then get his own house. It was possible. Look at Jimmy; soon he and Violet would be married. Trouble was would that be enough for him; should he go and enlist and do his duty? Mother wouldn't be happy, that was for sure, nor his father; and he would be away from Connie. But he would get some leave. He looked around and noticed the Smyth boys were not in the field.

6

10th September 1914

Moreton Village Hall was full of the noise of the villagers busy chatting, gossiping and catching up on business. Talk of the latest news from the front; and who had signed up? Connie knew there were less young men, the Smyth brothers and the Hansfords gone.

There must be fifty people all huddled together in the small wooden hut. It was too many for her liking. She didn't like being crowded together; she preferred it if she was talking to Violet. She searched through the crowd and found her standing with her parents, Oscar and Henrietta May.

Violet's father, a short man with sharp eyes, was disciplined and organised. He was already looking at his pocket watch to see when the evening would begin. His head was large with a big forehead. He hated the fact that the government was now in charge of his station. His wife, plump and short with a kind face, was as spirited as her daughter. Connie remembered her manners and greeted them before grabbing Violet to go outside.

'Come on, Vi, come outside; we can talk better there.' Connie led Violet by the hand and back through the crowd, down the wooden steps and into the autumn evening. The sun was on its way down; it still remained mild. They walked to the side of the hut, and away from the steps.

'Where's your father? I don't see him here yet,' Violet asked.

'He is getting washed up; he was late in. Some of the ewes got out of the football field and ran down Bull Lane. He chased them all the way to the Farmer's Arms before he and Jess got them back.'

'Here, Connie, I've had a good idea. Why don't we set it up for your father to sit next to Miss Appleworth? They'd have fun together, don't you think?'

'Violet, you're such a one! They'll know what we're up to.'

'Well, you don't want to have to sit next to smelly old spinster Miss Crabb, do you?'

'Look, Connie, you get talking to Miss Appleworth; talk about teaching and how you want to follow in her footsteps – something like that. She will talk to you for hours. Then when we go to sit down, she will naturally have to follow you. I will take care of getting your father to sit with us and keep a seat free next to him; easy!'

'Easy? I feel nervous as a chicken watching a fox! Maybe it's not such a good idea after all. Shall we just let nature run its course?' Connie said.

'Rubbish! We can do it,' Violet said, brushing some imaginary hairs from her dress as she got up.

'Oh, look, doesn't he look so handsome, Connie,' Violet said as she waved over at Jimmy and Redver as they approached the hut. Connie saw Jimmy and then Red enthusiastically wave back. They came together and Connie admitted to herself that the boys did look fetching, dressed in their Sunday bests. Red seemed a bit shy and was blushing; I know why, she thought to herself.

Violet grabbed Jimmy by the arm and slipped her hand through the gap between his arm and his chest; she leant into him. They all walked into the hut.

* * *

Connie stood with Miss Appleworth, whose hair dark hair was tied in a bun. She was tall and upright, her waist narrow. She stood straight in her plain black dress and sensible shoes, the same as she wore at school. She was strait-laced and proper. Connie thought she hadn't aged a day since she was her pupil; her face was free from lines. Miss Appleworth held onto her Victorian values, her discipline in school strict and military-like. Her pupils didn't misbehave through her threat of the cane. Even now as her colleague, Connie swallowed hard. Connie asked Miss Appleworth about her thoughts on the war, and how it would affect them at school, with Mr Martin leaving. Miss Appleworth talked about her father's view and how he thought there should be conscription for all the young single men; he couldn't see there being any other way. He kept saying they would need all the men they could get. Connie didn't like the sound of it. She hoped to herself that Red would not go, not as they were growing closer; she wanted to see where it would lead.

Vicar Thomas rang his hand bell and got everyone's attention. Connie knew it was the time to act on their plan. The villagers all began making their way to the two long trestle tables and chairs which lined the length of the hall. Where was Violet? She couldn't see her. There were too many people in the crowd.

'Miss Appleworth, come and sit with me and my father; you can tell me more about how you became a teacher.' Connie jostled her way past Alfred and Flora Crabb, Jimmy's father and mother.

'Of course, Miss Stevens; lead on.' Connie couldn't believe how easy Miss Appleworth was making it. It was going to work. Connie jostled past Jimmy's Uncle Walter Crabb. There was Violet. Why did she have to sit right at the other end? Connie walked quicker, turning behind to make sure Miss Appleworth was still following, which she was. It was difficult for her to move through the gossiping throng. She could see father; he was sitting with free seats to his right and Violet and her mother and father opposite. Come on, she thought to herself; let's get sat down quick. She didn't want anyone else to sit in that spot; it would ruin the evening. It would be months and months before there was another social evening where they would be able to play matchmakers.

'Oh, shittle bum hurdle,' Connie said under her breath, hoping it wouldn't carry to Miss Appleworth. It was the old spinster Miss 'smelly cat' Crabb: she was heading straight for the seat next to Father. The plan was going to falter before it even started. She watched helplessly as smelly old Miss Crabb with her hunched gait sprang forward like one of her old cats stalking a mouse. Redver stood up quick. He pushed in his chair and started to talk to Miss Crabb, her annoyance clear.

'So, Miss Crabb: I'm glad I spotted you. I wanted to ask you: I think you have some kittens? I'm after one to become a ratter for the stables,' Redver said.

Connie could have kissed him. She pulled Miss Appleworth by the hand and sat her down next to her father before any of the other old spinsters nicked the seat. Her father with his wide smile, his hair thinning. His beard grey and black, speckled and thick like sheep's wool. His face square, his arms strong and powerful; big thick fingers, making the glass he was holding look small. They all shared a toast before saying grace. Connie and Violet shared a knowing smile. Connie looked up the table and saw Red sitting next to Miss Crabb. She smiled and felt her stomach tingle.

* * *

'Thanks, Red; thanks for stepping in like that and waylaying Miss Crabb,' Connie said as they stood by the corner of the stage. The tables had been folded up and put away, the chairs lined the walls and there was room for dancing. Mrs Wrixon, the vicar's wife, went to the old upright piano that took centre stage. She was thin and taller than the vicar, her hair black; she wore spectacles and her eyes were small like a mouse. Her voice was full and harmonious.

'You're welcome, Connie. Mind you, she stank to high heaven,' Red said, smiling.

'Well, least you had a date for the meal,' Jimmy said. 'Shame it was my smelly old aunt.'

Violet pulled his arm that she was attached to and said: 'Don't tease him, Jimmy. She stinks, and her bloody house… My god: me and Mother went there once to get some hems stitched, and the number of cats she must have in that small dingy cottage of hers. We were only minutes dropping them dresses off. I must have seen twenty, all up on her kitchen dresser, drinking from the sink, on the table; ugh, and the smell of cat's pee, it was horrible.' She made a face.

'You don't need to tell me, love. Bloody hell! Can't believe I'm related to her! We hardly speak, and I did anything to avoid going there as a boy.' Jimmy held his nose. 'Think me mother and father tried to say something to her when I was younger, but she wouldn't listen; no, not my Aunt Bertha. She just said them cats were her family.'

Mrs Wrixon began to play the piano, playing *Sister Susie's Sewing Shirts for Soldiers*. Violet and Jimmy began to dance. To Connie they looked so happy and in love, their eyes trained on each other. She was glad she was there with Red and that they hadn't signed up. She saw the posters everywhere she looked now, the picture of Kitchener, "YOUR COUNTRY NEEDS YOU!" in the Post Office, at the train station. She didn't want Red to go.

'Red, you know about this war and everything we're fighting for – you know you don't have to sign up and fight, not even with what people are saying.' Connie looked at Red; she had to raise her voice above the music. 'My dad and your father both agree; you're needed here. You know, just because other lads your age are going doesn't mean you have to.'

'I know, Connie. It's – well, it's difficult, you know, when you hear about it and see boys younger than me going. Like Ken Smyth: he's so young and he's brave enough to go, you know, and do his bit.' She saw Red's eyes look down to the wooden floorboards.

'I know, but your family want you here.' She wanted to say she wanted him too. 'With your father not being well, your mother wants you around. You can't leave her with Edna; it will drive her mad.'

'Come on, let's go and join them out dancing, shall we?' he said. Connie felt Red's strong rough hand hold her lightly and gently tug her out onto the makeshift dance floor. Mrs Wrixon, seeing the floor fill, changed to playing a light two-step. Connie looked over and saw her father take Miss Appleworth's hand and begin to dance. She smelt Red's neck, musky. She felt safe, secure and content. He had a habit of making her feel like that. He could be the one for her. How should she know? How was Violet so sure Jimmy was the one and only for her? Violet always seemed to have so much confidence in her mind.

After dancing for an hour – which seemed like only seconds – the couples took a break, as did Mrs Wrixon, who went and talked to her husband.

'Oh, my feet ache,' Jimmy said. They went and stood at

the side.

The doors to the hut opened; everyone stopped talking and looked. Admiral Fox and his sons Theodore and Sampson walked in.

'Cor, them two sons have filled out, ain't they, Connie?' Violet whispered in her ear.

'Shh, Violet, we don't want them hearing.' She poked at Violet to be quiet. Theodore was dressed in his khaki army officer's uniform. Connie knew he was a captain, or something like that; she didn't understand the insignia. Sampson stood back from his brother, in clean navy jacket and dark trousers, his face round, less defined than his father's and brother's. His hair dark, he was an inch shorter than his brother.

'He's a captain now, you know. Who would have thought that bullying tearaway who plagued our childhood would be a flippin' captain who the country is depending on?' Violet whispered.

'I know; he and Red's sister made it a right nightmare for us; and his bloody gang.' Connie moved closer to Violet and spoke straight to her ear, watching as Admiral Fox went to the stage. She looked over at Sampson; he waved over at the four of them. They shared some good memories too: her, Red, Violet, James and Sampson, making hideouts in hedgerows and barns, being in their own little gang, trying to evade Theo, Edna, Thomas and David Smyth and their rival gang, them being that little bit older, thinking they could tell the young children what to do all the time. She had been so surprised back then how Theo was so vicious to his own flesh and blood; and Edna the same to Red.

The Admiral, dressed in his green and brown tweed suit, approached the centre of the stage. He was confident addressing his workforce and his village: the squire of all he surveyed. His white beard fell from his narrow, chiselled face. His white hair was confined by his hat. He stood no higher than the piano. His brown brogues were pristine clean. He stood with intelligent eyes, confident. He moved slowly and deliberately past the black piano and addressed the village.

'Thank you all for your efforts this summer, it has been a testing time for all of us.' He spoke with authority. 'I know many of you have loved ones away and that is hard in itself, but that has also left a burden on you that are here: more work to be done with fewer men. I know your country needs you but not all of you have to go and fight. We need to feed ourselves. I know only too well the threat there is out at sea; our ships are going to be under attack like never before. We import so much of our food there are bound to be shortages; that is why our work is so important. If you feel that you have to go, I won't stand in your way and I will always try and find a place for you when you return. But don't think that is the only way you can serve your nation. We have a responsibility to provide food, which is as vital as fighting.'

The Admiral stood back. They all clapped and cheered him from the stage. Connie felt goosebumps down her arm; the Admiral was speaking from the heart. For the first time, it brought home to her how much their lives were at risk, even here. If he was talking about food shortages then that had to be likely. She looked over at Theodore and Sampson. Theo was shaking his head from side to side, his hat under his shoulder, his eyes steely, his moustache cut and trimmed. He was tall and imposing, with thick blonde hair.

'There you are, Red: the Squire says you're as important back here as going to France,' she said, taking his hand.

'Yes, I suppose. It doesn't feel like it, though; and then you've got Brigadier and the vicar banging on about going and fighting.'

'But the Admiral, he's the one that matters.' Connie tried to push home the fact that she wanted Red to take in what had been said.

Sampson walked over. He wasn't handsome like Theo, but his good nature and easy way made up for it. Connie saw he was dressed in his blue university blazer with the Christchurch emblem and tan slacks. He stood shorter than Red. His brown hair was brushed back and his face was pale and withdrawn.

'Hey, Sampson, good to see you back,' Red said, and Sampson shook his hand. Sampson then shook Jimmy's.

'Yeah, good to see you. It's been too long,' Jimmy said.

'Yes, you boys too; I'm glad you're here,' Sampson said, shaking Jimmy's hand. 'And look at you two beautiful women all dressed up! Makes a change from the two skinny urchins with mud on their faces, and that was only a couple of years ago!'

'Oh, shut up! Flattery will get you nowhere,' Vi said, as the five of them smiled at each other.

'Well, guess the old gang is back together,' Sampson said. He patted Jimmy and Red on the shoulders. Connie sensed he had matured.

'How was university? Are you finished?' Connie asked Sampson.

'More or less; the war has put paid to that. I loved it, it's a wonderful place. It's such a shame you couldn't experience it,' Sampson replied.

Mrs Wrixon struck up the piano, and the dance floor filled again. Violet and Jimmy were the first to start moving. Sampson put out his hand and Connie took it; his hand was soft to the touch and clammy. She looked over her shoulder and saw Red standing, his face flushed and fixed.

7

12th January 1915

The horses were fed and cleaned out, the cows milked. Captain neighed and sighed; he was attached to the wagon and Red was up on the bench holding the reins. Jimmy was seated next to him. The sound of the steam engine driving the threshing machine was loud and carried to them. The air felt cold against his face; the sun shone through but was low in the sky, providing no warmth. Red called for Captain to walk on. They rounded to the rick of sheaves, the stack half its original height. Soon all the rats would flee their winter home.

Red brought Captain to a halt. George and his uncles threw down the sheaves and Red and Jimmy stacked; Red happy to be moving to keep warm. Red would be happier when spring came; two more months of cold. Father was out keeping an eye on things. He'd said he'd never missed threshing and he wasn't 'bout to start. He was bent double, coughing. He gave his instructions how things should be done. Slow and methodical, the same as usual. Red knew he was hiding how he ill he was; he'd seen plenty of sick animals. His father's back hunched, he spat, coughed, then spat again. Red hated seeing him this way. He looked at his father standing by the rick. He seemed thinner, even more so since Christmas. He'd been in and out of work, and his cough seemed to have changed too, reaching lower down in his chest. He watched as his father coughed, retched and spat out a sticky ball of phlegm.

The wagon was full, so Red and Jimmy took it back to the thresher and unloaded. There were half a dozen men, the gang of John the plough who ran the engine. Ploughing would begin once threshing was finished. Red loved the old steam engine: the noise, the smoky smell. It went back to when he was young, he supposed. He was always excited to hear the steam engine come to the farm, and John letting him drive it across the field; that made his day back then. Dust covered all the men from head to foot. The large belt ran from drive wheel to drive wheel, looking too flimsy for the power of the whirling maw of the thresher. The unmistakable odour of coal, grease and dried wheat filled Red's nostrils and reminded him of happy times working with his father. It saddened him to see him the way he was.

Mr Grey looked pleased; everyone working hard, the threshed grain being bagged up and ready to be taken to the mill. Then harvest would finally be done with, and they could get the land ploughed. John had told him they would be using the steam plough: John's big Forster's engine, Titan. There was more ploughing to be done this year; they'd even been told that Meadow Field would have to be done. It was needed for the war effort, and a crop of potatoes.

Red unloaded the last of the sheaves with Jimmy and made the shuttle back to the rick. He came around the bend and saw his father laid out twitching on the ground. George stood over him.

'What's happening? What's up?' Red shouted as he jumped down from the wagon's bench. Jimmy went with him.

'It's some sort of fit or summink,' George said, with deep concern in his voice. 'Looks like there's blood in his spittle.' Red knelt down to his father's side along with George. His father's eyes were blinking, his legs and arms twitching. Red took his handkerchief from his pocket and wiped the spit from his father's mouth.

'Get 'im on wagon, and back to the house,' Mr Grey said as he came up. 'It won't do him any good out here in the cold. I told him 'e should stay in. We could get on without 'im, but you know how stubborn he is.'

''Ere, I ain't dead yet, Mr Grey. I can still be of use. These youngens don't know it all yet, do 'em,' Father said as his eyes opened. Red felt relieved.

'Ay, they don't that,' Mr Grey agreed.

* * *

Mother stood at the side of his bed and fussed to make him comfortable. Red and George, covered in dust, caught their breath after having carried Father upstairs. The dresser stood against the far wall, hessian curtains pulled to dim the light.

It felt cold, not really any warmer than outside. Red and George looked at each other, not sure what to say. Red knew it was nature taking its course. Mr Grey had told him that he would fetch a doctor up from Bridport.

Father lapsed with another fit. Mother sat on the edge of the bed and tended to him. She held his hand and said, ''Tis going to be all right, Ham, it's going to be all right. Don't you dare die on me, you hear? I'm to be first, is that clear?' Red felt helpless; his father so withered; what could he do? He'd never heard his father tell him that he loved him, but whose father did? He was a good man, though, a good father. He hadn't beat him, not like some fathers in the village.

''Ere, young 'en, don't 'e go off joining up, not when I'm

gone, do you hear? You're to stay and look out for your mother, right, and make sure that ploughing is done right. I want them furrows straight and true, mind; and look after Captain. You treat Captain well; he's the best horse I've ever 'ad.' Father sighed, weak.

'Don't talk like that, Father,' George said, with tears in the corners of his eyes. 'You'll be there to keep an eye on us all!'

Red felt his sadness grow; he didn't like to see his father suffer in this way. If it was one of the horses suffering, Father would have the strength to put him down. It was the way nature was; there was no being compassionate if it had outlived its purpose, and if it was suffering it was the kindest thing to do.

'You, lad, Redver, you listen to me.' Red knelt down at the side of the bed. 'You're only young, lad; this war ain't no place for 'e. If you do go you'll be no more than fodder; you'll be no more than fodder for them guns, like oats for my horses; they'll eat 'e up and spit you out dead!'

Father tried to cough but his effort was weak. His breath slowed. Red watched as mother began to cry, and father took his last faltering breath.

'No, Ham, please!' Mother sobbed.

George went to his mother and put his large arm around her and said: 'He's gone, Mother; he's better off. It's for the best.'

'It's not best for me; he can't go! I don't know what I will do without him. I've never loved anyone so much. He always looked after me. I know I nagged him, but I loved him. I never thought he would go before me. He was always so fit and strong.'

'I know. He was for all of us,' George said.

Red felt his tears roll down his cheek; a pang of regret he hadn't told his father how he felt for him. He should have done. He wanted to help make his mother feel better but he didn't know the words. His tears stung his eyes. Mr Grey would want the two of them back out; the work wouldn't wait.

* * *

They were in the kitchen, home to so many fond memories. Mother sat back in the rocking chair next to the range. It was warm but she looked cold. She cowered under the blanket, pulling it up to her neck. She was lifeless.

Edna was barely being civil. She was in her work clothes of black full-length skirt and white blouse tucked in, her dark hair falling limp to her shoulders. Mother didn't bother much with anything since Father had died. There was no baking and not much cooking. She sat and rocked back and forth in the chair. She only talked when asked a direct question; then it was one word answers. When Charles and Mary came to visit with Dot, she couldn't even raise a smile. Red took some bread and covered it in beef dripping and ate it whilst he swigged on his tea.

Edna said, 'I'm to wed Sydney and you and Mother will be moving in with George and Dot. It will mean you sharing a bedroom with the children, but at least you will have a roof over your head.' Edna spoke with swift authority, sneering as she did.

Red could see she was glad about him having to share a room.

'When will the wedding be?' Red said with fake interest.

'Two weeks; and before you ask, we are moving in with his parents. It will only be a very short-term arrangement. We are planning on buying our own place very soon. We've saved up our wages. We like the look of the new houses they are building at St Michael's Lane off Ropewalks. They're not as big or fancy as them in Victoria Grove but well, it will do for the two of us. There's no garden to have to look after, only a yard for drying our washing. Oh, you'll be welcome to visit, you, Mother and George, once we're settled in.'

Mother nodded from the corner. Red knew this was for Mother's benefit; at least Edna was trying to make Mother feel better.

Two weeks to get out of the house! It was standard, but didn't make it any easier. Red was not looking forward to having to share a room with Charles and Mary; they could make a hell of a lot of noise.

Red went to the cake tin and found it empty, so he took a piece of bread and smothered it in butter. He washed it down with a mouthful of milky tea.

'Yes; when we are settled in, you must all come and visit,' continued Edna. 'I will put on a big Sunday tea and you can all come round; 'course you must. You will like that, won't you, Mother?' Mother nodded from the corner.

Red missed the presence of his father; he missed the banter. He missed the fun which was drained from the family. Mother was in her shell and Edna was busy with planning and organising her life as well as everyone else's, as if no one else existed; poor old Sydney.

He missed Mother's rabbit pie and fruit cake. He didn't have the energy to argue. He was working twice as hard, doing the work of Father. Mr Grey did say to him today what a great job he was doing with the horses.

* * *

Mother died in her bed in the night, broken-hearted. She wanted to join back up with Father.

Edna and Red went into the bedroom and said goodbye.

'I'll miss her,' Red said as he stroked her hair. 'She looks so peaceful. She will be with Father and Granfer. She's in the best place.'

'Yes. She loved the grandchildren,' Edna said. She came past Red and at the side of the bed, she slid Martha's wedding ring off her finger. 'She won't need this where she is going and I'm sure she would have given it to me.' She put the ring into her dress pocket.

Red was flabbergasted: 'That should go to George first! He can decide.'

'Oh, rubbish. I think she was about to give it to me.' Edna held her hand over her pocket, walked past Red and went to the chest of drawers. She pulled open the second drawer, Father's drawer, and took out his wedding ring. 'I'll take this one too. You ain't getting married anytime soon; me and Sydney can put them to good use.'

Before Red could answer, Edna was walking down the stairs, both rings in her hand. If Red saw his sister on his deathbed it would be one day too soon.

8

10th February 1915

'You know, for Edna to take the ring from my mother's finger: I couldn't believe that, not even of her,' Red said, finding it hard to fathom even now. He was talking to Jimmy as they rode on the wagon. Red had Captain and Tully harnessed together on the water wagon. The light, empty wagon jumped and rattled over the loose blue and black flint which littered the track. 'And it all so soon after Father died. Why does she have to be so nasty like that? I mean, I don't want them. But by rights, they should go to George, and if he didn't want them then she should have 'em, but then to go to the drawer of the dresser and take Father's ring as well. I don't get it; she had the same upbringing as me and George, didn't she? The same parents. Why on earth does she have to be so bloody nasty?'

'I don't know, mate; beats me. I'm glad Violet is so easy to please.' Jimmy smiled.

'There wasn't no way I was going to her bloody wedding. George and Dot went, well, George gave her away; but for Edna to wear Mother's and Father's rings... I couldn't face her,' Red said, shaking his head.

Red drove the wagon down to the stream and they filled

it with water, taking it in turns to pump. The steam engines pulling the plough would need filling soon. Before they finished Mr Grey came over with his horse and cart.

'Red, Admiral wants to see you; can you go and have a talk with him down at the Manor?' Mr Grey stood in his black top hat, with his watch pulled out studying the time.

'Now, Mr Grey?' Red said, as he looked down from the back of the wagon.

'Yes; I'm going heading that way. Jimmy, 'e can carry on here.' Mr Grey put the watch back in his waistcoat pocket.

Red got down from the pump and went and joined Mr Grey.

* * *

Dorothy let him into the Manor's kitchen. He stood by the range warming his hands. Fanny Hansford eyed him as she took her orders from Dorothy to go and clean the fireplaces. Dot went off to tell Admiral that Red was there. Mrs Fooks busied herself at the large range, stirring and adding to the pot.

Red was sure he would be given notice to leave the cottage. After all, with Father and Mother gone, it should go to a family. It would be sad to leave after spending his entire life there. Everything was changing and quickly. He couldn't have imagined six months ago being an orphan; it sounded funny to him, his parents both dead. He missed his father, having him around, having him to talk to, and having him to banter with. Connie and Stephen asked him in to share their meals as once Mother had to them. But it wasn't fair to ask Connie to cook for them both. Of course, George and Dorothy asked him over. He didn't see much of his uncles; they'd never been close.

'Admiral will see you now. You better take them boots off,' Dorothy said, pointing at his mud-caked boots. 'We don't want to have to clean that mess from the rugs.' His sister-in-law stood proudly in her white pinny and black dress; head maid, only taking her orders from the family and the cook, Mrs Flora Fooks. He undid his bootlaces and placed the boots next to the large range. The kitchen here was larger than the whole cottage; he felt intimidated. He followed Dot, glad of her presence.

'Don't worry; Admiral's kind. He won't be harsh.' Dot led him forward.

He followed Dot down the long passage. He felt naked in his dirty socks, sliding on the polished parquet floor. 'Course, he delivered milk to the back door nearly every morning as a child. But this was the first time he'd been this far into the Manor. He may have been friends playing with Sampson when younger but it never went as far as an invite inside. They didn't even play in the gardens; this was way out of bounds. Red looked into the large rooms as they walked slowly down the passage: the huge library, the dining room, and past the large ornate oak banisters that led up the wide staircase.

'In there, Red, that's his study. Knock on the door and remember to stand up straight. Admiral doesn't like slouches.' Dorothy left him as he faced the door. He felt his heart beating faster and his palms sweat. He knocked.

'Come!' Red heard Admiral bellow. He opened the door. The room had a large window looking down over the terraced garden; below that, fields of pasture with white dots grazing. Beyond that, the railway line cutting through to Bridport. The Admiral was sitting back in his chair behind the desk. He scratched his all white beard and ran his hand through it and looked at Red. Red tried to stand up straight. The walls, covered with oak panels, sucked the light in. The Admiral's tweed hat was on the desk. He was dressed in his green flecked suit and a crisp clean shirt with dark green tie.

'Good man, Red; I won't keep you. I know you are busy

out ploughing. Your father was a loyal servant to me all these years. He was a good, thoughtful, hard-working man, who spent his life here as the carter, and we are all going to miss him.' He looked Redver in the eye.

'Thank you, sir, Admiral.' Red couldn't think of anything else.

'I'll get to the point. You know the cottage is tied. I don't let single men have the house. It's not sensible. I've to put a family in, you know that, don't you?'

'Yes, I do, sir.' Red looked down at his feet. He hoped this wouldn't take long and he could get back out to work. He tried to stand up straight. He wanted to put his hands in his pockets but he resisted the urge.

'Good, good. Well look, I will be fair. Mr Grey says your father has trained you up all these years. He says you're the natural one with the horses and his word is that you should take on as carter. You're younger than I would think. But your brother and your uncles, they've not shown the interest like you have, so look, I'm happy to take Mr Grey's advice and offer you your father's position, the position of carter. Given your age I'll give you an extra shilling a week; it's not as much as your father but it reflects your experience.' Admiral looked towards Red from behind his long white beard. Red felt mixed emotions: so sad his father wasn't there to see him step into his shoes, but thinking how proud he would have been.

'I'll make a deal with you too, young Kingson: you can have a month in the cottage, get yourself engaged to be married, and you can stay in the cottage. It's more than I should because it won't look good me letting a single man stay on.' Red was speechless. To be offered carter and the cottage: it was more than fair.

'It's very kind, thank you, sir.' Red looked up and glanced at the Admiral who was sitting back in his chair.

'That's all I've to say. Be on with you; that ploughing is more important than ever. And listen: there is going to be more talk of joining up. At some point I'm sure the government will introduce conscription. Until then, your job is safe here, do you hear me? Don't go listening to the vicar or Brigadier; those two wouldn't be happy until every last man is gone. They've no idea about farming and what is needed. It's bad enough me having one son in the army. I don't want to lose more good men.' He shook his head.

Red nodded to the Admiral and left the study. He walked out to the kitchen and went about putting his boots back on. He was speechless; the Admiral being so fair on letting him stay on, if only temporarily.

9

20th February 1915

Connie and Violet got off the train at Dorchester station. The station was much grander than Moreton, with the whole platform under the large cast iron roof. Pigeons roosted on the heavy beams and cooed. Smoke from the engine was slow to float away, shrouding passengers in smoky fog. The station was busy, and their carriage had been full with most heading for the market. The khaki uniforms of the soldiers were dull in the winter light. The camaraderie was clear to see as mates jostled, played, laughed and bantered together. Connie watched as they ran from the train, looking to catch the next, heading for camps in the south-east. Outside the snow was melting, turning to slush underfoot.

Connie, with her bonnet pulled down tight, held Violet's hand as they made their way to the High Street. The wind, funnelled by the street, whistled down, pushing Connie and Vi as it funnelled down through the shops on either side.

'I see your father was out walking with Miss Appleworth last Sunday,' Violet said. She was wrapped tightly in her warmest coat. 'Seems like we may have done some good.'

'He likes her. It can't go anywhere; she won't give up

teaching. It's a stupid rule, to think you would be any different teacher just because you're married.' Connie walked around a couple who had stopped in the centre of the pavement.

'They can be of some company, even if they can't sleep together,' Violet said as they walked fast down the street.

'Violet, shut up. You can't say that.' She told her friend off. 'Look, Vi, it's Sampson. I've not seen him since harvest festival.' Sampson strolled over. Connie could see he walked with confidence.

'Good morning, Constance; morning, Violet. It's good to see you. I'm sorry I haven't seen more of you two, but I had to go back to Oxford and tie up my loose ends before I could come back for good.'

'Oh, so you're back for good. I thought you would be away to London or somewhere fancy,' Violet blurted.

'Haha! No, I did think about following Theodore to the army and all, but Father has insisted I come and learn the ropes on the farm. He says giving one son to the war is more than he owes his country, after the service he gave, and he is so desperate for men, he insisted,' Sampson said, looking from Violet to Connie. Dressed in a navy suit and tie, he looked smart. A proper gentleman, Connie thought.

'Oh, we are going to see a lot more of you from now on,' Violet said. Connie felt herself blush.

'And I should say you two have grown into two fine young women. I think we were all little urchins back then, weren't we?' Sampson stood tall with his shoulders back.

'We were, Sampson. Look, sorry; we've so much to do. We've all the shopping to do for the wedding,' Violet said.

'Oh yes, of course: the wedding. Why don't we meet up in a couple of hours? We can have tea and I can drive you back in my new motor car; then you won't have to wait around for the train and you can have more time.'

In Fields of Gold and Red

'That's very kind, Sampson, but I don't...' Connie was interrupted by Violet.

'Oh, yes, Sampson! I've never been in a motor car before.' Connie felt herself blush again. Why was Violet always saying the wrong thing and at the wrong time?

* * *

The tearoom was full but they found a free table in the bay window. They looked out, watching the market day throng. Connie noticed more soldiers darting from shop to shop.

The waitress took their orders for tea and went to fetch the freshly made pot from the kitchen at the back. The walls were decorated with ornate oak panelling and made most of the room dark.

'I was at Christ Church College. Believe it or not, that was where the vicar went. He's an absolute legend there even now. They talk about his achievements as a boxer and footballer; he won so many contests, he won so many competitions and was unbeaten against Cambridge.' Sampson looked at Connie with his soft brown eyes as he talked. She noticed his lips curl into a smile.

'What were you like in the ring, Sampson?' Violet asked.

'Me? Oh, I was useless. I should have gone to his boxing club in the hall like Redver and James did. Father didn't think I should, and sports has never been my thing; I preferred to read and to study.'

'What did you get your degree in, Sampson?' Connie asked.

'It was in History. I love reading the classics too, and Shakespeare; and of course I've had to study Latin since Eton,' he replied, looking from Connie to Violet and then back to Connie.

Connie sipped at her tea, careful not to gulp it.

'I've never read any Shakespeare. Of course, Miss

Appleworth says I should.'

'Yes, you should. I must admit I like *Macbeth*; that's my favourite.' Connie noticed how his mannerisms were so different to her father's, precise and quiet, as he sipped at his tea and didn't speak until his mouth was clear. 'You know, Connie, I'm sure Father and Mother would be happy for you to come and spend time in our library; the books hardly get looked at these days, and we have so many.'

Connie's palms warmed and goosebumps broke out on her arm. She held her cup by the thin ringed handle. She didn't know if she was holding it in the correct way. She cast her eyes around to see how the other ladies were holding theirs; she seemed to be doing it the same. She hoped Sampson wouldn't notice.

'If they wouldn't mind, I would love to.' Connie looked over at Violet and could see her eyes glazing over.

'So are you going to give us a ride home in that motor car of yours. like you said you would? Or was that all talk?' Violet said. Why on earth couldn't she be more subtle? Connie bit down on her lip.

'Of course, of course. How rude of me! Follow me, ladies.' Sampson settled the bill and left a tip on the table. Connie and Violet picked up their two shopping bags. They walked briskly. The sun was poking through thin grey clouds; there were signs that the grey cloud was lifting as pockets of blue filtered through. They walked through the slush of melting snow and Sampson took them to West Street where the motor car was parked.

'This is a Morris bullnose; we should be able to get up to fifty miles an hour,' Sampson said, his enthusiasm clear. 'Squeeze in.' Connie and Violet put their shopping in the back and shared the passenger seat. The Morris's bodywork was bright yellow with an up-and-over black canvas roof. Sampson pulled the roof back. 'It's more fun in the open air.' On the running board were the spare wheel and petrol can.

Connie was impressed. She'd heard all about motor cars. Motor cars and motorbikes were all Red, James and Father wanted to talk about when they were not discussing the latest football results. They always thought them so exciting; but she didn't really give them a second thought. She would be getting the first ride.

The Morris made a funny wheezing and blowing noise, not unlike the big steam engines but smaller. It was cold, moving in the open air; she pulled her bonnet further down. She noticed Violet do the same. The front window gave little protection from the wind. It was much faster than a horse and cart; it could be as fast as the steam train. She didn't know if it was right that smoke was pouring from the back as they made their way through Askerswell. Even so, she thought it better than having to wait around on a windswept railway platform, waiting for a train that half the time wouldn't be on time and the other half didn't turn up at all.

As they came out of the village, Sampson swerved to miss the coal wagon. Coming down the slope and around the left bend, the wheels lifted on Connie's side.

'Agggh!' Connie shrieked with Violet. 'Watch it, Sampson! I don't want to see my breakfast again!' Violet shouted. Sampson laughed loudly. 'It's all right; that's nothing.'

The Morris jostled and bumped its way along the rutted lane, rounding the right turn into Yellow Lane, the sandstone banks high on either side. It struggled slowly up, wheezing, the white smoke thicker behind creating a fog of its own. Connie was sure it was moving slower and slower and the wheels struggled for grip. When they reached the bottom of Snowdrop Hill the Morris bullnose ground to a halt on the icy lane.

In Fields of Gold and Red

'Sorry, ladies; that's the trouble with these new contraptions. They often come to a stop with no warning. You wait here. I will go and get some help from the farm.' Sampson ran off up the hill. Connie looked at the bank, grass poking through the melting snow. They were at the bottom of the steep gradient of the hill. On her left, out of the motor car window, she could see Dorset Horns grazing on bare patches of pasture that were islands in the snow, their white coats making them partially invisible; their full winter wool looking warm. On the bank, the white drooping heads of snowdrops were on the wane.

'So what do you think? Connie, he's quite a dish now, don't you think?'

'He's certainly, em, matured. He's smart, too. He'd never look at the likes of you and me though, would he? And you know his father is just like Miss Appleworth's. He would never allow him to marry below his position to the likes of you and me.'

'Shut up! I saw the way he looked at you, and it's different to Miss Appleworth. After all, he's a man of age; he wouldn't need his father's permission.'

'Yes, but still his father could disinherit him, couldn't he? Anyway, this is stupid talk; I don't even like him,' Connie said.

'Oh, yeah, you like him. I know you too well! You were smiling when he was going on about those bloody plays and books. Come to my family library, Miss Constance; oh, Mother and Father won't mind,' Violet said, mimicking Sampson's voice.

'He sounds nothing like that, Violet.' Connie felt her feet and hands getting cold. 'He was only being kind, and interesting; they're good plays, I'm told. I was only smiling because I was learning something; you should try having an open mind, Violet,' she said, and poked her friend in the ribs with her finger.

'Oh get off! Anyway, why are we waiting here like this? I'm getting cold. Why don't we walk home?'

'Good point; come on, let's walk,' Connie agreed. They got out and hitched the hems of their dresses up and began to walk. They reached the brow of the hill and saw Sampson on his way back.

'Are you two deserting me?' he said, out of breath.

'Sorry, yes. We were getting cold waiting,' Violet said.

'We weren't sure how long you would be, Sampson,' Connie said.

'I understand. I don't think I would have waited if I was you. I did mean it about the books; we have a large library hardly anyone ever uses. Connie, if you wanted to you'd be more than welcome, anytime.' Connie saw his brown eyes watering with the cold and exertion.

'Yes, I may take you up on that.'

Connie saw three shire horses walking up the lane with Redver riding sidesaddle; this must be the help that Sampson had organised. She smiled up at Red as he controlled the horses and brought them to a stop. She saw the lead shire was Captain. She went over and stroked and scratched his nose where he liked it. He gave a friendly snort.

'Hey, you two, how's your day?' Red said.

'Good, thank you, Red,' Connie and Violet said, smiling up at him.

'Red, the car's down the bottom. Come with me and pull it back. Sorry, ladies, we better get going,' Sampson said.

Connie could see a frown and look of annoyance on Red's face.

'Yes, sir,' Red said. Then: 'See you later,' he said to Connie and Violet before commanding the horses forward.

Connie and Violet walked off in the opposite direction to

the two men and the horses.

'Why are you blushing again, Connie?'

'Oh, I don't know why. Shut up, will you?' Connie strolled off away from Violet.

10

7th March 1915

Redver walked up into the old copse above Ashcombe that nestled under Ashcombe Beacon. He watched as a goldfinch with its red cap and sleek body flitted from one fresh green bud to another. He breathed in the woodland air which smelt of pine, ash and hazel. He had an hour before he was to meet with Connie down at the bridge in Meadow Field. He felt so under-prepared. He'd been thinking about what to do since being called in to see Admiral Fox. He thought of Connie, how happy they could be. He felt he should go and do his duty; even though his father had told him not to on his deathbed; but now he was gone. Shouldn't he go and do his duty? Fight for his country, do his duty, like Vicar Wrixon preached?

He could hardly think straight. His mind was clouded by his sadness, his ache for his family. It felt suffocating. He wanted it to be back as it was. 'Course, things couldn't go on forever, but his Granfer had seemed to; why not his own father? How unfair was it that they were gone, that they weren't here to give him advice? Granfer would have known what to say. He walked through the clearing, and thin shards of sunlight fell on the woodland floor. The old oak trunk, more weathered, provided a handy place to sit, a place he had spent so much time with Granfer.

What should he do? If he was to marry and to keep the house, it would be more or less everything as normal, he could see it now. He could marry Connie and soon they could have children. He would work all his life on the farm, doing his father's job; then when he had children he would teach his son like his father had taught him. That would be easy, except would Connie agree to marry him? She liked him and she liked Sampson; he knew that. Why had Sampson come back? It made things more complicated. What did she want? Why were women so hard to work out? If he was going to ask Connie to marry him, it would have to be this afternoon. It would be the last time they could spend time together before Admiral's deadline was up. How should he do it? What should he say? He didn't even have a ring! Jimmy and Violet would be happy to share their day; they could make it a big double wedding; it could all work out.

If he was married, he wouldn't have to go and fight. Connie might even marry him to stop him from going. He didn't want that. He wanted her to marry him for love.

* * *

Redver stood next to Jimmy; the church was full behind him. The whole of the two villages inside; every pew was filled with friends and family. Red looked up at the high vaulted ceiling and followed the curved stone with his eye. He let out a huge breath, and took another, deeper and slower; he tried to calm himself. He looked at the face of Vicar Wrixon, who gave him a reassuring smile back. Jimmy moved from one leg to the other. They were both dressed in their Sunday suits. Jimmy took a deep breath; he was nervous too.

Mrs Wrixon sat at the organ, waiting for the signal the

bride was about to enter with her father. Red remembered last Sunday afternoon.

* * *

It had been warm for spring and the daffodils were in full bloom by the bridge, their deep yellow flowers contrasting with the shades of green ferns and rushes on the bank. He was late and Connie was already there. She looked so pretty in her blue bonnet neatly tied, her blonde hair spiralling out.

'I'm so sorry I'm late, Connie; I thought I should wash before I came down.' He couldn't help but smile and look her in the eye.

'You don't have to apologise. It's such a beautiful afternoon, and it's warmer than it's been for so long.' Red felt his body ache. When had she grown so beautiful? Her smile crossed her whole face, her lips attractive and wide. He wanted to kiss her like he'd done so many times. Surely they should have done more by now? He was sure Jimmy had with Violet, even before they were engaged.

'Let's walk down by the river,' he suggested, as he took Connie's hand in his. Her skin felt so soft and warm. He wanted to touch more of her.

They crossed the bridge and into the grass of the pasture. The dozen or so shorthorns grazed at the far end, chewing slowly. Red breathed in and smelt the lush fresh grass, and Connie's lavender. He thought over the words he should use. They walked to the bend in the river where the bank was high from the water, and sat down.

'Connie, I've been wanting to talk to you. I've decided on something. You know, this isn't easy for me to put into words.' Connie looked at him; he could tell she wasn't sure what he was about to say. Nor was he.

'You know, I've been thinking a lot about the future, and – well – you know with the war going on and all, everyone's saying that young single men should go and fight.' He found it hard to talk about how he was feeling; it was so easy when he practised up in the copse. He looked down at the river; it was shallow but ran briskly. In places, it bubbled up whitewater over underwater stones. Opposite them, the bank rolled to a beach of shale and larger stones, dragged there by higher waters in winter. He felt his throat tighten; it was important for him to say this right.

'Red, you don't have to. You know your father and mother, they didn't want you to go. Admiral has said don't go. You're too valuable a worker to leave. What will you be? Another Tommy going off, fighting for your country. Don't listen to the vicar or the Brigadier.' She held his hand when she looked him in the eye. Red felt as if his emotions would run free, like the river below. He should pull on his reins. This was so hard. He could change his mind and propose, change what he was going to say; he could just come out with it; it would only take seconds, seconds that could change the rest of his life, seconds that could mean his life went on, went on with Connie.

'Red, what are you thinking? You know, just because others are signing up, going to fight, it doesn't mean you have to. You don't. I know it's hard for you losing your father and mother so close. You're grieving; it must be hard to think straight.' Red looked at Connie; she looked so beautiful. He would do anything to be with her. He didn't want her pity. He wanted to make her proud. He wanted to impress her and show he was worthy of her love. 'You know, Red, we've known each other so long, you can tell me anything; you can talk to me.'

'I know, Connie, I know. I'm confused. I've been so happy, happier than I can ever remember, and then Father and Mother died and it feels the world has changed. I have to sign up; it's the right thing for me to do. I can't stay here, you know, not whilst the war rages and men my age and

In Fields of Gold and Red

younger are giving their lives.' He felt his eyes well up with tears; he tried to suppress them.

'If that is what you feel you have to do, I won't stand in your way.' Red looked at Connie; their fingers were twined together. She wasn't smiling; her face was fixed. 'When will you go?' she clipped.

'I thought I would stay for haymaking; you know, help get that in, then go after that.'

He was brought back to the present when Mrs Wrixon started playing the wedding march. He looked over at the bridesmaids, and Connie smiled back. Jimmy and Red looked back together and watched as Violet walked down the aisle with her father Oscar. Red noticed Violet's mother Henrietta was weeping and smiling at the same time.

Oh, why had he said what he did? Why hadn't he asked her to marry him?

* * *

Connie looked at Violet; she was looking so pretty in her mother's wedding dress. Violet was in all white, the brightest in the dark oak panelled bar of the Farmer's Arms. Oscar, her father, had never looked so happy. Mrs Wrixon, smiling, went to the old upright piano. The villagers gathered around, led by Oscar, his face beaming. Mrs Wrixon began to play and led the singing. Her voice was full and steady.

'For to plough and to sow and to reap and to mow.' Her voice boomed out in the bar. More joined in; they all knew the words. Connie held Redver's hand as she watched everyone sing.

'And to be a farmer's boy, boy; And to be a farmer's boy.' It was sung with passion. She heard Red's voice beside her.

She danced with Redver. Time stood still and speeded up. At first, it felt as though the evening would never end, being held in his arms, and she wished it would continue forever.

His smell so musky; feeling his arms holding her close. She and Redver went outside. He led her to the garden, the darkness lifted by the large shining white moon. It seemed close enough for her to touch.

Her breathing was fast. She could see the outlines of couples among the ash trees. There were soldiers back on leave, waiting to go back or to go for the first time. Soon Red would be one of those; he would be one of the anonymous soldiers in green khaki.

The sound of the party spilled from the bar. She could feel her heart beating fast. She stood up against the tall trunk of the ash tree at the far end of the garden. She should persuade Redver to stay; to stay, to get married. She could; she felt she could; should she do it? Violet had looked the happiest she had ever seen her, and Jimmy too. They would be happy together, starting their family in the cottage by the green. Connie thought Violet might even be pregnant already; her face was giving it away. Would she tell her tomorrow when they were alone? Life seemed to be moving faster than ever.

She kissed him. She felt his tongue touch hers. It felt divine. His rough hands moved delicately down her arm. She felt warmth she'd never felt before. Why had he decided to go? He wanted her. She pushed herself against him. She felt his tough body push back. She felt herself being consumed by pleasure. She could easily give in. His hand moved from her arm to her waist. He stroked his hand from her waist to her hip, and gently up her side. His hand moved from her side to her cheek, as he pulled away. His hazel eyes glimmered in the light of the low moon, and she saw the stars reflected in them. Should she stop? Could she stop herself? It wasn't right. But these were different times. He would be gone soon. What if she never got the chance? What if this was it, what if he never came back?

She felt their lips touch as he cupped her face in both hands. The warmth flooded her stomach and moved to her groin. She felt the heat like never before. The passion was overwhelming. She felt his hand move to her breast; her nipples became hard as he caressed them through her dress. She felt carried, her head light.

She put her hands on Red's shoulders and pushed him back. 'It's time we went home. Will you walk me back?' She said she didn't mean it; she wanted him, she wanted him so much. To sleep with him, to wake up with him, to have him take her; but she couldn't, she could only do this with her husband. How lucky Violet was to be on her wedding night.

* * *

The walk back to Kingcombe Cottages was the fastest she ever remembered. It wasn't that they walked any quicker. She tried to savour the moment. They held hands all the way. She didn't notice them walk in the gate or close it behind them.

'Red, can we sit on the wall?' She felt more in control and didn't want to say goodnight.

'Connie, I'm sorry, I have to do it.' They sat on the wall together. She could make out the outline of the trees over the far side with the moon behind. How easy would it be to make love to him? Father would be out till late; the cider was flowing freely. They could go up to her room; she could have Red in her bed, they could make love. It was a tempting thought, that it would change his mind. They watched as a red fox with white patches on its forehead slinked around the edge of the field.

'You know the Admiral wants the cottage back,' Red said.

She felt comfortable, secure, his arm around her shoulders.

'I thought he would.' She rested her hand on his thigh and felt his body heat next to her. 'It's going to feel weird not having you next door after all these years.' She felt a pang of loss strike her.

'Old Admiral said to me if I got engaged within the month I could keep the cottage.' She felt him tense.

'What? He said what?' How could he not have told her, or discussed it with her?

'He said he couldn't be seen to let a single man live alone, not in this big old cottage, but if I sorted myself out, got engaged to be married, well, he could let that go, said he would turn a blind eye till we got wed.' He averted his gaze.

'Why didn't you tell me before, when we went to the meadow?' She knew it; she knew there was something else he had wanted to say. Why hadn't he? She would have said yes, she would have done it, to keep him safe, to keep him by her side, to keep him from having to fight; she would have done that; she would have given up teaching for him. She didn't pity him, she didn't hate him. 'You could have stayed in the cottage?'

'Yes, he said so. But Connie, I want to do something, something more. You know my father gave his whole life to the farm, from child to man; he worked all his life for the estate. It was all he ever knew. God, he's never been out of Dorset. It was the same for Granfer too.' She wanted him to touch her, to kiss her; she'd never known him talk like this before; it was liberating.

'I see. My father's the same. I do understand; it's just that… it's so hard to be losing you.' She could feel her tears rise from below.

'I know, but I wouldn't be any good staying, thinking I've let people down, thinking I could have done more, and I didn't want you to do anything you'd regret, giving yourself to me because you wanted to keep me safe.' He stroked the top of her shoulder and squeezed her close.

'Oh Red, you're a silly gallybagger, aren't you?' Connie

could feel the tears roll out from the corners of her eyes. She could see the same on Red's cheeks.

'I'll write to you. You might have to correct my spelling, but I will write, I promise.' He laughed as he wiped his face with his free hand.

'You better, Redver Kingson, or else you will be in trouble!'

11

10th July 1915

Red was seated on the rickety wooden seat; he'd stuffed an old hessian sack underneath as a cushion but still he felt every stone, every bump; his spine ached. The weather was warm and dry, and with a light breeze, it was perfect for haymaking. Captain and Tully were on the ends of the reins, glad to be exercised, happy to be pulling the mower. Red hoped Mr Grey was right with his forecast, that they would have three clear dry days to get the hay in.

Red breathed in the smell of the fresh cut grass and felt the sun on his face and arms. The smell was so good, and would be even better when the hay was dry: sweet and earthy. Could this be the last time he ever did this? Could he change his mind after all he'd told Admiral and Constance? Admiral wasn't happy; he couldn't believe Red was giving up the chance of the cottage. Connie wasn't pleased but she'd gone along with him; after all, she said she understood why he was going. He wouldn't change his mind; Kingsons never did. His father always said a man was only as good as his word, and once said you had to keep your word.

Red reined back at the corner: 'Whoa, Captain, whoa boy.' He clicked his tongue. Captain and Tully slowed; Captain shook his head and led Tully in the turn.

Red looked out and watched his uncles, George and Charlie, and his brother George, who along with Jimmy were scything the headland. The grass was tall and weeping. The mower handled it, throwing the cut grass to the back. The sky was clear but the breeze was picking up.

The horses were used to Red's kind, gentle, encouraging way, the same as Father's. They seemed to remember this field. He got the mower moving and the horses were soon in rhythm.

Red was happy he was out working the horses and they were in their stride; they more or less did it themselves. He needed to make the turn at the headlands. Red checked to make sure that no stones clogged up the knife.

He noticed Mr Grey in his black hat moving the horse and cart into the field, Sampson and Theodore in the back. What did they all want? Perhaps Mr Grey would ask him to stop if he thought the weather was going to turn. There were no rain-carrying clouds above Ashcombe Beacon, from where the wind was blowing.

They pulled up the cart; Theodore jumped down, in his captain's uniform, his peaked khaki hat on. He stood with authority. Red didn't much like the look on his face.

Mr Grey, who was wearing his tall black hat, got down from the cart and went up to Red and said: 'Er, Red, can 'e let Sampson take on? His turn to learn. What with you leaving us and all.'

Red reined in Captain and brought him to a stop: 'Whoa, whoa there, Captain.' He got off the wooden seat and walked down; he nodded to Sampson. Theodore ignored him, staring at the men working the field.

'Red, you come back with me; we've to sort out which horses we gonna have to send to the army.' Red watched as Sampson gingerly got on the mower; he was unaccustomed to working the horses. Red felt he'd lost his position; he supposed it was his own fault.

It wasn't hard to decide on which horses to send after all was said and done. He had to keep Captain, Tully, Trudy, and Duke. The other eight all had to go. It wasn't fair; they would struggle, down to four horses to do the work of twelve, and him leaving. He felt guilty, leaving them like this; but he had to. He was doing it for himself. He was being selfish. His father had given nearly fifty years to the farm; what had he done? He hadn't even made ten.

After leading the horses to the old artillery yard in Bridport, he walked to East Street and caught the train back. Now he was walking up to the Piggott Field. His hobnailed boots cracking stones underfoot scared the fighting male blackbirds from the hedge.

He walked into the field; he couldn't believe what he was seeing. Sampson and Theodore were fighting, rolling and struggling on the ground, rolling through the drying rows of hay. Jimmy was there, trying to pull them apart. Red sprinted as fast as he could from the gateway.

His uncles and brothers were on the far side of the field and he could hear Sampson screaming in pain as his brother punched him.

'What the hell is going on, Jimmy?' he shouted as he approached.

'They've been at each other all afternoon; couldn't agree on what field to do next, or if we should stop as it feels like rain. Help me get 'em apart,' Jimmy said.

'You two leave us alone. He needs to be taught a lesson, ' Theo said.

'I'm here on the farm, you're not here most of the time; don't think you can still order me around,' Sampson said as he pushed his elder brother away.

'I'm the oldest and I can still tell you what to do! We

should get on and cut the next field.'

'It could rain any time! We should get this cut grass stocked; that way it can dry.'

Jimmy got behind Theodore and pulled him back. Theo's face coloured, his eyes staring at his brother. Red pulled Sampson back.

'Leave us, you two!' Theo shouted. He broke free from Jimmy; he came at Red and Sampson. With Sampson in front and Red still holding his arms, Theo punched Sampson. He caught him on his jawline. Sampson slumped to the ground; Red, unable to hold him upright, let go. Theo glared at him.

'Are you next? Do you want to take me on?' Theo's face was red and blotchy; grass stuck to his uniform. His eyes were wild.

'Sampson has a point; it's clouding in,' Red said. Jimmy went to Sampson and tried to wake him.

'Don't you bloody start arguing with me. You should have signed up ages ago, dodging your duty just like him.' He pointed down at Sampson who was coming round.

'Well, even your father says we should stay, that it's no good fighting a bloody war if we all starve to death,' Red said as he faced Theo.

'Shows you're weak. Men your age should be fighting; it's the decent thing to do.' Theo came up to Red, standing taller than him and in his face. Red pushed him back in the centre of his chest. Theo came forward. He threw a right-handed punch. Red blocked, then jabbed out his right hand. It connected with Theo's chin, who didn't flinch. He stared at Red and leaned in, retaliating with a punch to Red's solar plexus. Red, bent double, swung his left, an uppercut under Theo's chin. The taller man fell back. Red, winded, looked down at both his master's sons in the hay. It was time he left.

***

Once at Maiden Newton he got off the train and headed to the small café; he bought a pasty and a cup of tea. He scoffed the pasty down. He felt he could eat two but he should keep his money. He was one of seven people, three women gossiping and drinking tea on their way back from shopping in Dorchester market and three soldiers off back to barracks.

His train wasn't due for another half an hour. It was odd for him to be sitting still for so long on a working day in summer; not done since he was at school sitting next to Connie when he was twelve. He was filled with excitement, exhilaration and nervous energy and was fearful of what was to come. He was leaving the farm and his life; a chance to see something different, heading towards war. At least he was going to do his bit, whatever that turned out to be. Perhaps he would be killed like so many men in the village already; this didn't frighten him as much as the idea of being maimed or feeling pain, of being shot and surviving or being gassed in a trench. That seemed so much worse than dying. He touched the papers handed to him by Brigadier Appleworth, signed up and off.

He closed his eyes and began to daydream. Seeing Connie: walking, talking, being together up on Moreton Castle, and sharing a passionate kiss. He so wished he could say goodbye to her, his one regret leaving so quickly. He felt sure he was in love with her; he would be so happy if she felt the same way. He wanted to kiss her again.

He opened his eyes, and there she stood looking beautiful in a blue summer dress. 'Hey, Connie, what are you doing here?' He couldn't believe it and thought he was still in a dream. Connie was smiling at him. The sun dazzled in through the dirty windows of the café and illuminated her face.

He couldn't believe his luck; he stood up and gave a huge smile. His stomach flipped; there was so much he wanted to say but his mind was blank.

'Hey, Connie, you look amazing,' he said as he touched her on the shoulder.

'How are you? What are you doing here? Is everything all right?' she said.

All he wanted to do was kiss her beautiful mouth and look into her big green eyes. If only she wanted to do the same it would make him the happiest man on earth.

'I'm going today,' Red said. He looked down.

'You're what? I thought you were staying till haymaking was done! I thought they were short-handed! Why on earth are you going now?' she said with a concerned look on her face. She sat down opposite.

'I've got to leave; me and Theo have had a fight. I was trying to protect Sampson; you know how he and Theo always end up fighting, you know what Theo is like.' He rubbed his face with his finger.

'Yes, I do; but that's no reason to go. Stay two more weeks, please,' Connie said, looking him in the eye.

'It's too late; I've signed up with the Brigadier. I've my papers now.' He sighed.

'Train for Dorchester now at platform one, train for Bridport at platform two,' the announcer said over the tannoy.

People were running out of the café doors on both sides for their trains.

'But Red, I want you to stay! I don't want to lose you; I want you…' Her face was drawn.

'I'm sorry, Connie, I feel this is what I have to do. Don't worry; I promise I will come back, and you'll get my letters.' He stood up.

'It looks like it's time we both have to go.' Connie said,

taking her red and black dotted handkerchief and giving it to Red.

Red folded the hanky into his pocket. She does care about me, he thought. He hugged her and didn't want it to end. He held on for a few seconds, feeling her warm body beneath her summer dress; she smelt so sweet and clean. He wanted to better himself and win her heart. He wanted to make her proud and he wanted to make her happy.

All too soon they had to break their embrace, say goodbye and make their way to their trains heading in opposite directions. Already he missed her. He looked back just as she did, and they waved. He never wanted to forget how she looked.

12

14th September 1916

Connie woke with a start; she knew it was early. She could hear the chatter of magpies and the chirping of blackbirds and sparrows. The light was dim.

'Oh, fucking hell.' The voice of her father interrupted the dawn.

'Father?' she called back as she raised herself out of bed. She picked up her dressing gown from her chair and wrapped it around over her plain nightdress. Her father's knees were much worse; it was the damp autumn that did it. He stumbled around most mornings. Old Miss Bertha Crabb told him he should eat plenty of boiled onions. Connie couldn't stand the smell of them cooking in the kitchen. It was worth a try, though, if it made Father feel any better. She didn't have to get up for hours yet; Miss Appleworth and she wouldn't need to be at school before eight. It was hard without Mr Martin, but the two of them were coping; Connie looked after the children eight and below and Miss Appleworth the rest.

She found her way downstairs by instinct as the stairwell had no windows. Father was slumped in his chair in the corner of the kitchen next to the range with Jess lying out by his feet. Jess wagged her tail and looked up at Connie, wanting to be stroked. Connie knelt and pushed Jess's fur back from her eyes.

'What's with all the swearing?' Connie asked.

'Oh, nothing. Banged me knee on the kitchen table. Nothing to worry about; just a stupid old fool.' He grimaced.

She could see he was hiding the pain from her. She said: 'Do you want boiled eggs?'

'You don't have to; I can see to myself. You go on back to bed.' Father scratched his knee. She looked at him and realised how old he was looking, his beard whiter. There were wide furrows on his forehead and his eyes were dark and sunken. His trousers hung from his waist, and when he walked he did so with an awkward gait, having to swing his right leg.

She hoped today would be the day she got another letter from Red. She wanted to hear how he was; his last letter was over a month ago. Where was he? Was he in France? Had he been in action? And was he safe?

Father ate his breakfast of boiled eggs and buttered bread and washed it down with a mug of tea. He put his smock over his shirt, black waistcoat and corded trousers, picked up his crook from beside the door and headed off to check on the ewes.

Connie went to her stationery drawer in the large sideboard in the front room and returned to sit at the table and write to Red.

Dearest Redver,

It has been so long since I last received a letter. I know I am impatient and I know there is such a delay as you had in getting mine.

She paused and sipped from her mug of tea.

I am back to school teaching the under eights, I do love it. They absorb all the information and I get enormous pleasure from seeing their faces when they answer my questions.

Harvest festival is coming at the weekend and I know it will not be the same, I miss seeing you so much. Life is quiet without you and Jimmy around, and Vi and I keep each other company. We've been volunteering handing out tea and cake at the station to all the soldiers passing through. I wish you could have had some leave; there is so much I want to say to you. I keep thinking of you, and of last summer. I regret we didn't do more. From your last letter I understand you will be crossing the Channel soon and although the distance looks so short I know the difference will be huge.

I get so much pleasure from your letters and I hope you do too. I'm sure Captain is missing having you around, and Jess. Father says to keep your chin up and your head down. We heard that Ken and Thomas Smyth have been killed on the Somme; their father is distraught in the forge, as you can imagine. Vicar Wrixon is trying to get a memorial organised for all those who don't come back. I hear your sister has moved into her house in Bridport. I did pass her but she didn't speak to me, she was too busy rushing off. Violet is loving the cottage but of course is sad that Jimmy has not got back to see his bouncing baby boy; he is so lovely and looks like Jimmy. He must be so proud. He is just like him in the face. He smells so gorgeous, and he gurgles away when Vi lets me hold him.

It's hard to put into words how I feel. I miss you and I do love you; it has only been by your absence I've come to realise by how much I do. Please be safe and make it home. I promise you I will wait for you.
xxxxxx Your forever loving, Connie xxxxxx

She wanted to write more; she wanted to write that with every day that passed her love grew stronger and stronger for him. That she would promise to marry him when he got home. How holding Vi's little boy William was making her think of having her own children. How she would think he would be such a good father. How she wished he would make it back, and how she wished she had made love to him the night of Vi's wedding. No one but them would have known, no one would have had any idea, who would have cared? Even the vicar would have understood, wouldn't he? Who could stop them having a small amount of pleasure when there was so much death and destruction taking place?

* * *

Connie sat with Violet in the front room of Vi's cottage. Violet held William in her arms, with her hand supporting his head. The afternoon light fell through the window panes. The room was sparse, wooden floorboards under the red and green patterned rug; two wooden chairs and a small round table on which the teapot stood.

'Vi, have you had a letter today?' Connie could smell her tea; she hoped Vi would let her hold William soon.

'No, nothing. The post office is going to go mad with us all clamouring for letters every day,' Violet said as she rocked Billy back and forth. Connie noticed how much fluffy blonde hair topped his head.

'You know, Vi, I'm really sorry; if I'd done more to convince Redver to stay, Jimmy would never have gone, would he? We all know he only signed up after Red to stick with his mate.'

'Don't be sorry, Connie; he'll be back and at least there was time for us to marry. It was such a good night, Connie; I've never been so happy. We made love all night! It was so passionate and loving; oh, it was so wonderful. I'd never been so happy; and look, I have this bundle of joy, don't I? We have to have them home; we just have to,' Violet said looking at Connie from above her cup.

'Yes, but because of Red…' Connie said, her eyes looking down.

'Don't say that. We knew Jimmy and Red would always stick together. And look, they're not even fighting.' Violet sipped at her tea. 'They will be training for ages and ages; they will get back on leave. Don't feel guilty; there was nothing you could do. They have their own minds. You've got to let them get on with it, work it out for themselves. We've got to believe they will be back. You know they've always been quick on their feet and lucky; yes, lucky is what they are! We've got to believe that.'

'I guess, Violet; I know we have, really I do. It's so hard at the moment; you know, reading what you do in the papers, everything that's happening. I don't understand why they don't get more leave. Bloody old Theodore Fox always seems to be back here swanning around, doesn't he?'

'We've each other, we've got to stick together,' Violet said, putting her teacup down with her free hand and reaching out to touch Connie.

'You're right, Violet. I know you are. It doesn't make it any easier,' Connie said, looking out of the window, hoping the postman would be dropping a letter through her door.

* * *

She came out from Violet's cottage into the small triangle of Ashcombe, where the lane from the Farmer's Arms came to the junction of Bull Lane and Castle Mill Lane. The rain drizzled down. She would have to move quickly if she wasn't to get soaked walking back to Kingcombe Cottage.

She walked into Bull Lane and coming down the path from Chapel Cottages was Fredrick Dunn. He was older than her father. He walked upright and with purpose. He was wearing his dark blue peaked cap, dark blue trousers with red stripe and dark blue overcoat. His cap was emblazoned with the badge of the General Post Office. He looked smart. Connie's heart skipped.

'Ay, young lady, before you ask, I've good news for 'e today,' he said as he saw her rush towards him. 'I've just come from your place and there's a letter waiting for 'e.'

'Thank you, Mr Dunn, thank you!' She touched him on the arm as she passed. She hitched up her skirt; she didn't care for the rain or how she looked; no one was watching her; well, apart from Mr Dunn who she could sense was smiling and shaking his head.

She ran up Bull Lane and then turned right into Farm Lane. Dirt, mud, leaves and twigs washed down the side of the hedge and splattered on her blue dress. She didn't care; there was a letter; it must be from Redver. She felt her legs tire as the lane's gradient increased. She didn't stop. She ran all the way past the pasture and the entrance to the farmyard. She opened the gate and left it open. She sprinted as fast as she could around to the back door and in. She went in through the kitchen and down the corridor. It was there, below the letterbox of the front door. She picked it up and walked back to the kitchen, tearing her bonnet from her head. She sat down at the kitchen table.

What would he say? She held the letter. It was his handwriting. She would have to teach him how to write better. Now she had it here, she dared not open it. She wanted to savour the moment to make it last. Once opened and read, she knew the waiting and anticipation would build for the next letter. The longer she could make it last... She breathed in deeply. She took her shoes off and placed them by the back door. The kettle came to the boil; she made the tea and sat back down. She used the kitchen knife to slice open the envelope.

My Dearest sweet Connie,

Oh, what fun we have been having at training. It's so much better than basic from last year. I can't tell you all that has happened, or what work we are doing in this regiment it is so new. But the friends me and Jimmy av made, there is one who has become our firm mate, his name is William Tucker, but we call him Geordie, cos he's from Newcastle, he's funny and his hair looks like that of a badger. He loves his football as we do, oh we've been having a time of it alright, we can hardly understand a word he speaks, and he can't us. He's always up to summink. If we were not soon to be over to France this would be the best time of me life.

My job is gearsman in the girt machine, Jimmy is same on opposite side and Geordie is a gunner are commander is a nice officer, very polite and proper and is Jackson. We've ad to train on all parts. I've been signed off on all roles, gunner, driver and Jackson said my driving is the best after Stone. I like driving and me an Jimmy go out in the evening too to do extra. Young man by the name of Guppy, isn't old enough to be out of school e passes shells to Geordie and fires the Hotchkiss. We are short coz man called Greening couldn't stop being sick and passed out. One downside and Jimmy and me were gobsmacked I don't think you will believe it. I'm only ended up in the same bloody regiment as Captain Theodore Fox, aint I. Trust my bloody luck not to escape them Fox's! Good news is that are Captain is Mahoney and he seems fair. Geordie got me and Jimmy in a bit of a scrape one night pinching carrots from some old boys vegetable patch. Course Captain Fox found out and made sure our leave was cancelled. So I won't be back before France.

I hope you and Vi are well, and all the animals too, Captain and Jess, how be they? You and your father, how is things on the farm, how was the harvest did e get it all in before this weather?

I do miss e, so much my darling. I wish I could hold you in my arms like I did after the wedding, I hope it can all be over soon, that the Bosche don't give us too much trouble. Geordie says the front is no place e want's to be. He should know, him and driver Henry Stone, they says training's hard but wait till your under fire. I aint looking forward to it, but we are all in good spirits and Geordie, tells us he is lucky and we are all going to make it home.

I do so miss e, my darling buttercup. After basic training back last year, this now all seems to be such a rush. The food aint too bad, mind you that tinned meat is awful don't think Jess would touch it, and me and Jimmy have been keeping Cookie supplied with plenty of rabbits from our snares.

I hope to be back to you soon sweetest buttercup, how is the weather there, it's been so hot, and the camp was run over with earwigs, poor old Geordie screamed like a girl when they were in his bed! I better go we've more practice. I miss you so much, I think about you every day, and how beautiful you looked in the summer, pass on my best to me brother and Dot, and all in village.

xxxxx Your loving Redver xxxxx

Connie felt her tears boil up from deep within her soul. She couldn't help but cry out. It was the longest letter he'd ever written; he was happy and in good spirits. But she couldn't help but fear for him. The *Daily Express* was full of news of the horrendous death toll and casualties from the Somme. The village was suffering badly with news of men being killed coming ever faster, every day. It seemed to her no one was going to be spared. She prayed for Redver and Jimmy. She prayed they would come home; she needed him, she wanted him, she wanted him to be with her. She read the letter again. Oh, how she prayed for another letter. The wait, the expectancy, the flicker of hope, it squeezed in on her.

* * *

She was sitting in the kitchen with her father at the kitchen table eating breakfast. She heard the drop of a letter on the mat at the front door; without pause, she looked at her father with a smile. She leapt from her chair and raced to the letter. It was, it was, it was! She ran back with the prize in her hand, sat back down, took the butter knife, wiped it on the tea towel and sliced the envelope open. Her father grinned at her from behind his mug.

My Dearest sweet Connie,

I'm so happy to have got your letter today. You don't know how much me spirits are lifted when I see your letter. Jimmy cannot stop talking about his baby William, little Billy Crabb he swears he is going to teach im to be a great footballer and runner! I dream about you every day, seeing your smile and your deep green eyes, I think I would stare in them all day if I ad half a chance and get no work done at all. When I get home, I'm gonna make you the happiest woman in all of Dorset, I swear!

I tell e France do look like England in places where there is no fighting, it is green, they have tree's the same as we, sept the land be flat and where there is fighting I be sure it looks like craters on the moon.

We've been practising and practising, more drills every day in the girt machine. We are so used to the smelly fumes, even young Guppy ain't sick no more!

I do miss Captain and Jess, but would e believe it, there are so many animals here tis like a farm, anyway, horses, chickens, pigeons, even cows I did go out and help with milking too! I've also found me self a pet aint I, well e found me truth be told. We were having games like at the fair, running, tug of war. Course Jimmy e did win the running, I came in second tripped up by a spotty grey mongrel of a dog. I've called im Barty boy, all the crew love em and e don't mind being inside with us all. He's only one who will eat that Maconochie's tinned stew, it's disgusting, so e eats darn well. I prefer the corned beef, it's bloody lovely. Geordie does say Barty boy be are lucky mascot, it might be true coz are crew won the tug of war and we was declared winners of the games. Lieutenant Jackson was very proud of us and gave us extra rum. It did give me such a headache, I had to give me paybook to Jimmy to get my wages, e still ain't given it back! Mind I better see e' does else e' will have my money too!

'What you grinning for so much? Tell I, will 'e?' her father said. 'Don't keep me in suspense!' He slurped from his cup.

'In a minute; let me finish in peace,' Connie said, concentrating.

Course that Fox still has it in for me and Jimmy and tried to get us in trouble with the Major, lucky Captain Mahoney and Sergeant Nicol did stand up for us, it was all to do with the fishing we went and did. You would have loved the lake, twas massive, larger than all of meadow field and flat and full of fish! Me and Jimmy tried to tickle the trout out of the stream, lied down on are tummies, we woz there for hours, course Geordie got bored went back to camp, we couldn't belive it when water, gravel and stones came flying down on us, we thought it a shell, but twas Geordie letting off grenades in the lake, bloody hell e must have killed a thousand fish. Course Fox wanted us court marshalled or sent into town to be strung up, but well Cookie, the Major and Captain Mahoney, were so happy to having something to feed the men, we was all forgiven and treated as hero's sept for Captain Fox, you should have seen the look on his face!

I love you Constance Stevens, my darling little buttercup I can't wait to be back and have you in my arms. I know I aint romantic or anything like Jimmy, but when this darn thing is all over, I do so hope we can be together for ever I think it's all I've ever wanted.

xxxxxx Your Loving Redver xxxxxx

She beamed across her face, put the letter down, then picked it up again, not quite believing it.

'Come on; your smile is bigger than the moon! Wass up?' He smiled over the table. She clutched the letter to her chest.

'Oh, it's nothing. Oh, Father, he's got to make it back, he has to.' She took the letter and read it again; she dwelt on the last paragraph.

13

23rd November 1917

'Listen up, boys: our orders have changed, again. We are to head for the village of Fontaine-Notre-Dame, instead of the Bourlon Heights as we were told yesterday. I know things change but this is the target. Zero hour is ten thirty,' said Jackson. He put his hat under his arm. 'Our objective is to knock out machine guns placed in the houses of the village. I've been up and done a reccy and we are likely to come under heavy fire from a battery in La Folie Wood; it's plumb in line with our attack.' He paused and took in a deep breath as he addressed his tank crew. Drizzle fell on his blonde hair. He was thin and his accent clear, his hair short, his neat moustache wide above his top lip.

Red looked at his crew, all dressed in their brown boiler suits, covered in grease and oil. There was driver Henry Stone, short and intense. Geordie, William Tucker, with his black hair swept back, with a streak of badger-like white. Guppy, the youngest at fifteen who shouldn't be there, not old enough for face hair; and Shepherd, who was the same age as he and Jimmy and had to crouch over; he was on the gun on Jimmy's side. They were still short one man, Greening never replaced since training.

'We will need to try and take a less direct route, move to our left and come down the back gardens of the houses, hopefully missing as much fire as we can. As our start point is further up at the mill, we leave here at ten. We will have covering smoke from ten-thirty. Until ten, rest up, check the equipment and be ready. We follow the tape I've laid.'

Red hated the wait, the downtime. He checked David over, running his eye over the engine and chains, checking the tracks for any loose bolts. He made sure to fill the radiator. Geordie checked the Hotchkiss gun again and applied more grease. Shepherd did the same. Red took the crumpled letter from his inside pocket and read it again, for the fifth time that morning.

Dearest dear Redver,

Oh Redver yes, yes, a thousand times yes. I promise I will be here waiting for you; there is nothing more that would make me the happiest I could ever be. Your friend Geordie sounds good fun, but you make sure he doesn't get you in any more trouble, do you hear. Do I sound like a nagging wife? I don't mean to, but it is good practice.

Young Billy is a chip off the old block. Violet is so happy, but of course misses Jimmy like I do you.

When I hold young Billy, I do think I might like children of my own, he is so cute and warm and he smells so nice!

Violet and I have been out giving tea and cake to all soldiers on the platform. I can't help but think of you and hope you are eating well and are well looked after. At least you've had plenty of fish! Father is not so well lately, his knees aching all the while.

Course we all read the papers, study them we do to hear of any news at all we can glean. Miss Appleworth tells me I'm doing well at the school; she is very happy with me. I still can't believe that I'm teaching when only a few years ago I was the pupil. Miss Appleworth still scares me now!

Mr Grey and Sampson are running the farm as best they can. They have more women who work but everything takes longer. Would you believe Meadow Field is awash with potatoes? It makes a funny sight. The weather has been hot and sunny all these last few weeks. When I've spare time I like to walk up to the castle and remember the fair, the ride in the swing-boats and the picnic under the oak tree, and remember all the fun we had as children running and playing in the river in our little gang, making dams and larking about. It seems so long ago. I wonder if our children will do the same; I do hope so, don't you?

Make sure you keep safe and come back to me. I can't wait to go to the old castle like we did at the fair. I will make you the best picnic ever! My heart is yours, my dearest.

xxxxxx Your forever loving yellow buttercup, Connie xxxxxx

He was feeling ten feet tall; they would be together. He fed the pigeons and recalled their successful mission in Albert two weeks ago.

* * *

The two other tanks in David's formation this morning were the Divinity and Damnation. Red looked around checking for loose bolts, making sure the tracks were secure; he checked the oil and water levels. He took out a pigeon from its wicker basket and stroked it before putting it back.

Brigadier General Hugh Elles had written the rallying call that Lieutenant Jackson delivered.

The Tank Corps will have the chance for which they have been waiting for many months – to operate on good going in the van of the fight. All that hard work and ingenuity can achieve have been done in the way of preparation. It remains for unit commanders and tank crews to complete the work by judgement and pluck in the battle itself. In the light of past experiences, I leave the good name of the corps with great confidence in their hands. I propose leading the attack of the centre division.

Red noticed the difference in the air this morning: there was no smoke and there were no guns going off in the background. This was part of the plan to leave the bombardment to the last moment to reduce craters so that the tanks could have a more or less clear run at the trenches; this had been learned from the early battles. Red saw Captain Fox hurry through the crowd looking important; he didn't notice Red, his head in the air. Red guessed all the privates looked the same dressed in their drab brown boiler suits, their faces covered in smoke, dirt and grease.

Red and the crew got in the tank. It was five forty-five. Ten minutes later they got David cranked over, it taking him, Jimmy, Guppy and Shepherd to move the crank. The engine screamed into life; the vibrations, smoke and fumes filled the compartment. He tied Connie's hanky over his mouth. The noise, the smoke and the fumes didn't bother him. He gave a thumbs up to Jimmy, Jackson, and Stone. They were on the left flank within a group of twelve tanks, the infantry instructed to follow at a distance. It was still dark outside and darker still inside the compartment. David moved forward in line with Divinity and Damnation following at 3mph. Driver Henry Stone skilfully kept in line, even with his limited view. There were little turns to be made, which the team managed. Red patted and stroked Barty on the head to keep them both calm.

Six-twenty and they were in no-man's-land; clear of craters they made good progress. Red heard the barrage from their guns begin. David moved along the ridge, the shells hitting home on their targets. Divinity crashed the barbed wire. Red was instructed to make a turn; this moved David out from behind and to the left of Divinity. Damnation moved right so that David and Damnation formed the base of a triangle with Divinity leading the way at the point. Slow but steady. There was some enemy fire that peppered the exterior of David, nothing too heavy. Divinity came to the first trench and dropped its fascine. It immediately went over the trench and turned left and put down suppressing fire.

Damnation went over the fascine that had been laid and David followed. The next trench, more fire. Damnation lowered its fascine, pulled left and put down fire; Divinity left its position and followed David. David came to a halt in front of its trench. Red saw Commander Jackson pull the chain. God, he hoped the fascine would drop without problem, or him and Jimmy would be up for it. Success: the bundle of tied sticks fell down the front of the tank and rolled effortlessly into the gap of the deep trench.

Henry Stone gave the instruction to go forward. Red engaged first gear, David dipped nose down into the massive trench and moved slowly forward; it was working. Stone pressed the accelerator. Even with the fascine the Hindenburg line was deep and the edges up and out were steep. The tracks slipped on the muddy bank. Stone pushed down on the accelerator. There was nothing Red, Jimmy or the rest of the crew could do. The tracks slipped and looked for purchase. Stone had to correct a slide, which he did nonchalantly. Red held his breath. David needed to make it up and out. He could hear the sound of Divinity up behind them.

David's engine was strained to its limit; Red waited for the order to get out, but finally David gained traction and exited the trench. It moved forward and turned left to put down fire on the machine guns. Divinity entered the trench but became stuck; it was unable to get out of the trench. Commander Jackson gave the order to engage reverse to go back and to help; Red selected reverse at the same time as Jimmy, the Commander navigating through his periscope. They lined themselves in front of Divinity. It would be Jimmy or Red who would be ordered out to attach the big chain. Jimmy was ordered out. Red was not happy. Jimmy ran as fast as he could, grabbed the big chain, ran down and attached it quickly to Divinity. He signalled the thumbs up.

All the while, Geordie and Shepherd fired the six pounders on enemy positions. The chain attached, Jimmy sprinted back, climbed up the tank and dived inside. Red could finally breathe a sigh of relief. They engaged gear and began to pull, putting more strain on the engine. The pitch changed; Red winced. Even with 105hp would it be enough? It strained and pulled. Divinity was revving the bollocks of its engine, too. Finally, it was free of the trench and out. They released the chain, and Jimmy darted out using all his speed to pull the chain up and onto the back of David. They drove to the rallying point and held their position; they were joined by eleven of the twelve tanks. The infantrymen followed on, securing their targets. The brown line was secure; it was time to move into the village.

The ground was dry and they could move at top speed. When within range, David came under fire from the houses. Geordie fired the six pounder; he blew great holes in the buildings. Moving through the village, it was eerily quiet until the machine guns started again. Commander Jackson was looking for the railway line. He found it and instructed Stone to follow it. It took several turns with Red and Jimmy alternating between selecting gears; eventually, they got onto the tracks. The vibration rattled through the hull. Red could feel every sleeper as they banged their way down; it must be damaging the spuds on the tracks, Red thought. At least there was no enemy fire. Divinity had turned right down the lane and they were on their own, each tank with its own objective. David – if Red remembered correctly – was heading for the bridge over the canal, which they were to secure.

Eventually, after an hour they came up to their bridge. The German infantry was laying wire to explosives. Shepherd fired the Hotchkiss air-cooled machine gun: *rat-a tat-tat, rat-a tat-tat.* Empty casings littered the floor. The noise inside was constant. He fired in twenty second bursts, the Hun diving for cover in the rubble of the demolished building.

Commander Jackson ordered Red and Jimmy to go out with him, with the intention of cutting the wire. Red jumped out; Barty went to follow but Red tied him up.

They ran quickly to the bridge, keeping low for cover, but this wasn't much: just an old brick wall which was shattered and low. Running hard and with Geordie, Guppy and Shepherd providing covering fire, they made a dash for the bridge. Rifle fire attacked them from the third storey of the wharf. Geordie let rip with a six pounder; it burst the building, knocking it tumbling; and the rifle fire ceased. Red ran in front, quickly followed by the Commander and Jimmy. He found the wire; his heart in his mouth, he cut it whilst Jimmy and Jackson kept fire at the entrance of the window. The wire cut, they made a run back to David. Just as they made it back, Divinity came along the railway track and put more fire down. Back inside David, Red felt safe. Stone moved David off towards their next objective.

Stone brought David to a stop and Jackson gave them the order to disembark. The village was finally cleared of Fritz, all captured and taken prisoner or killed at their posts. Red opened the sponson door and gingerly put his head out; Barty jumped down and Red joined him.

The air was thick with the smell of carbide, and smoke drifted on the breeze. Red looked around at the picture of devastation. Buildings lay in heaps of rubble; he counted only three or four that had survived intact. Trees were shattered at their trunks, cut down in their prime. Stone had parked David in front of one of the standing buildings; the sign hung down damaged and dusty. The rest of the crew shimmied and crawled out of David. Red saw the dead bodies of German soldiers, limbs separate from their owners, blood-covered, mangled and motionless, except for crows and magpies taking a meal.

Jackson got out and perused the situation. 'Stone, Guppy, Shepherd, you come with me. I want to do a recce to the north of the village. You three stay here and guard David.'

'Yes, sir,' Red said.

Jackson led the three soldiers through the fallen rubble.

'Hey, 'bout time for a brew and a bacon sarny,' Geordie said, rubbing his stomach. 'Come on, Red.'

'Yeah, come on, will 'e? Get a move on and something to eat; I'm bloody starving,' said Jimmy as he peed against the front of David.

Geordie brought out the bread and they pulled out their old crates to sit on. The smell of bacon wafted from the engine plate. When the bacon was cooked they sat on upturned crates and ate it, and washed it down with tea and condensed milk. Barty sat at Red's feet. Red tossed him a piece of bacon rind, which he swallowed.

'That wasn't so bad, was it,' Geordie said as he took a cigarette from behind his ear and lit it up. 'Reckon we did all right; and the best thing is, like I told you, we're all in one piece. Ain't we?'

Barty sniffed the loose stones and broken timbers.

'This place ain't looking so good, is it,' Jimmy said.

'Ain't, is it,' Red said. The three of them got up and wandered around David, taking in the view of rubble and the smouldering wreckage of devastation. Barty ran from one pile of rubble to the next. He scraped at it with his paw; he couldn't find anything of interest.

'Reckon this place was once quite beautiful,' Red said.

'They're going to need some building done after the war, ain't they? Reckon when I make it out, I will bring my Eliza and my sprogs back; I'll make a bloody killing,' Geordie said.

'You'd come back? But you can hardly speak bloody English, can 'e! How you going speak bloody French I don't know,' Red said as he scuffed his boot in masonry dust.

'When they see how quick I can throw up them houses, they won't worry about whether I can speak bloody French or not, will 'em?' Geordie said, picking at his teeth.

'I think if I make it back to England I want my own business; I don't want to be taking any orders any more,' Red said, patting Barty and stroking his fur from his forehead and down his back.

'You're right there, Red,' Jimmy said. 'We could go into business together: Crabb and Kingson.' He smiled.

'Nah, Kingson and Crabb; got a better ring to it,' Red said.

'Where are you two going to get the money for that?' Geordie laughed. 'You ain't going to be able to buy much for your shilling a day you're getting paid here, is you!'

'You forgot the extra penny we get for being in 'ere,' Red said, tapping the hull of David.

'Ay, and you two can't even agree on the name, can you, lads?' Geordie said as he slurped his tea.

'We will work it out, won't we, Jimmy?' Red said. He scratched Barty behind the ears.

'Yeah; maybe we can race for it or have a bet on it,' Geordie said.

'Crabking, Kingcrabb, Crabson, RedJim, Redcrabb,' Jimmy said.

'Don't think any of them sound like world beaters,' Geordie said. 'And what you going to do, anyway? You only know farming and catching rabbits.' He picked up a stone and lobbed it; Barty gave chase.

'Maybe you should come in with me: Tucker, Crabb and Kingson.'

'Nah, Kingson, Tucker, Crabb,' Red said.

'No, Crabb, Tucker, Kingson,' Jimmy said.

Barty brought back the stone and Red threw it for him to fetch.

'Don't think I want to come to France; there's a girl back in Dorset for me,' Red said.

'Yeah, he's in love, Geordie,' Jimmy said as Barty returned. Jimmy threw a stone and Barty sprinted after it. 'And I don't think my Vi will want to come. She's always been happy working in the station café with her mother and father; she's a real home bird. Think we will spend our lives back there.'

'What about you, Red? You and your sweetheart. What's her name, Connie: reckon you might come out and help your old mate?' Geordie said.

'Nah, don't think so. I want to marry my Connie and have a whole clutch of children, maybe more even than you.'

'Sounds like I will be making me fortune on me bleedin' own then.'

'Where's Barty disappeared to?' Red said, looking around. 'Barty! Barty! Here, boy!'

'Bet he's smelt something in the hotel. You know what he's like,' Jimmy said.

They all ran into the hotel, shouting for Barty. 'Barty boy, Barty! Here, boy!' Red shouted. He looked at the large open staircase on his left and the table of red roses on the side table. The floor was thick with dust, white and black tiles only visible in places. He walked past the entrances to the bar and restaurant and down the steps to the kitchen. Geordie and Jimmy followed.

'This place looks good, don't it? Did you see the bar back there? I bet...' Geordie said.

'What the hell...!' Red said, as he saw the man pointing a shotgun at him. The young woman was on her knee patting Barty; she smiled up at him. He smiled back.

'Papa, Papa, put the gun down.' She got up, walking to her father. 'They're English, they're Tommies.' She was dressed in a flowing white skirt and white blouse. Her dark brown hair fell in waves down to her shoulders. She was short, young and her smile was wide. Her hazel eyes shone up at him. Her waist was thin, her cheekbones sleek; her face glowed. Her father was dressed in a plain striped shirt and black trousers, his belly full and falling over his belt; his hair grey and thin and his eyes full with large dark bags under; his nose red and puffy.

Red put his hands up. Barty ran back to his side.

'*Bonjour, bonjour,*' Red said.

'*Bonjour.* We speak little *anglais*,' she said. The man put the Winchester shotgun down and went to the far corner.

'*Le chien*; good, good dog,' she said in broken English.

'He is that. He's Barty,' Red said as he looked at the girl, noticing her dark face speckled with dust and her hazel eyes, sharp and inquisitive.

'Barty, *le chien, le chien* Barty,' she said. 'You like some *frites* to eat?' She motioned to the kitchen.

'Not bloody likely; I ain't eating Jerry,' Geordie said.

'You silly gallybagger, she means chips! Even I know that!' Jimmy said as they all laughed.

'We would love *frites*; *frites* and *overs*?' Red said. He clucked and made a chicken impression. The girl, Jimmy and Geordie all laughed.

'*Oui: oeufs. Frites et des oeufs!*' She laughed and went to help the old man prepare the food.

* * *

Red went behind David and took a pee; the last thing he wanted on his mind was when he was going to get to go again before the end of the battle. Red hoped today would go as well as the last mission had. They got in and Jackson made the order to start and they cranked David over. It was all instinct. The tank rumbled up the lane. Red, accustomed to the fact he couldn't see out, concentrated on watching the Commander, the driver and Jimmy, so they could synchronise. Choking, suffocating smoke filled the cabin.

Barty sat obediently at his feet, keeping his tail underneath, his grey and white spotty coat clean and damp from the drizzle. He kept one eye open, watching the pigeons in the wicker basket.

The convoy of tanks set off at a slow and steady pace. By ten thirty they were passing Cantaing Mill. David was third in the convoy. Jackson ordered a left turn with the normal hand signal; Red, without thinking, took his track out of gear. Jimmy moved in unison.

Red could hear the machine gun fire as they moved up the rise; it must be Damnation and Divinity coming under fire from the battery in La Folie Wood.

They moved into range, coming up the ridge out of the cover of the lane. The bullets pierced David's armour. Jimmy screamed, hit; his arm began to bleed. He tore a rag with his teeth and tied it off. Geordie was grazed on his leg. David kept creeping forward; more bullets pierced the tank.

Jackson ordered Geordie and Shepherd to commence fire on the enemy positions in Fontaine. With their limited view, it was hard for them to find their targets. They knocked out one machine gun post. David edged forward, inching into the narrow streets; turning was ever more difficult with the houses close, Geordie and Shepherd finding more targets and creating bedlam. Driver Henry Stones dropped the speed.

Rounds and rounds were let off; Red could hear the damage and destruction as the shells found their targets. They inched their way into the village. Machine gun fire let rip on David's rear and more bullets flooded the compartment. One of the pigeons was shot and Guppy was hit in the arm; he screamed in agony, his arm shattered. Red got up and went to him, trying to put pressure on the wound, but Guppy was rendered unconscious. Red moved him from the Hotchkiss gun and dragged him onto the floor. He stepped into his position, looked through the small slit and aimed at a machine gun that was firing from the house next to the church. He hit and the machine gun was silenced. David still crawling, Red saw more fire coming from the other side of the church; he aimed, but failed to silence this gun. At less than walking pace, they were an easy target for the machine guns firing from behind.

These damn Bosche; I want to shut you bloody bastards up, Red thought. Geordie kept firing, shell after shell, again and again, hitting targets and missing others. There was no sense of time and Red did not think to be scared. There was no halt to the constant machine gun and rifle fire; it was piercing the tank all over. How long would their luck hold out? Where was the bloody infantry? They were meant to be right behind them to clear up. Red had to move back from the machine gun, so as to be able to navigate some more turns in the village. They went past the inn and the village crucifix, heading out of the town at the opposite end. There was a lull in the din on the exterior of the tank. Barty was cowering and whining to himself. An armour-piercing round set light to one of the accumulators; Jimmy covered it with an old blanket, dousing the flames.

'Be all right, Barty, soon be back.' Red tried to reassure his dog, not believing it himself.

They were heading back down the ridge and the safety of the mill when Stone pushed the clutch and indicated they come out of gear and stop.

'What the hell we stopping for?' Red shouted over the engine noise.

'It's Captain Fox and Cinnamon,' Jackson said looking

around.

'Oh shit, what does he bloody want?' Geordie said.

Jackson climbed past Geordie and over Barty. Red opened the sponson hatch and Jackson clambered down. Red watched as he kept his head down and walked over to Captain Fox. Jackson waved his arms, indicating back to camp. Fox shook his head and pointed back to the village. Jackson came back after what seemed like hours but was actually only two minutes.

'He only wants us back into the village; told us to use up all the bloody ammunition before we head back, the fucking twit!' Jackson said as he pulled himself up into the tank.

They turned David around and headed back into the village, Red finding it hard to fathom where the attacks were coming from; there was smoke and noise and fire.

The tank was riddled by more bullets and molten splash. David went back up the lane to the church but the way was blocked by another tank; it was Divinity. It was impeded by a telegraph pole and wire. The wire had become wrapped around it. Divinity reversed, then moved forward. They were still entangled. The engine revs whined to a high pitch. They reversed, then moved forward, pulling on the wire and wooden pole. The engine shrieked under strain as the tank failed to be released from the trap. Heavy fire rained down. Then Divinity exploded in a huge fireball; shrapnel flew out in all directions.

Stone pulled David to a stop. Red opened the hatch and leapt down, running towards Divinity. Machine gunfire cracked and the bullets peppered the ground in front of him. He stopped, then started running as fast as he could. He looked back and saw that Barty had followed him.

'No, boy, go back!' He waved at Barty to go back.

Barty didn't obey him but followed him. He reached Divinity and felt the heat of the fire on his face. He could smell carbide and petrol mixed in the air. The left track had been blown clean off. Divinity had a massive shell hole, clean through its armour. He pulled the arms of his boiler suit down and took his handkerchief from around his mouth. He put this in his hand, then pulled the lever on the hatch of the sponson. The handle was hot to the touch through the material. He opened the door. Hot air from inside blew out, scorching his hair and eyebrows. The smell of roasted meat filled his nostrils.

He got up into the tank. The gearsman on his side had life, although he was slumped against the engine, holding his arm which was badly torn at the elbow. He pulled him by the ankles out of the tank, banging his head on the side as he dragged him. Jimmy came up to help.

'There's another, I think another alive, inside; see if you can get 'im.' Red moved back, pulling the survivor. Barty tried to help, biting hold of the man by the trouser leg; he pulled with Red. Red could see he thought it was a game. They got back to the cover of David, and Geordie and Shepherd dragged the injured man aboard.

'Don't go back, lad, don't risk it; Jimmy will make it!' Geordie shouted. Red ignored him and made a run for Divinity. Barty followed him. Red could see Jimmy struggling out with his casualty. A machine gun started firing from his side of the street. Jimmy didn't stand a chance and was mown down. Red ran with all the speed and energy he possessed. He got to Jimmy and bent down over him, the machine gun raging at him. Dust and earth were blown in his face. Divinity was burning, with explosions going off as its ammunition was ignited. Red knelt down, holding Jimmy's head in his hands.

'Don't you leave me, you lummock. We're in this together, pal.' Red felt the intense heat coming from Divinity. Machine gun and rifle fire filled the air, the smell of carbide, oil, smoke and fire were all around. The wounded soldier murmured. Geordie was out, waving at him. He couldn't hear him over the burning flames and machine gun fire. David fired shells on the enemy.

'Tell Violet I love her, won't 'e,' Jimmy whispered. Red wiped the blood from Jimmy's face as life left him.

Red got hold of the other soldier and began to pull him back to David. Barty took a bullet and yelped, limping back to David. Under fire, Red managed to drag the man back. He left him and ran back to Jimmy; he took the heart necklace from around his neck and closed Jimmy's eyes with his hand. He took a deep breath; he grabbed Jimmy's body under the arms and began to pull. More machine gun fire came down. Jackson was out. Shouting at him to run, to get back; German troops were advancing out of the church doorway, making their way forward, firing as they ran. He could see anger in their faces as he stumbled back, pulling Jimmy with him.

Bloody Captain Fox, he thought. He pulled Jimmy's dead body to David, the German soldiers giving chase.

Getting in, they laid Jimmy down. Red had tears running down his face, mixing with blood and sweat. Jackson took over on Jimmy's gears. They went to make the turn. David turned slowly, and they escaped the confines of the village. They headed back down the open field; three hundred yards and they should make the relative safety of the cover of the sunken lane. The noise was intense; enemy fire fell on them, worse than any thunderstorm. Molten metal flew in the compartment.

There was a huge explosion; it came from a shell. The fuel tank went up and fire engulfed the compartment. Stone, Guppy, Jackson and Shepherd were killed. Red felt his head ringing. Geordie was next to him and they bundled themselves out of David and down onto the ground. Barty kept close to Red, hopping on his three good legs.

'Jimmy, Jimmy! We can't…' Red said.

'He's gone, lad, he's gone!' Geordie shouted.

They held each other up, Red's vision a blur, his head numb. He could make out green-grey uniforms: maybe six or eight men with rifles, heading out from the village. He and Geordie ran and stumbled. Red felt as if he was in a drunken three-legged race and couldn't move his feet fast enough. The two of them limped, stumbled and struggled towards the cover: a bomb-blasted house. The Germans fired on. Red felt his leg shot away and fell. He heard Barty yelping.

14

22nd December 1917

Connie helped Violet set up the stall on the platform. Moreton Station's platform was short, not like Dorchester or Bridport, and it wasn't like there was a huge amount of passengers, but they would make the effort. Soldiers passing through would get tea and cake; it might help lighten their burden for a few minutes at least. She wouldn't have wanted Red or Jimmy going hungry waiting for a train. The stall was an old table of Oscar's used at the fair, or when he wanted to put out his vegetables to sell to passers-by. He'd been disappointed the government inspector hadn't let him put it out in the summer.

Connie was wearing a large overcoat of her father's over her dark green winter dress. She must look a right sight. She and Violet had been baking fruit cakes since dawn, the ingredients donated by Tom Fooks, the baker in Moreton; he'd been ever so helpful in giving them the recipe and advice on cooking times. It took forever in the small range, but Miss Crabb came to the rescue, bringing three cakes of her own. She didn't even smell of cats, this morning; the smell of well-done fruit cake stuck to her, overwhelming any unpleasant odours.

There hadn't been any letters this week. None to Violet, none to her. She hoped the boys were safe. Henrietta stayed inside the café to look after her precious grandson William. The sun made an appearance, but it failed to warm her. The first train pulled in with its white billowing cloud of smoke. Passengers got off to stretch their legs, and soldiers in khaki, heading to Dorchester, came and took the refreshments. Connie poured from the large teapot, and there was fresh milk brought from the farm by Mr Grey.

They worked all morning, feeding troops as they passed through: some off to the front, some returning on leave. Connie noticed those returning, their heads tightly wound in clean white bandages, arms in slings, hobbling on crutches. There were few who were in clean khaki unencumbered by injury or wound. She thought and prayed to herself: *please keep the boys out of any trouble; please may they be the ones who stagger back onto the platform.*

The last soldiers embarked heading to Bridport. Connie and Violet packed the tea things away, all the cake gone.

They sat together in the warmth of the small kitchen, happy to be out of the cold and having a chance to rest their feet. Henrietta came in and handed William to Violet and said: 'He's been as good as gold; pity your father can't behave as well as 'im.'

'Haha! I thought you had Mr May all trained up, Mrs May!' Connie said.

'Well, he's learning, but not as fast as I'd like.' She walked out and headed for the station café and to find Oscar. Connie didn't doubt she would be telling him how she should be doing something around the house whilst he was waiting for the next train. No wonder he hated having the government telling him how to run his trains; it was the only time he was in charge of his own kingdom.

There came the sound of knocking on the kitchen

window. Connie and Violet jumped. It was Fredrick Dunn, peering in from under his post office blue peaked cap. He waved up the paper in his hand. Connie was first up; Violet laboured to her feet with William cradled in her arms. Who was it for? Was it for Connie or Violet, or both? She so hoped it was another letter; but so soon after the last? Red wouldn't have had time.

'No, no, no!' Connie screamed out, realising that the thin paper Fredrick waved was no letter; it was a telegram. Was it Red or was it Jimmy? It was too bad to contemplate. She hoped Fredrick would go away. Panic flooded her body. She felt sick. She swallowed. How could it be? Not Jimmy – he hadn't even been back to see his own son. She didn't want it to be Red, and she didn't want her friend to lose her husband.

Violet, realising the same, stumbled to the door. She opened it to see Fredrick, his smile absent, his face solemn.

'I be sorry, ladies. So sorry to have to bring 'e this. I've been out with so many this morning. You should both sit down. I'm so sorry.' He handed the telegram to Violet. Violet burst into tears. Fredrick walked out, his bag over his shoulder, and closed the door.

Violet stared at the telegram. Connie felt her throat tighten and constrict. She felt for her friend. She could see pain etched across her face. As deep a wound as any of the returning soldiers.

'Connie, you read it, please.' Violet handed her the slip. She pulled William close.

Connie took a deep breath and said: 'Regret to inform you, Private James Crabb killed in action France, November 23rd.' She uttered the words, trying to soften them but unable to do so. She couldn't think straight. Her friend crying, cradling her baby boy. Connie drew a short breath, seeing her friend devastated. Holding her son who was not yet two; weeping for her husband.

Oscar and Henrietta came into the kitchen; seeing their daughter, they put their arms around her and held her. Connie stood back. She didn't get a telegram; where was Red? Was he in the same action? Wouldn't he have been with Jimmy?

'I can't believe it. I'm never going to see him again. He never got to see his son; William will never have a father. I'm never going to feel his face again, hold his hand, listen to his rubbish jokes.' Violet sobbed as she talked.

Connie began to cry with her friend. Oscar pulled his wife to him; he held her hand and took her to the living room. Connie knew there was nothing she could say, nothing she could say to make it any easier, nothing she could do that would relieve her friend's pain or give her any sense. William sensed the sorrow and began to cry out.

'It's so unfair. He should have got to see his son!' Violet cried, wiping her tears. 'I don't know, I don't know. Why did they have to go?' she said, her head in her hands.

'It's what the pair of them wanted; there was no stopping the pair of them. Not once they decided they wanted to go, Vi. You know that he loved you so much; it was so clear, Violet; he loved you.'

'He was so lovely, Connie. He was so loving and so special. I adored him; he was the love of my life. I swear, Connie, I will never have another man. He was the only man I ever slept with and will be, Connie. I will take his love to my grave, I swear it, Connie; I swear that to you; do you hear me?' She looked at Connie and Connie could tell she meant every word.

'Don't say that, Violet, you're in shock. You don't know what you're saying. You have William to think about ...'

'He will know all about how brave his father is. But I do mean it; I'm not just saying that; he was the only one for me.' She touched William's face. 'You know I was so happy, as much as I'd ever been; he was always so funny, so jolly; you know he was.'

'It's all right, Violet, it's all right,' Connie said, and couldn't stop herself as more tears rolled down her cheek. It was so painful, so crushing to see her friend like this, and all the while wanting to know if Red was all right or was he dead with his friend. Was the telegram on its way, or… Oh my god, she realised; a fresh wave of panic swept through her forcing its way from her stomach. She wouldn't have got the telegram; it would have gone to his next of kin; maybe it was with George. What had Fredrick said? He'd been delivering out more telegrams that morning.

* * *

Connie walked straight from the station and up Farm Lane. The light was fading fast on the cold December day. She didn't like leaving her friend but she had to know. Did George or Dorothy know anything about Red? She walked into the farmyard, looking for George. She heard the horses neigh and sigh from the stables.

She found George putting the harnesses away. The barn smelt of fresh straw.

'George, wait! George!' she shouted.

He turned around. 'Connie, luv, what's up?' His face set; what did that mean?

'Have you heard anything, any letters and any telegrams?' She hoped there was none.

'Nah, nothing, Connie, nah, nothing at all. We haven't a clue. As soon as we hear we will tell you.' George shook straw from his head.

'Oh, I was hoping he might have sent you a letter?' she quizzed him.

'There is no telegram. So I'm taking that as good news,' George said. 'He was never one for much letter-writing was my brother, was he?'

'No, I don't... I suppose not.' Connie knew that wasn't true. Red had got quite good at writing. 'Yes, but him and Jimmy were together always, and in their tank.' Panic was etched on her face.

'We don't know that; he may not have been.' George went out to fetch the milk churn to begin milking. Connie followed him out.

Connie thought he might be trying to ignore the facts. How likely would it be for them not to be together? After all, they were inseparable. The not knowing was unbearable. Her breath was short, the air squeezed from her chest. If Red never came back it would be the end of her world as she knew it.

'Don't worry, Connie, I'll let you know, soon as I get any news.'

'Thanks, George, I'll do the same if I get a letter.' She walked out of the barn and headed across the road to home.

* * *

Stephen was bed-ridden. He had been there for the last three weeks. He was so ill; he hardly moved his head when she entered the room. She was fed up with cleaning his soiled sheets.

She looked after him as best she could; Miss Appleworth came and sat with them, as did Violet. When Miss Appleworth left, the two of them sat in silence, conversation exhausted. Jess lay at the bottom of the bed, sensing her master's discomfort.

The doctor came and went. His only words to Connie were that her father's days were limited; if she wanted to say anything to him, she should do it soon. She didn't like seeing her father suffer. Bringing her up on his own he had been so dedicated to her; she owed him everything; but what words could do this justice?

Violet came and sat, three women and Jess. Jess whimpered as if she was feeling the pain.

Stephen stopped breathing. Connie held his hand and wiped his face. She touched his soft wool beard and remembered the good days.

* * *

The rain was whipped up by the strong south-westerly wind as it swept across the graveyard. Vicar Thomas Wrixon finished blessing the grave and the mourners followed him into the Norman church with its high vaults and wooden pews. It was no warmer inside but at least it was dry. Connie was thankful for Violet; she held her hand throughout as they sat on the wooden pews, all in black. They sang two of Stephen's favourite hymns: "All creatures great and small" and "The old shepherd". Connie could not hold back the tears and they streamed down her face. Violet cried for Jimmy. Admiral and Mr Grey went to the lectern one after the other, dressed in all black suits. Connie found it hard to follow their kind and grateful words for the dedicated work he had carried out on the estate.

Afterwards, Sampson came up to Connie and Violet and said: 'You know, take as long as you need; take your time moving out. We will give you as long as you need,' Sampson said as he walked on.

'You must come and stay with us,' Violet said, looking at Connie.

'No, no, it's not fair on your mother and father.' Connie couldn't impose on her friend and her family.

'Where else will you go? I know he's said you can stay as long as you want, but they will want that cottage for the new shepherd.' Violet placed her arm on Connie's shoulder.

'I don't want to stay there without Father. I keep expecting to see him sat in his old chair, or coming down the stairs or coming in the back door. Even Jess is unhappy,'

Connie said. 'Miss Appleworth has been so kind and she has room, so I think I will go and stay with her. It seems the sensible thing to do. There's no point hanging around; I'll move over the weekend. That way I will be out of the cottage.'

'You know you are always welcome at ours. Mother would love you to stay, you know that, and we would talk Father round; he wouldn't mind, of course,' Violet said, holding out her hand for Connie.

'No, no, that's fine. Miss Appleworth has set out rent; and working at the school I know I can afford it. Thanks all the same, Violet,' she said, hugging her friend.

She gave Jess to George. It wouldn't be fair for her not to work.

15

14th January 1918

Constance looked out of the classroom window as she paced between the flat wooden benches and the two rows of sloping desks. The children were quiet; she had set them a spelling test so she could have space for her thoughts. She daydreamed as she watched golden leaves blow and dance across the yard.

'Oh no,' she said under her breath. Coming in through the school gates was the loping stride of George Kingson; Jess walked at his side.

She left the children and ran out to meet him in the schoolyard. It was cold, one of the coldest of the winter so far; at least it was bright. She immediately wished she'd pulled on her coat.

'Here, Connie, this has come. You better read it; my reading is not so good.' George handed the telegram to Connie, his face etched with dread. Fearing the worst she read the telegram. She knelt down, stroking Jess's fur from her forehead and down her back.

'Regret to inform you, Private Redver Kingson, missing in action presumed killed France November 23rd.' Their jaws dropped.

'That's it? That's all there is?' Connie said, looking bewildered. She stood up and Jess nuzzled her leg.

'My, it's so short! God, is that it?' George said. His face stayed set.

'Presumed killed? I can't believe that it's so short; no information, no nothing,' Connie said, her alarm rising.

'Well, I s'pose they know best; we have to accept it.' George looked puzzled.

'I'm not; I'm not accepting that. It's two months since Jimmy died. Why do they send it now? Why's it dated the same? What do they think they are doing? If they knew he was missing... They must have known. They must have known at the same time. No, I'm not putting up with that. Someone must know. Their commanding officer? Someone in authority must know! God, they can't give up on their men, can they? I've got to find out what's happened.' Connie left George and went and explained to Miss Appleworth. She called in at the house and picked up her bag, some money and a change of clothes, stuffing them quickly into her small suitcase.

She wrapped her coat tightly around her and walked down School Hill. She took the short cut across the bridge and into the field over the second bridge and through the sheep field, up the hill and into the road. Mud covered her dress. She kept her head down. She was in no mood to slow down; she was going to get some answers. She practically ran the last three hundred yards to catch the train. Oscar called out to say hello. She waved; she didn't have the time to chat. She caught the train to Dorchester with seconds to spare.

At Dorchester she went straight to the army office, which was manned by a stout Sergeant Major with a moustache.

'I can't tell you any more than the telegram. Look, they all come from London; we don't have anything to do with

them. If you want answers you will have to go to London.'
It took the wind from her sails, but she wasn't to be denied; she would head for London. She went back to the station and got a ticket for the first train to Waterloo. She felt nervous; it would be the first time she'd ever been to London.

* * *

The train arrived in Waterloo in the afternoon and she felt intimidated by the number of people; the noise, the smell, the unknown. She walked out of the station with no idea where to head. Her mind full of the sounds, of horses, carts, motor cars hogging the street. She walked in a haze, bumping into strangers. She found herself at the Houses of Parliament.

'I'm looking for the War Office,' she told the guard.

'You want Whitehall. Keep walking straight down this way.' He pointed the direction as he spoke.

Connie followed his direction and found the Whitehall War Office. She was tired and hungry. It was a long time since her breakfast of bread, butter and tea. She knocked on the door; a grumpy, bald, portly man answered, wearing a suit and tie.

'We're shut; we closed at five. Come back in the morning,' he stated, not wanting to enter into conversation. She saw the time was five past; she had missed it by five minutes. Did he not know how far she had travelled?

She found a small bed and breakfast back near Waterloo. The bed linen was dirty and she shared a nasty-smelling bathroom. It smelled of a blocked drain. She was relieved at least to get in from the evening cold. To try and keep warm under the thin blankets, she slept in her coat.

In the morning she was up early. She washed as best she could and paid the landlady, then she walked back to the office in Whitehall. It was six o'clock. She stood outside, waiting for someone to arrive. She wasn't going to give up, not with being so close; she was sure to get some answers. She wanted to know for sure. She couldn't believe Red was gone.

A small man in a navy suit and blue tie opened the office door.

'Excuse me, sir. Sir, please can you help me?' She looked him in the eye. He wore glasses; his eyes seemed to be kind.

'What is it?' he said. Connie thought him very abrupt.

'Please help me; I'm trying to find out…' She tried to hold her tears back.

'Look, we can't tell you. I get asked all the time. I want to help, I really do; but look…'

Connie burst into tears, the stress of the last few days boiling over.

'I'm sorry, I'm sorry! I didn't mean to snap. Come in out of the cold.'

He took her into the office. The walls were painted white. He sat her next to the white radiator; she could feel the heat. She took out the crumpled telegram and handed it to the official.

'Please, can you help? He was in one of the tanks; I think it was D Company or something like that,' Connie said, trying to convince the man to help.

'Mmm… Give that to me; I will see what I can find out, see if there is a report.' He went scuttling off out into the corridor.

She sat, pleased to be in and out of the cold. The chair was covered in green leather. When the secretaries arrived they made her a cup of tea with lots of sugar.

The civil servant came hurrying back into the office.

'It's sometimes the information is not there; it is confusing out on the battlefield. It depends on the officers' reports. It's hard to tell what happens; names, dates and times can get mixed up. I've still got a few friends; I will speak to his battalion commander. He might help.'

Connie felt for the first time she was getting somewhere. After an hour the civil servant returned.

'Yes, I've spoken to your man's commander, Brigadier Billington. You're lucky: he's back in Bovington. That's not far from you. If you can get there tomorrow he will speak to you. You don't realise how lucky you are; it's not many he will speak to.'

* * *

Connie felt exhausted but at least she could reassure herself with the fact that she would be getting answers. She was sure it was all the bustle of the city; it was like nothing else in her world; the motor cars, the people, the pungent air. It was all this that took her energy. The dozens and dozens of people crowding in, the smell of sweat and dirt: it was suffocating. She was glad she was only here for the day; and tomorrow she would breathe the fresh Dorset air and the people in the village would be back saying 'hello' and 'good morning', something the city people didn't value.

The train out of Waterloo back to Dorchester took forever, stopping at station after station. She was glad to be back in Dorset. At Dorchester she caught the branch line to Wool; here she got off and walked the two miles to Bovington in the pouring rain.

The camp was not what she had expected at all. There were no buildings as such, just a group of four tents. There were not many guards on duty at the makeshift entrance, a small hut and an old wooden five-bar gate. Still, she needed to persuade the guard to let her through to see the Brigadier. She could see the look on his face and it was an accomplishment in her bedraggled state to get let in. He pointed in the direction of the tents and said if she wanted to try her luck she should report to Sergeant Nicol.

She made her way through the ruts and the mud towards the tents. Connie heard the noise of shells exploding as tank crews practised on the heathland; she then saw two tanks slowly drive towards and over the barbed wire, then over the deep wide trench. She was pulled out of her haze by a man in green uniform with three stripes on his arm. She tried to stand up straight and put her shoulders back. He was short and stocky and with a moustache.

'I'm here to see Brigadier Billington,' Connie mustered with as much confidence as she could find.

'Oh, is that right, lassy?' he said, standing straight, his face used to being obeyed.

'Yes, he knows I'm coming,' Connie said. She felt her confidence ebb away.

'You better come with me. We don't get many lassies down here, I can tell you; and even less get to see the Brigadier.' He strode off, heading towards the tent.

Connie continued to worry. It was very intimidating: all the noise, the large tanks and the self-important men.

The Sergeant took her into the tent and gave her a seat. 'What's your name? I will go find the Brigadier.'

'It is Miss Constance Stevens.' She took a deep breath and tried to relax.

'I'm Sergeant Nicol,' he bellowed.

He made a brew and gave a cup to Connie, keeping one for himself before leaving to find the Brigadier. Connie blew on the tea; it was dark and bitter and didn't have fresh cream.

There were fires burning in braziers outside the tents, but it was cold. She was glad to have the tea to hold warmly close to her chest. She wished for a book to read to pass the time. She thought of Violet back home and hoped she was all right. She dared not hope she might get her own good news about Red in a matter of minutes. She looked out through the gap in the tent, watching the soldiers walk from task to task. Seeing the backs of soldiers, she felt they looked familiar. At first, her eyes would deceive her: it's Red! The thought would pass to her brain, the brain would pass the message on to her stomach, and there a small butterfly would stir before being stopped dead by a new signal from her brain: no, it's not.

There were noises of soldiers shouting. It looked to Connie as if they were refuelling one of the massive tanks with the small cans of petrol.

Connie sipped at her tea. It was really disgusting. She hoped the Brigadier would be nice after all the miles she had travelled to get to see him.

He walked in briskly and straight. He looked domineering and was wearing a huge handlebar moustache.

'I'm Brigadier Billington. So you are the young lady who has set the cat amongst the pigeons up in Whitehall, are you?' His voice was deep and authoritative.

Connie didn't know what she should say or how to address him.

'I must say I'm impressed,' he said, looking down at her.

'Um… yes, sir. I suppose I am,' Connie said.

'You're quite a lady. I don't think I've ever seen anything like this before.' He pulled a chair and sat down. 'I've been expecting you.'

'Thank you, I think,' Connie said, blushing.

'I wouldn't have even seen you, but I think you know old Brigadier Appleworth; we went to Eton together. I can tell you we got into some japes when we were younger! Don't think they ever did find out we were the ones who did it. Oh, that was another life! Think the old bugger still wishes he was fighting. He was in the cavalry, you know.'

'What… how did he…' Connie muttered and she caught her breath.

'Think it was that daughter of his; must have pushed him into it. He always did what his wife told him so now he's listening to his daughter. Got his telegram, asking I help you. I tell you, you've got some very persuasive friends down there. That's very important; you need your close friends in wartime. Sorry, I'm waffling on. So this is all about your fiancé, is it? He's a very lucky man to have such a beautiful young lady as you chasing after him.'

Connie was flattered but she wasn't here for compliments.

'Er, Brigadier Billington, can you...' She had to get to the point.

She took the telegram from her purse and neatly unfolded it from the four folds. She handed it to the Brigadier.

Billington read the telegram and said: 'Ah, yes, sounds like the battle for Cambrai. A damn place that was, all open space surrounded by woodland, several villages. He was probably near Fontaine. One day we would take ground, next day we would lose it again. Sounds to me as if he was lost round about there. Don't get your hopes up; we do know that some prisoners were taken and held behind enemy lines, though I'm sorry to say that the Bosche shot a lot of our men rather than feed them,' he said, looking at Connie. 'You should be prepared for the worst. – Sergeant Nicol, go and find Mahoney and Fox and bring them here.'

Nicol was gone for no more than two minutes when he returned. The two Captains followed him in. Connie was disappointed to see that one of them was Theodore Fox.

Captain Fox nodded at her and she nodded back. He stood tall in his army uniform, his blonde hair showing at the side of his peaked hat, his narrow pursed lips closed.

'You two know each other, that I can see,' Billington said.

'Yes, sir, we're from the same village before the war,' Fox

said sternly.

'Look, come on you two; don't take up the lady's day. She is itching to know what you two know.'

Captain Mahoney started, telling her about the operation and what the objectives had been.

'They were successful; they completed their primary objectives. They were spotted helping Divinity. This is where I have to hand over to Captain Fox; he was in Cinnamon and was the last on the scene.'

'This is not easy to say. Connie, David – which was their tank – was a fireball. By the time we got there it was a burning wreck. There were bodies everywhere. But we counted seven, seven bodies; we all knew they were one short and – well, I found this.' Captain Fox took from his pocket an army paybook; he handed it to Connie. 'We use it as identification.'

On its front cover, Connie read 'Private Redver Kingson'. It was true: he was dead. Tears flowed down her cheek in torrents. The officers, embarrassed, didn't know where to look or what to say.

'Come on, Miss Stevens. Here, have my handkerchief,' Brigadier Billington said. He handed Connie the pristine white cotton square; she took it and dabbed at her tears, unable to stop the flow.

16

15th January 1918

Redver felt the intense pain. It shot through him like lightning. Then the images came. Death, fire, machine gun fire. It all blurred into one. Running, running from the gunfire. The shots ringing out. Then the physical pain in his leg. The thought of Jimmy dead. It was excruciating; however much he tried to forget the feeling, it would come back, again and again. The nurses were few, far too few for the number of casualties. He struggled to move his arms under the tight grey blanket, so tight was it tucked under the mattress. He looked up and saw he was under green-grey canvas. The voices echoed in his head and mingled with his nightmares. Time passed but he wasn't sure how long. It seemed like days. Then the pain returned, more forceful than before.

The nurses walked from bed to bed in a hurry. Their uniforms light blue like spring sky, with once white pinafores, white banded hats wrapped around their heads no longer clean, splattered with blood, their eyes in shadow. He could smell blood and urine; he could hear shells in the distance.

Did Geordie make it? Where was he? What about Barty?

He remembered the machine guns, being cut down, falling, being chased, Geordie helping him. It was coming back to him but he didn't welcome it. Then the soldiers, chasing, shooting, captured.

They gave him morphine. It was then the doctor came. He spoke, and looked decisive; but Red didn't understand him; what had he said? Then without hesitation, the doctor had picked up the large saw, and began to cut his leg. He remembered that; the feeling was dull. His memory flaky, but he remembered that, thinking, *he's about to saw at my leg.* Thinking *no, don't do that, what are you doing to me? Leave it; I'm going to be wanting that.* He didn't feel it; he passed out.

Jimmy's dead. He was gone. His best friend gone in an instant. Weren't they all meant to make it? His body with the others, in David, no burial, no funeral.

He looked around the tented field hospital; there were rows and rows of beds. He craned his neck but the rows went as far as he could see. He heard British voices, screams and shouts. There was one doctor. The nurse came to change his bandage. She had soft eyes, with dark shadows below.

'*Guten Morgen.*' She didn't smile.

Red replied: 'Do you know where my dog is?' – hopeful he was safe.

'*Was?*' the nurse said, in a heavy German accent.

'Dog, woof, woof. Where?' He pleaded with her. 'My friend Geordie; where are they?'

'*Hund?*' she said, looking bewildered.

'Yes, hound; my hound,' Redver said, his frustration causing him more pain.

'*Nein, nein; kein Hund.*' She shook her head. She busied herself removing the blood-soaked bandage from his stump, which ended above where his right ankle used to be.

'My friend, Geordie,' Red said, pleading.

'*Freund?*' The nurse took away the old bandage and began to wrap the clean white bandage. Red didn't feel anything.

'Yes, *Freund*, Geordie.' Redver nodded.

'*Kein Freund*, Geordie, *nein*,' she answered.

'Oh, I see.' His mind was still foggy on morphine. 'What's your name?' Red asked.

'*Mein Name?*' the nurse said. Red nodded.

'Helene,' she replied.

'Helene, my name is Redver. Where is my friend?' he said.

'*Ich verstehe sie nicht.*' She shook her head from side to side.

This was hopeless. Helene tucked his arms back under the mattress and left him. His leg gone, his friend dead, Geordie missing, and Barty dead for all he knew. God, why had he come to this war? Why hadn't he stayed and been happy on the farm? He could have been in the arms of Connie. How he would have made love to her, kissed her; they would have been happy. He dropped off to sleep and began a new nightmare.

He was on a big steam engine, bigger than Titan; then he was with Geordie back in the tank. It exploded and everyone was dead. He floated up to the clouds, floating up over Ashcombe, flying with the crows. He looked down and he could see St Mary's Church. Vicar Thomas was there and lots of villagers, watching and cheering. He flew down and found a branch which made a good perch. A second crow was there and it was Jimmy. They sat there watching and worked out they were watching a wedding. It was a sunny spring day and the warm breeze made it comfortable. He was shocked when he saw the bride arrive; he couldn't see her face, she was behind a veil; but it was unmistakably Connie. He willed himself to be the groom. Her dress was all white and followed the contours of her slim figure. She lifted her veil and he could see she wasn't smiling; she looked sad. Barty was at the bottom of the tree barking up.

Connie looked over at the tree and seemed to look him straight in the eyes.

'You know, old mate, you don't have much time; you should get back as soon as you can. She loves you. You don't have any time to waste,' Jimmy said.

He woke with a start. A hand was on his shoulder. His sheets were soaked with his sweat.

'Tommy, Tommy, you wake.' It was a nurse. 'You wake, Tommy.' She wore a blue tunic edged in dark red. '*Sie kommen draußen,*' she said. Helene came and joined her with a wheelchair. They manhandled him out of the bed and wheeled him outside. The smell was as horrendous as in the tent; and even with the blanket wrapped over him he felt the chill wind. He saw the large number of tents, which the nurses ran in and out of. He saw German soldiers, walking and wounded the same as the British. Battle weary.

'*Was? Was?*' Redver said.

'*Freund, Freund,*' Helene replied.

It was sunny if cold. Helene wheeled him through the six other field hospital tents. They came around a corner of a green tent. Standing there was Geordie, his arm bandaged; and on a length of string, Barty. Helene left them and returned back to her patients.

Geordie let go of Barty and he ran straight to Red's side by the wheelchair.

'You saved him, Geordie, you bugger.' Red smiled as he scratched Barty behind his ears. Barty wagged his tail from side to side.

'Ay, did that, and you too, mate,' Geordie said, walking over.

'How did you find me?' Red said as he looked up at Geordie.

'Looked in every bloody tent, didn't I, when I came round, and kept hold of Barty. They wanted to take him from me when I was lying there so I thought I better bloody well get up and find you else you would never talk to me again,' Geordie said as he lit up a cigarette.

'You're feeling well enough for one of those, then! Have you seen anyone else? Did anyone else make it?' Red said, trying not to breathe in Geordie's smoke.

Geordie pushed Red out from the tents. Red could see the high wire fence and sentry posts, manned by Germans with fixed machine guns.

'Nah, sorry, we seem to be the only ones who's made it. We was the only ones captured. You better get yourself out of that chair, swift like; the word is we are to be moved to a bigger camp.'

* * *

Redver looked out from the back of the horse-drawn wagon, with no idea where they were. He held Barty close to him; they had tried to take him from him at the hospital. He'd shared his meagre rations of weak broth and black sawdust bread. But he wasn't going to let Barty suffer. The wagon was so full, they huddled close. It kept the cold away.

The sun was up, moving across the sky as they headed eastwards. They travelled on rough lanes, passing German troops whose eyes were hungry and desperate, and standing trees shattered in two. The voices different and distinct, the ravages of war the same.

'Don't like the look of this,' Geordie said as he pointed at the high wire that appeared on the horizon. It must have stretched hundreds of yards in all directions. The fence was nine feet tall and towered above them. Red saw machine gun posts high in the wooden sentry boxes. The camp reminded him of training camp at Elveden, the massive area sectioned behind the fence. They came up to the wooden barrier and were led through by the guards. There were rows and rows of green-grey tents. The wagon moved down the long drive, at the end of which was a large chateau; four floors high, with two round towers at each corner. The drive ended at the bridge to the moat.

Red looked at the soldiers who stood to attention. The soldiers guarding them on the wagon ordered them down. Red clambered down with his wooden makeshift crutch. He and Geordie had fashioned it from a discarded tent pole.

He was lucky. Many men were worse off than him; and other prisoners told him about their friends who had got killed rather than being taken prisoner. Barty stood with him, obedient for Red.

The commanding officer came from the entrance of the chateau. When he got closer Red could see he had a birthmark on his cheek. He was tall, dark haired. Thin, with his hair groomed back. He removed his grey-green hat with its black peak and red band and placed it under the crook of his shoulder.

'I am Major Von Achterberg,' he said in perfect English with a German accent. 'You prisoners of war,' he continued, as he eyed the prisoners. 'You will obey me and my men. If you do this and work hard, you will not have anything to worry about.' He paced in front of the prisoners. Red felt worried. He seemed to have no mercy in his eyes. 'I tell you, if you try and escape, my men have orders to shoot. If you cause me trouble of any kind, I will have you shot.' He stared.

"'E sounds worse than bloody Sergeant Nicol, don't 'e,' Geordie whispered to Red.

'If you work hard and follow orders, then I will make sure you get fed.' The Major stopped in front of Red and Geordie. 'Is that clear?' he shouted.

'Yes, sir.' The prisoners replied as one.

'We are short of food; there is not a lot to go around.' He shook his head. 'You there; step forward,' the Major ordered, pointing at Red.

Red hobbled forward on his crutch.

'Bring the dog.' Red pulled Barty forward with him, with a growing sense of despair.

'We have no room for dogs; we have no food for dogs; we only have food for men.' He unclipped his holster and took out his Luger pistol. 'Hold him.'

'No! Don't do this! I can share my food! I won't eat any more than anyone else, I can catch my own, don't worry, I won't take any...' Red pleaded and stood in front of Barty.

'*Nein*, you do not disobey me! Is that clear?' The Major nodded at his Sergeant who swung up his rifle and brought the butt down on Red's cheekbone. In the same movement, he knocked Red's crutch away. Red fell to the ground. Before he could stand, the Major fired one round of his pistol. Barty slumped to the ground, dead.

'See what happens if you disobey me? I don't make, what you say, empty threats.' He moved away.

* * *

Geordie and Red were seated outside the tent on old crates, close to but not touching the burning fire in the brazier. Red felt despondent. His friend Jimmy gone. To see Barty shot, stone cold dead. How could a man do that? Why hadn't he listened? He would have fed Barty; it wouldn't have been a problem. Why had the Major been so cruel? He must find some paper, something to write with, and get a letter sent to Connie. He must let her know he was alive.

'Think of it like this: it's Elveden all over. This time we have that bloody Major instead of Sergeant Nicol bawling at us. And least we ain't having to ride round in that poisonous ol' tank. Thank god we ain't going be doin' that again,' Geordie said.

Simple beds lined each side of the tent: too many, cramped together. Their hair, clothes and beds were full of lice and the smell of shit blew over from the latrines. Red ran his hand over his wooden peg of a foot. He itched at the leather straps that held it in place. At least this didn't get cold, not like his left foot. He could get around, not like some of the more unfortunate.

'The food's not so good, though, is it? It's a shame Cookie wasn't captured too,' Red said, adjusting the leather straps to his peg leg.

'I've been thinking about that.' Geordie warmed his hands in front of the brazier, rubbing them together.

'You bloody would, wouldn't you? I'm surprised you haven't done something already. Don't tell me: does it involve some kind of wager?'

'I'm offended, Red! What do you take me for? The way you talk it makes me sound like I'm forever making a bet.' Geordie smirked.

'Me? I never said such a thing!' Red said, keeping a straight face.

'Look, the old Bosche: they're short of everything, we can all see that. They don't have enough to eat; and look, the Major doesn't know that in our midst we have one of the best poachers in the business. Don't we!' Geordie patted Red on the shoulder. 'We should talk to the old Major, tell him if we can set some snares, we can get him a dozen rabbits or so. Once he is on our side, he won't be able to stop lavishing us with praises.'

'He ain't going to want to speak to the likes of us! And why should I bloody help him out anyway? Not after he shot Barty.'

'I know, I know. Well, it would be helping ourselves, as much as him. 'Cos we would keep a couple for ourselves, wouldn't we? Keep 'em down our trouser legs. Every morning, that Major goes for his walk; we could see him then. It can't fail!'

'I'm sure to regret this; why not?' Red let out a sigh. 'I ain't going to forgive him, though, not even if he agrees and gives us the wire. He was cruel.' He shook his head.

'Good lad, good lad.'

* * *

Red sat on the corner of the bed. Geordie had managed to get hold of some paper and a pencil; it would do. He leaned on his thigh and began to write.

Dearest love, my darling Connie,

I hope this letter finds you well. I'm sorry not to have written sooner, I'm so sorry I was not able to save Jimmy, I know how she must feel and how much you must have been worrying about me, but I am well, I have survived and I am now a prisoner. We do eat, not that well but if we keep to the orders I think we will be alright.

I love you, I love you and thinking of you helps me get through it all. I don't know when or how I will make it back but I will I promise you.

I want to marry you Connie my little buttercup, will you ask your father for me. I want to marry you the day I get back if I can! I know that may be too soon. I promise you I will be with you soon as I can.

xxxxx your love Redver xxxxx

Redver folded the letter, put it in the envelope and addressed it. He took it straight to the post point. He kissed it and handed it in.

17

16th February 1918

Connie and Violet sat together on the St Mary's Church wall, looking down over Moreton Hill. The old yew tree was full of tree sparrows; their morning song filled the graveyard. Henrietta was babysitting William, letting Violet get some air.

'I love him, I loved him, Violet. Why didn't I tell him? Why didn't we get married like you and Jimmy? At least then we would have the memory of being together.'

'Don't think like that. Remember the great time you did have. How much fun there was. That's what I'm trying to do with my memories of Jimmy.'

'It's so hard, Violet. First Father, now Red; both my favourite men are gone, and even Jess my old dog, too. Oh, Violet, why?' She looked down School Hill as Fredrick Dunn in his uniform struggled up the hill. Vicar Wrixon walked out of the church gate.

'Hello, ladies.' He nodded and walked past.

'Hello, Vicar,' they said.

'I know, Connie. I understand. It's what I've been asking myself every day for the last two months. It's so hard, but you have to get up and get on with it.'

'Yes, but I never told him how I felt. I never gave him the words he wanted to hear. We have the letters, but it's not the same. I thought we would have the rest of our lives to work it out, not a few months. I'm sorry, Violet; I should have been more supportive. I didn't understand what you were going through; not really. It's so hard. I didn't know how deep my feelings for Red were. We don't even have their bodies to say goodbye to, do we?'

Fredrick Dunn walked past, saying good day as he continued on his round.

* * *

She walked and walked on through the pouring rain; she came to the river and then continued on up the path. Torrents of brown water cascaded over her feet; she didn't feel or notice. She was thinking of reaching the top. Her legs ached and the backs of her calves were sore with the effort. It didn't matter and she didn't care. She walked through the natural tunnel.

She put the faded maroon blanket down on the spot where she and Red had picnicked in the ramparts. The maroon blanket was already wet; even so, she sat down.

Tears and rain mingled on her face. She remembered that summer how warm it was; the sun on her face; how tactile and gentle he was. She felt alone. Violet had William and her family. She had none. No father and no husband. She'd never felt so lonely.

She watched the magpie stand and peck for a worm and then, successful, fly away. What would Red's Granfer have said? 'One for sorrow.' Her heart felt drained and empty; the sorrow dragged on her like a ship's anchor. She felt exhausted.

* * *

She threw herself into work at the school. She spent her spare time with Violet, consoling each other. Time went by slowly. She would often visit the library in the Manor House; here, she found it easy to lose herself in her reading. Books she never imagined she would get to read: *Middlemarch*, *Great Expectations* and *David Copperfield*. Often she would sit and read by the large window, glancing up to see trains passing on the railway line below. To Connie, it looked as if the trains appeared every minute, so absorbed she was in her reading. Spencer, the butler, would come in with a blanket to keep her warm, along with refreshing cups of tea. His grey hair was thin and his chin sharp. He stood straight and walked deliberately.

She liked it when the sun warmed her. On Sunday, she wore her blue striped dress. Sampson came and sat with her and they discussed *Pride and Prejudice*. He wore his dark hair short; his kind, honest eyes looked at her.

'I like the colour of your dress, Connie; it's such a good match for the colour of your eyes.' He glanced up at her, his eyes soft and gentle.

'Thank you, Sampson that's kind of you to say,' Connie replied. It wasn't often anyone in the village said anything as nice. She was surprised; he could spend time with a far more sophisticated woman than her.

'There's a dance Saturday night, in the Masonic Hall. We should go. You could bring Violet along; it will do both of you good.' He smiled.

'Oh, I don't think so; it's not me. Thank you anyway.' She looked down at the book in her lap.

'Go on! Look, it's time you enjoyed yourself; think of it as exercise. I'll pick you up at seven,' he insisted.

'Go on then, all right.' She pushed her hand through her hair.

She didn't believe she was agreeing, but if she didn't, Violet would never let her hear the end of it.

* * *

'He's such a good dancer, Connie,' Violet said.

'I suppose; he moves well. Why don't you dance with him next time he asks?'

They were in the Masonic Hall; a charity dance with the entrance fee donated to Coneygar Hospital for wounded soldiers. The band was set up on the wooden stage at the far end of the hall.

The band was a mix of servicemen home on leave. The hall was dimly lit. Connie and Violet sat in the back corner, as far away from the dancing as they could.

They were both asked time and time again. Connie did have to concede that Sampson was by far the best male dancer there: his feet precise in their position, his timing and rhythm impeccable. He was also showing huge perseverance. She thought she had better accept his next invitation; it would be the fifth or sixth time of asking. She'd lost count.

'Are you going to dance with him or not? The poor soul; he's asked you six times already,' Violet said as she looked around the room.

'Is it?' Connie looked away from Violet. She played with a stray strand of hair.

'You should dance with him; and after all, we do want a lift home, don't we!' she giggled.

Connie watched as Sampson glided over the floor, taking his female partner back to her seat. He walked with his shoulders pinned back and his back straight, his head high. She tried to look elsewhere, at those still dancing or at Violet or at the wall; but she glanced back to see him advancing towards her.

'How about it? Will you give me the pleasure of the last dance, Miss Stevens?' He bowed his head down.

'Yes, Sampson, why not?' She breathed in deeply.

'Thank heavens! I thought you'd never say yes.' He held

his hand out.

He took her by the hand and led her to the centre of the floor. She felt him pull her close. He smelled of clean, fresh aftershave. She conceded he looked good in his suit. She couldn't help but think of the last time she danced with Red, all that time ago at the harvest festival. She tried hard to put it out of her mind.

She didn't notice the tears running down her face until they touched her lips. They continued dancing. He pulled her closer, she feeling embarrassed. She didn't know the moves as well as the other woman.

She looked over at Violet, who was smiling, and gave her a small wave.

* * *

Sampson drove them back, the yellow Morris bullnose making light work of Lee Lane and Snowdrop Hill. He dropped Violet off first at the station. He then drove back through Ashcombe, down Palmers Hill, before driving up School Hill. Miss Appleworth lived in the first schoolhouse on the left. Sampson parked, applying the handbrake. Connie heard the owl call out from the tall pine trees that stood opposite. The moon was bright, and she could see hundreds of stars. She thought of Red being one of the stars shining down.

'Connie, I've become very close to you this last month.' He looked over at her from the driver's position. Connie thought she could see the small boy in his face.

'Sampson, I've enjoyed your company. I don't want any more than your friendship at this time. I've too much work to concentrate on.' She couldn't get Red from her mind.

'I understand. I've never lost anyone like you have. To lose your father and a friend, so close together… I'm so sorry.' His eyes conveyed kindness.

'You're very kind to say, Sampson. I know you mean it. I

mean, you're an honest man.' The owl hooted again. It was late; she should get in before Miss Appleworth came to find them. 'I should be getting in.'

'Red was a friend to me as well. He was standing up for me to Theodore. I can't ever thank him for that. And well… to lose Jimmy as well… I wonder some days if we will have any of the men return.'

'Your brother always seems to make it back, doesn't he? It was him who told me, you know, and he couldn't disguise his contempt. I'm sorry, Sampson; he's your flesh and blood and all, but that man, he is repellent.' She felt herself losing control.

'It's all right, Connie; I don't have much time for him myself. He is my brother and all; but I have to say, I don't want to see him again.' He placed his hand on hers; she pulled it away and into her lap. The touch seemed to give her energy, a feeling of intimacy, a bond she had felt emerge when they danced together. Red was gone; he wasn't coming back; she should move on with her life. Sampson put his hand to hers again. She held it; it felt warm and secure. He moved his hand to her arm and stroked her. His hands felt soft and gentle.

'No, Sampson, I only want us to be friends.' She blushed; she should get out.

'Connie, Red would have wanted you to be happy. He wouldn't want you to be sad. He would want you to get on with your life, to enjoy it, to follow your dreams. He loved you so much; that was clear to everyone. I don't want to replace him. I don't want you to forget him; I want you to be happy too, and I think I can help you be happy.' He looked her in the eye as he spoke. He was speaking from the heart, he was deliberate. He spoke with honesty and feeling. He was right, Red would want her to be happy; he wouldn't like seeing her like she was, not like this, all morose.

'Drive, Sampson, drive the car.' She looked at Sampson, her arms in her lap.

'What? Where?' he stammered back.

'Anywhere away from here, from the front door. I don't know. Up to the beacon?' Sampson obeyed her and drove the Morris up the hill. He turned right at St Mary's Church and followed the lane right up to the beacon. They didn't meet any traffic; it was getting late. She should really have gone into the cottage, gone to bed. But what would she have done there? Would she have been able to sleep? She hadn't for the last weeks. Why not stay out? Why not? Her Red taken from her; why shouldn't she? Violet was always on at her to enjoy herself to have fun, wasn't she? To do something spontaneous, to let herself go. Well, this would be something to tell her friend, wouldn't it.

There was no one else in sight. Sampson pulled the car off the road. She looked down over all of Ashcombe and Moreton, the moon casting shadows. Down in the field, Connie could see the herd of deer, some feeding whilst others slept.

'I'm sorry, Connie, I didn't mean to make you feel bad.' He put his hand out; she met his hand with hers. It was good to feel his soft hands in hers. She tightened her fingers around his. His voice was soothing and calming. 'It will take time, time for the grief to heal.'

'It doesn't feel like it will ever leave me, Sampson. I don't sleep at night. I'm wishing he would come back, that he would be with me again.' She couldn't believe she was telling Sampson of all people. Shouldn't she have said this to Violet?

'I know, I know, but eventually, I don't know when, or how long it will take, but you will come back to yourself. You will in time. You will feel better and you will remember those fantastic memories you had with him.' He gave her a look of support and understanding.

'Thank you, Sampson, you don't have to say that.'

'I mean it, Constance. It's so unfair, this war. We're fighting for our freedoms but it only seems to be taking away. We are gaining so much in that we are not oppressed and largely we can continue with our lives. One day it will all be over and if we win, then we will live in freedom; if we don't win, then life will not be as we know it and everything that our loved ones have done will be in vain.' He paused; he took his hand out from her fingers and stroked her arm, from her shoulder to elbow. It made her feel secure and comfortable.

'Constance, Redver and James: they died for a cause, they wanted to do their duty, they have given their lives so that we can live free, that we can live our lives. And they loved you and Violet so much; that can't be taken away, even with their deaths.' He was right but it didn't make it any easier to hear. His hand lingered on her shoulder before he moved his fingers, so soft and so gentle, to the back of her neck. She felt his fingers touch the naked skin on her nape. Her senses awakened. She could smell his sweet aftershave. His fingers, so soft and callous-free, warmed her neck as his light touch caressed her. She should tell him to stop, to behave himself. She didn't have the will. Why was she letting him go this far? She should stop. She couldn't; she needed his touch.

'Connie, none of us are perfect, we all have our faults. God knows I have so many. I will never try and be Red, you know. I know you will always have feelings for him. I will always do my best for you.' His fingers stayed on the nape of her neck. They were warm and comforting. How could this be wrong? She wanted his lips on hers; was this wrong?

'Sampson, your words are so kind. I don't know why you say them?'

'I mean them, Connie.' He stopped and brought his hand back to hers.

'But why me? You could have your pick of any woman.' She held his hand and rested it on her thigh.

'I hate seeing you make yourself suffer like this when you were always full of so much light.' It was the nicest thing anyone had ever said to her. He leaned over, put one hand on the base of her neck and moved the other to the side of her head. Her mind screamed at her to put a stop to it. She couldn't; her body was aching and empty and desired it.

He moved his lips to hers, soft and gentle, his fingers moving to her back. He met her lips with his. She felt the intensity ripple through her body, like waves on a shore. She felt herself being carried out to sea. His lips were warm on hers. He kissed her, she reciprocated. His hand was in her hair, stroking her head. She wanted to feel more of his skin on hers. His hand moved down to her shoulder. He moved his head up and away; *no, don't stop*, she thought. He then moved back; this time, his lips moved to her neck. He kissed her on the side of her neck and nuzzled into her. She placed her hands on his head and held him there. She could feel his intensity. She could feel the pleasure through her entire body. He kissed her neck slowly, holding her hand as he did. He moved to her ear and nibbled gently with his teeth. He stopped.

'I shouldn't; I'm sorry.' She looked at him; he looked as if he was going to cry. 'I shouldn't take advantage. You're vulnerable; you're not feeling yourself. I don't want it to be this way,' Sampson said.

She didn't want him to stop.

'Constance, I know the timing isn't good; and look, I want you to know I don't ever want to trample on the memories you have of Red. I think there is no one else who can be as good for you as I can. I've thought about nothing else, nothing else for so long now. It isn't something I've just thought of; will you marry me?' He held her hand. 'I don't even have a ring or anything. This feels so right to me, I promise you I will do my best to make you happy and give you everything you ever want.' He paused for breath. 'You don't have to answer me.'

'Oh, Sampson, I don't know; I don't know how I feel.' This wasn't entirely the truth; she did feel something coursing through her. Her body was telling her but her mind was trying to block it. 'Why not?' She couldn't believe what came from her mouth.

'Is that a yes?' A smile so wide appeared on his face.

'Why not? We have a lot in common.' Her confidence grew; she could do this; she was alone and this way she wouldn't be, not any more; and he was a good man. 'Yes, Sampson.'

'Oh, thank you, Connie, you've made me happier than I've ever been in my life.' He took her hand, then kissed her. She kissed him back, wanting more. 'I promise you, Constance Stevens. I will never let you down, I swear on my life.' She stopped him talking; she put her hands around his neck and pulled his lips back to hers.

18

2nd March 1918

Had she done the right thing? Her mind raced with twenty different thoughts at the same time. She sat on the wooden pew at the front of St Mary's Church. Walking up from school, the air had felt warmer, the sky was clear. The sun was shining, the hazel and ash were in bud and sparrows and blackbirds were singing. There seemed to be more hope.

Why had she said yes? Should she go through with it? She had to now; she had given her word. She looked around the church, the altar in front of her, to her left the pulpit. The vicar had told her to wait for him. Whilst she waited she closed her eyes and prayed for Red, god rest his soul. God be kind; he was in a better place. She hoped he hadn't suffered in his last minutes. She was going to be married on May the eighteenth; she would be Mrs Sampson Fox. God, how strange it sounded! She would be married to the squire's son! She couldn't believe it. It didn't sound like her; she would be his wife. She would be related to the Admiral and Josephine; she would live in the Manor. Live in the Manor! How could that be, the shepherd's daughter living in the Manor House? Would her father have been proud of her? She hoped so.

'Sorry to keep you, Miss Stevens. Come in, come in. You know, there is so much work for me in the parish,' Vicar Wrixon said as he opened the vestry door. He beckoned her over.

She got up and walked to him. She came into the vestry and noticed newspapers and the Reverend's papers piled on his desk. His glasses were on the end of his nose, his squashed nose; and she noticed his thick black eyebrows. She hadn't really looked at him this close before. Looking at him up close was different to seeing him perform his sermons on Sundays. He looked more approachable, more friendly. His face was round, the top of his head bald, with hair only on the sides covering his funny shaped ears. She noticed his boxing prizes in the cabinet behind him.

'Connie, thank you for coming up.' He looked at her from above his spectacles, his dark eyes sharp and intelligent. 'I hear you've been doing such good work at the school. Miss Appleworth is always singing your praises. I can remember when I first came here what terrible business it was getting you children into school. It was so rough back then, and you've kept that work going.' He sat back in his chair.

Connie wondered what he was going to talk to her about. It must be something to do with the wedding.

'Thank you, Reverend, I enjoy it, I find it very satisfying and rewarding seeing them improve.' She smiled at him.

'Yes, Miss Stevens, good. And you've set the date and I'm very pleased for you. He's a good young man; I know he's doing good work on the farm. I would have liked him to be in the army like his brother, but... well, the Admiral has his reasons, and I know that we've lost so many men: poor James Crabb, Redver Kingson, Ken Smyth, Thomas Smyth, Charles Fooks, John Hansford, Thomas Gale, Robert Gale. I know Redver and James were your friends, and you've lost your father too. But your friends have given their lives for a great, great cause, and now they are in heaven,' he said. She felt as though he was giving her a sermon. She felt her hairs stand up on the back of her neck at the thought of Redver and James.

'They wanted to go; I didn't think they should.' She bit her tongue to stop herself.

'It was the right thing for them to do. I'm sorry they had to give their lives but it was God's work they were doing.' He couldn't have called her in for this. 'I'm going to make sure we never forget them, Connie; we will remember that they have given their lives so that we can live ours free from tyranny.'

'Yes, Reverend.' She could have argued that they could have served their God just as well making sure there was food on people's plates.

'Look, Connie, I've been meaning to talk to you, now you're going to be married. I'm going to have to ask you to leave your post. Not straightaway, but once this war is over, which I don't think from the reports I've been reading is going to last much longer. Look, when it's over I'm going to have to have this position open to give your teaching post to someone who will need it. After all, you will be well provided for, what with being in the Fox family.' Her face dropped. She'd expected something like this; after all, Miss Appleworth had never married. But now with the suffragette movement, she thought times might be changing.

'But Reverend, I was hoping that maybe you could turn a blind eye. I do so love it, and like you said, Miss Appleworth is so pleased with me. I was hoping that perhaps you could let me carry on past the end of the war, if you're right and it ends soon.'

'Look, it's not really the done thing. I don't know of any other school in the area which does let women work on once they are married. You have to think of others, Connie;

you know, those who survive the war. They will need the positions; it won't be easy for them. We have to give them the chance. I'm sure you can understand that, can't you?' He took his pen and made a note on his papers.

'I do understand that others will need the opportunity, but I've lost so much too and teaching is the one constant that I can always lose myself in. Please, will you consider letting me stay on?' She swallowed hard; she had said too much. The vicar sighed and pushed himself back in his chair.

'Miss Stevens, I know you care about the children and you love this role. Look, you can continue, as I said, till the war is over; and who really knows how long that will be? Look, I will say this to you: I will not make you any promises, but if you carry on as well as you are doing, I will consider it again. It is no promise, but... well, I will think it over. I can't be fairer than that, can I?'

'Thank you, Reverend, thank you.' She had known it would be the case: be secure and be married, or have taught all her life.

'And Miss Stevens, I'm sure you will have more than enough keeping you busy once you're married bringing up your family. So it's not like you would have enough time to dedicate to your role, like Miss Appleworth.'

'Yes, Reverend.' She chewed her tongue and hoped he wouldn't notice. 'Is that everything?' She stood up and went to walk out.

'Yes, my dear. I will see you in church on Sunday.'

19

18th May 1918

She headed to their bedroom. The day had been beautiful; the sky clear and dark blue with only the odd white fluffy cloud. Violet, with William in tow, had been her bridesmaid and she had been glad that she was by her side. George Kingson had walked her down the aisle. It was painful to see the likeness of Red in his face. His memory strong; and if the pain had dulled since January, then it was brought back to the surface with the thought that she could have married him. If only they had been more decisive. It could have been him she was walked down to marry. Sampson: he was a good honest man, he was, and she must make him as happy as possible. It rankled that Reverend Wrixon insisted she would have to leave the school after the war. What an attitude! It was all right for women to work when needed with all the men away, but as soon as they were back then they could go back to breeding children.

She walked up the landing with the train of her dress flowing behind her. She was happy to be alone and to herself. Who would ever have imagined that she would end up married and in the Manor? She couldn't believe it. It was so large. She headed down the corridor and opened the door to their bedroom. Connie could feel her heart race, and she would be making love for the first time to her husband Sampson Fox, and she Mrs Sampson Fox. It was kind of Sampson to let her come up before him. She undid her dress and slid from it. She hung it in the large wardrobe. She had never had such nice clothes and such ornate furniture. The dress had been made in London. She picked up the blue silk nightdress; Fanny Hansford had laid it out. It felt so luxurious as she dropped it over her head and onto her naked body.

She heard footsteps on the stairs: Sampson's, her husband's. He walked slowly along the corridor. Her heart beat a little faster. He was coming to her. She got under the covers and waited for him. She hoped it wouldn't hurt.

'Hello again, Connie my wife,' he smiled and joked. 'How is your nightdress? I hope you like it. Violet helped choose it, you know.' He went to the dresser and began to remove his trousers. Connie rolled over and faced the wall.

'It is so very nice, thank you, Sampson. I don't think I've ever owned anything so beautiful.' She sighed.

'You are more than welcome; it's nothing. I am going to make sure you're the best-dressed woman in the village.' She could sense he was naked but she dared not look.

'You know, I'm not fussed that much about clothes; I'm happy with those that I have. They're not that important to me.' He walked around to his side of the bed; she felt him get in. He put his hand on her back, he slid closer to her and she felt his warmth through the silk as their bodies touched.

'Yes, I understand, but now you're my wife, we can afford them. It will make me happy to see you and see you enjoying them.' He spoke slow and soft, his voice deep and controlled. She felt reassured and secure.

'It's kind of you, Sampson. Look, I don't want you spending money on me unnecessarily.' He stroked her arm as his body moved against her. Her body began to warm.

'Yes, Connie, of course, whatever you want. And look, I know the Vicar has said you can keep working until the end of the war, but you don't have to. You can leave now, or in the summer. After all, you don't need to, do you?' She turned over on her back.

'Sampson, you know I enjoy it. I don't want to give it up any minute sooner than I have to.' It annoyed her. Why did all men think that as soon as women were married they would give up their passions? 'I love doing it; I don't want to have to give it up, ever.'

'Yes, but you want your own children; I mean we want our own children too, don't we? After all, Father and Mother are expecting it. We will be expected to.' He stayed on his side; his hand went to hers. She sighed.

'I don't know, I didn't think I did want children. I'm worried, Sampson; my mother died giving birth. What if I'm the same? What if I can't have children?' She took in a deep breath and looked at the top of the four poster bed. She thought Sampson might have been different; that having been to university, he would be more enlightened, his views more modern. 'You know not all women can, and women are doing more and more these days. Look at what they have given to the war effort. Look at the women who work on the land, those that fill all the positions producing ammunition; you've seen it yourself.'

'Yes, yes, Connie, I know, and I want you to be happy. I'm sorry; I'm sorry I've said the wrong thing. I didn't mean to upset you. Of course, keep teaching for the time being, as long as the vicar lets you.' He took her hand and squeezed.

He moved his mouth to her neck and kissed. His hand then moved from hers and stroked her down the arm. She began to warm to him. She felt her body tingle with desire. She raised herself to her elbows. Sampson leant over and pulled her nightdress off over her head, then threw it to the floor. She lay back down.

Sampson kissed her neck, then moved his lips to meet hers. She felt his tongue penetrate her mouth; their tongues touched. Her desire was building within. His hands traced down her neck to her breasts, where his finger circled and teased. She felt her nipples harden and she kept kissing back. He moved between her legs and she felt the weight of his body. She held his back. She felt the anticipation building.

Her body wanted him. She tried to put all thoughts from her mind. She tensed.

'It's all right, Connie, we don't have to do anything if you don't want to.' He propped himself on his arms, his blue eyes closer than anyone she'd seen.

'No, carry on; I want to. I'm scared it might hurt.' She blinked.

'Don't worry; if it does, I will stop.'

He kissed her, more intense than before. She put her hands through his hair. His hands moved over her breasts, his fingers touching her nipples. He moved his head back to her neck and kissed, moving to nibble her ear. She felt him hard against her as he lowered himself. He pushed himself inside. She muffled a cry of pain and bit her lip to stop herself from screaming. He penetrated her and thrust hard.

'Is it all right?' he asked, as he continued, propped on his elbows above her.

'Yes, Sampson.' She couldn't tell him the truth, not on their wedding night; she wouldn't spoil it. The pain lessened as he continued thrusting. She could see the excitement build on his face. He began to moan to her. She breathed heavier and this heightened his excitement.

'Oh, Constance, Constance, thank you.' He rolled off and lay on his back. She couldn't help but wonder why it was that she so enjoyed the anticipation more than the act. She lay back and tried to fall asleep.

20

8th November 1918

It wasn't a bad day at all. They returned to the tent as the sun went down. Red undid his trousers and pulled them down. There, bound to his leg, was a dead rabbit. He took off the string and went about preparing the rabbit to cook. Once gutted and skinned he skewered it with the piece of hazel.

Geordie copied him. Soon the air was full of the smell of fresh roasting rabbit; it spilled into the surrounding tents. They were soon watched by hundreds of hungry eyes.

'Form a queue, boys. A piece of delicious rabbit. What have you got to offer? All considered; what do you have?' Geordie was in his element with everyone watching and listening. 'Have you a cigarette, a bit of baccy, some rations, chocolate from home? What do you have?' He grinned.

Red pulled a piece of tender meat off the bone; he popped it in his mouth. It melted as he chewed. He savoured the taste and closed his eyes. He thought of the family kitchen, all of them sat together eating rabbit pie, of the times he and Jimmy went and set snares at Elveden, all the good times with Jimmy back in Ashcombe. It seemed so far away. He thought of Connie, and dreamed of sitting next to her on the riverbank and getting married.

He took another piece and handed it to the soldier next to him, then another and did the same, then again and again and again, stripping the rabbit to the bone.

'Red, stop! What do you think you are doing? These are bloody priceless.' Geordie scratched his head; he got up, holding his rabbit over the fire. There was pushing and shoving as more prisoners congregated, attracted by the aroma of roasted meat.

'We have to, don't we? We can't profit, not when there are so many going hungry, can we?'

'Oh bloody hell, it goes against everything I believe in.' Geordie took one mouthful of lean meat and then passed it out.

* * *

There was silence at dawn, no shell fire. Later a ripple of anticipation spread through the prison camp. The Germans surrendered; there was bedlam, great roars and cheers, and rum was found; British soldiers at the gates. The handover was peaceful. Red and Geordie watched as Major Von Achterberg was loaded up on the back of a British truck and taken away with all the German officers.

The prisoners were formed into units and were ordered to march back to Cambrai. Red and Geordie stepped in line. The sky was grey and low and they took the ancient Roman road. The noise of a thousand hobnailed boots on cobbles rang out above the squawking crows. It seemed the entire traffic of the army was on the road and heading west. Their orders were to move back to the camp at Albert; here, they would be held awaiting instructions to return to England.

'We've bloody dun it, we 'ave bleedin' gone and bloody dun it, ain't we,' Geordie said as he lit a cigarette.

'Yep, I can hardly believe it; we have, mate, we have,' Red said. 'I don't know how, but we are here. If only Jimmy and the others were too.' He looked out over the horizon.

'I know, I know. But look, they wouldn't want you going all maudlin.' Geordie adjusted his backpack.

'That's true, that's true, they wouldn't; but I can't help thinking. You know, about all them back home; they're going to miss him.' He wiped his face with the back of his sleeve.

'We have to live our lives. I'm going to make sure I bloody well do. I am, I am; I'm going to live every last minute to the full. I'm going to do it. I'm going to bring out Eliza and my sprogs and build a new life, where I can be anyone I want and not take orders from any bleeder except my missus!' Geordie said, smiling and patting Red on his back.

'You know, Geordie, that sounds perfect, perfect for you,' Red said as he looked out over the desolate landscape, at crater after crater of devastated farmland. 'Me, I'm going back home and I'm going to Constance. I'm going to sweep her off her bloody feet I am, take her down the aisle and have enough children that I can make half a football team. That's what I will go and bloody do.' He smiled with his whole face.

After two days of marching, they made the holding camp outside Albert.

* * *

There was a huge celebration in the Hotel de Madeleine. It was packed full of allied soldiers singing, dancing and drinking. Red and Geordie shared a bottle of red wine and sang around the piano.

Red went to the courtyard and out to the garden and looked up at the bright full moon and shining stars. He remembered the night of Jimmy's wedding. He tried to remember the look on Connie's face and the feel of her touch.

He was woken from his daydream as Marie sauntered over to him. Her brunette hair flowed over her shoulder. The white apron was tied at her slender waist and worn above the grey work dress. He breathed in her sweet scent. Her hazel eyes looked up at him.

'*Qu'est-ce que tout cela veut dire?* What?' Marie said. He didn't understand. She placed her hand in his. 'What you think?' She smiled.

'I don't know; we are free, I suppose.' Red felt her warm hand in his.

'*Et que ferez-vous? C'est fini, la guerre*, war.' She looked up into his eyes. He understood *fini*: the war finished.

'*Oui*, war *fini*, me returnee home.' He looked at cute Marie. Her hazel eyes so welcoming, so expectant. He felt the heat of her body close in on his chest as she touched his arm.

'*Rouge, embrasse moi*,' she whispered in his ear.

'I don't understand.' As he looked at her face, she tiptoed up to his height and kissed him.

21

12th November 1918

Connie stood in Moreton school hall for the last time as a teacher. She looked at the ceiling and remembered the times she had enjoyed, seeing the looks on the faces of her young pupils. It didn't seem that long ago that she had been a pupil. How scared she had been of Miss Appleworth! Even now as her headmistress, and her landlady for a time, she was still a little scary, her intelligence and confidence intimidating.

The hall felt cold and empty, the children sent home to celebrate the end of the war. Of course, Connie felt glad it was over, that at last those that had survived were able to return to their families. The temperature outside was cold; the winter evening was about to draw in after another short grey winter's day.

'Ah, Miss Stevens, I'm glad you're still here; I wanted to have a word with you and ask you to wait on for a while. The celebration in the village hall is not due to start until later anyway. Is that all right?' Miss Appleworth said. Connie wasn't sure how old she was exactly; she was upright and her face was delicate yet chiselled, cast from marble, good-looking yet hard-wearing. Her figure was slender and tall,

In Fields of Gold and Red

her hair tied tightly. She was paler than most women in the village.

'Yes, of course, Miss Appleworth; I've some cleaning up I can do.'

'Good, thank you. I've some matters to discuss with the vicar when he gets here. He should have been with me by now; you know I can't stand lateness.' She looked up at the school clock. Miss Appleworth walked out of the school hall and went to her office.

Connie entered her classroom and took the slates from the sloping wooden desks. She took the old rag and began to wipe down each of the slates in turn. She walked around, looking at the familiar pictures on the wall and the old world map, her eye drawn to France. She looked out of the large arched stone window, out over the yard and down School Hill. It was misty, grey and dark. A few villagers walked past. She saw the vicar bustle into the yard, his glasses on. He must be coming to make sure she would finish today. She went to meet him at the entrance.

'Hello, Mrs Fox, and how are you today? I expect you're glad that you're finishing.' He looked at her, his mouth open.

'Hello, Vicar. Not really; I'd much rather carry on.' She was careful how much she said. She took a deep breath.

'I would have thought you would have changed your attitude, now that you're married and expecting your first child.' He looked down at her from above his glasses and stared at her belly.

'Miss Appleworth will see you in her office; I'll take you through.' She walked in front of him through the hall and to the small office at the back of the school. She knocked on the door. Miss Appleworth was seated behind her desk, with a photograph of her father in military uniform on the wall behind her. She got up and greeted the vicar.

'If you don't mind, Vicar, I'd like Mrs Fox to stay for this meeting,' she said, holding his eye.

'Well, I don't know; it is not the done thing now really, is it.' He blustered back, his cheeks blushing, his thick eyebrows raised.

'Look, it's not up for discussion; she's to stay and that's that. Mrs Fox, sit there.' She pointed to the chair in the corner. Reverend Wrixon made himself comfortable on the seat in front of Miss Appleworth.

'Miss Appleworth, I want to get straight to the point. Now we have had the news that war is over, I see no reason for not getting back to normality straightaway, and that is that no married woman will continue to teach in one of my schools. Is that clear?' He looked Miss Appleworth in the eye.

'Yes, Reverend, I understand; you don't have to tell me.' Connie watched as Miss Appleworth's steel-grey eyes faced the vicar. Connie felt nervous; they were going straight to the point, and being in the room with them made her nervous. She felt a twinge from the baby inside, as it kicked. She moved her hand down, to ease the tension.

'Look, I have given her the start of the new term; I kept my word. You don't realise how much the Bishop has been on at me to remove her from school.' He moved on the chair, and his finger went to his lip.

'Yes, yes, Reverend, and I am very grateful; you have given her the extra time. But where am I to find her replacement? What have you done about that?' She sat upright and didn't move, her back straight. 'What have you done, tell me?'

'Well, look, I've been busy, you know. It's the principle: there will be men back soon. I'm sure those leaving the army will need work.' He squirmed.

'Yes, yes; but none that can teach. Not like Mrs Fox.' Her face was a picture of calm.

'Look, there will be many officers being decommissioned that will be more than capable. After all – and I don't mean any disrespect – but if Miss Stevens, I mean Mrs Fox, can do it, well then...' He moved again in his seat.

'And how would you know? Do you not realise that Mrs Fox here has been one of the best teachers I have ever worked with in my forty years as a teacher, thirty of them as headmistress of this school? Do you know that teachers of her ability are rare, that teachers of her dedication and perseverance and quality are as rare as albino deer? I'm sorry, Vicar, but to have you say that is condescending and an insult, whether you mean it or not.'

Connie held her breath, and felt she shouldn't be in the room. She could see the vicar squirm in his seat. Connie had never seen anyone take him on and win; never had she seen someone question his authority. It was liberating as well as daunting and she was glad she was not on the end of Miss Appleworth's tongue. The pride with which Miss Appleworth was talking of her made tears come to her eyes.

'Yes, yes, and that is credit no doubt to you, your teaching and the way you have mentored Mrs Fox; but now she is with child there is no way she could continue anyway, is there?'

'I will ask you, Vicar, to look in your heart. Mrs Fox wishes to continue as long as she can; I need a quality teacher. I will not beg you, but I ask you as a man of God to look inside yourself. The children need her, I need her support. Please let her stay, at least until you find a replacement.'

'I've already given her an extension; how would I ever convince the Bishop?'

'You're a bright man, Reverend, and you're a fighter, I know. She's not taking the job from anybody else; there isn't anyone, is there? You agree on that?'

'Well no, not immediately.' Connie sat stock still; the baby stopped kicking.

'So it's best if we compromise, isn't it? Why don't we say she keeps on working until she has the baby?'

'Well, I suppose. I can see when I'm beaten.' He stood up and shook Miss Appleworth's hand. He turned to Connie. 'I can see you impressed Miss Appleworth; that's enough for me.'

Connie breathed a huge sigh of relief as the vicar walked out of the office.

'Thank you so much, Miss Appleworth.'

'That's enough, Mrs Fox. It's only what you deserved; and I meant every word of it. Now get on home with you; and don't be late tomorrow.'

* * *

'What have you done?' Sampson said as he sat at the large oak table in the dining room of the Manor. Connie was sat to his side; Admiral and Josephine were not yet at their seats.

'It was Miss Appleworth. You should have seen her! I've never seen anyone speak like that to the vicar in all my life.' She felt so proud of the way Miss Appleworth had stood up for her, she couldn't wait to tell Sampson; but his face…

'Connie, how can you? You're to have the baby in a few months. You can't go to the school! What will people think of me, letting you go out like that? Not to mention what Father and Mother will have to say!' Her face dropped and her smile evaporated. It was like putting her hand in a bush of nettles.

'I don't look at it like that. The school needs me, there is no one else who can do it, and Miss Appleworth says I'm good at it; why shouldn't I?' She tried to stay calm as Miss Appleworth had done, but she felt blood race through her veins.

'Because you're pregnant! You should take it easy, to make sure of the health of the baby, and your health,' Sampson continued, his voice raised.

'I will be fine. There are many women who work on through pregnancy. Look at them at harvest time! You wouldn't have been able to get many harvests in without women and there were some who were carrying babies, too.' She calmed herself back down.

'That's different. I wasn't married to them, was I.' His frown was deep on his brow, his fingers touched his mouth and his hand moved to the back of his neck. Connie could feel the heat reaching her cheeks.

'You said you love me, that you would do anything to make me happy when we married, didn't you?' She tried to catch her breath.

'I did, Connie, and I meant it; but this is a step too far, this is beyond reason. It's as if you are not thinking straight.' He got up and pushed his chair in. 'You can't do this for the health of the baby, for your health, going down to the draughty cold old school, carrying our baby. Yes, I know you enjoy teaching, but you enjoy writing, reading, you love the library here; Spencer, Dorothy and Cook can keep an eye on you. You know, to make sure you have everything you need.' He paced in front of the long curtains in front of the window. The dim gaslights were not strong enough to show the look on his face.

'Please, Sampson, please let me continue; it's only up until I'm ready to give birth.' She put both hands on her tummy.

'I don't know, Connie; it's so much to ask, and how ever will Father and Mother take it?' Why was everything such a battle? She'd been so happy coming back from school, feeling proud that Miss Appleworth had stood up for her; now she was being dictated to by her husband, a husband who had promised to make her as happy as she could be.

'If I do this, if I let you do this, you have to promise me it's the last time, that when you've had the baby, you won't go back teaching at the school.' He came to his chair, placed his hands on the top and looked down at her.

'Yes, all right, yes, I promise you,' Connie said. She rotated her wedding ring and gritted her teeth.

22

11th February 1919

They had a paddle steamer back from Cherbourg to Southampton. Red found it horrendous; hordes of soldiers all rushing and scrambling to get trains home. He wished Jimmy was with him. He clasped the heart necklace. He and Geordie got separated before they could say goodbye.

The excitement of seeing Connie so great; time itself seemed to be stalling. He was dressed in his army greatcoat. He finally got on his packed train for the West Country; it was standing room only. He stood for most of the journey. He could have joined the other soldiers; there were enough out drinking and revelling in their freedom, but he wanted to get back and see Connie. To see her face and to feel her in his arms.

The train seemed to lurch and strain under the load, its carriages bursting with cargo. As it got closer and closer to home it seemed to go slower and slower. This was worse than in battle; at least there he was in action. He had a phantom urge to scratch his missing toes. Finally, he was able to change at Dorchester for Maiden Newton. At least it was quieter with fewer people. The rain kept falling, heavy and incessant without pause. The station master came out of his cubicle and told him there were going to be no more trains going to Bridport. It felt like a big kick in the teeth.

'Sorry, lad, I bet you want to get home and see your loved ones and all. Well, yesterday afternoon, what with the non-stop rain, there's been a girt landslide; 'tis three miles from Moreton Station; darn hard place to get any wagons to, to shift it all,' the station master said.

It would take days if not a week to clear. Red decided the best option was to get back on the train to Dorchester where he hoped he might find a lift. He found a room for the night at the Market House. The fire was in a big open hearth, with big chairs in a semi-circle around it, the smoky aroma telling of a winter's day.

* * *

In the morning there was more rain and it felt colder too. It was set for snow. The wind was coming from the east. Red thought he would head for the market and look for a friendly face.

The market was filled with the familiar sounds and smells of animals. He saw maroon shorthorn bulls penned behind the hazel hurdles, ewes bleating and wooden crates of chickens. He saw old Walter Crabb, Jimmy's uncle, inspecting the shorthorns.

'Hey there, young 'en!' He took his pipe from the corner of his mouth.

'Ah, Mr Crabb.' Red looked up as he hobbled over.

'Woz happened to yiz foot?' He pointed his stick.

'They took it off 'cos of the gangrene.' Red pulled his coat closer to keep out the driving rain.

'Sorry 'bout Jimmy; it was terrible,' Walter said. 'It was that. 'Tiz harder for young Violet. We've all been round and that.'

'Wondered if you could give me a lift back to the village?

The trains are all cancelled due to the landslide.'

'It's a bit more than just a landslide; half the bloody hill has come down over the track. It will take them bloody weeks before it's clear. It's those bloody navvies; didn't cut it right, did they. 'Course you can have a bloody lift, lad. You know you're as good as family, boy. Come on, lad, you can help me with the horses.'

They set off from Dorchester in the afternoon. The rain was turning to sleet, the two horses finding it tough-going on the rain-sodden road, with Red leading them around the deepest puddles that blocked the road. Along the long straight after Winterbourne Abbas, the road was flooded. Red would have liked to pass. Walter insisted they double back and rest at the inn.

* * *

The rain stopped in the night. Red and Walter were up at five seeing to the horses. It was a lot colder; the wind rattled through the old stables. Red smelt the cosy smell of warm straw and horse sweat. By six they were on the road. The puddles were ice. Progress was slow, Red leading the horses around. They got up to the heights of the chalk ridge heading to Askerswell looking down to the coastline on their left. It wasn't long before the first flutters of snow came, then heavier. By the time they got to Wellbourne the snow was up to the shire horses' fetlocks.

Red made sure the horses were comfortable at the inn's stable. It was very cold and the white of the snow made it feel worse. He felt happy again with the animals and gave them oats. He breathed in the fresh smell of the oats and straw. He was so excited: only five miles or so from Connie. Excited and frustrated; he could have been in France, he still hadn't seen her. It felt as though he would never get back. Looking back out of the stable he saw his footprints were covered with another layer of snow. He walked briskly out and into the bar of the inn. The fire was lit and the bar smelt of smoky sweet apple and pear. He thought of the anticipation, of smelling the lavender on Connie, of seeing her smile, of holding her in his arms. He felt like he did as a child, full of excitement for the steam engine to arrive for threshing. He would see, hold, smell and touch her soon. He carried the anticipation like a full bag of grain.

Walter swigged on a measure of rum and lit his pipe.

'You know, lad, there is no way we can take the horses today. Best we stay put and have a couple of drinks.' He puffed up a cloud of smoke.

'Walter, I'm going to make a walk for it; if I take the short cut across the fields it will be half the distance,' Red said as he looked at Walter. He took his greatcoat from the stand.

'Are you sure? It's going to blow up into a blizzard.' Walter puffed on his pipe, then it hung from the corner of his mouth.

'It is, but I've faced far worse. I ain't going to let a bit of bloody snow stop me.' Red did up the buttons and braced himself to face the cold.

'Wait another day. I know you want to get back, but another day won't make any difference, will it?' Walter's pipe hung from the corner of his mouth.

'Nah, I've made up my mind. It won't take me long if I get going, and I should miss the worst of it when the wind gets up.' Red headed for the door.

'If you must, you daft gallybagger! Can't understand why you don't have another rum!'

Red turned and came back to the bar and said: 'Here, you have one on me, for giving me a lift.' He put two shillings down on the counter. The tall landlord pushed them back.

"Ave these on the house, mate. You're all bloody heroes to me.'

The rum gave off the odour of deep dark cherry; he

swigged it back. It lined his throat with a coating of warmth before cascading to his stomach, where it exploded with heat. His stomach warmed and his mind fortified, he walked out into the snow. Walter was right: the wind was getting up and blowing strongly. It whistled down through the birch trees that lined the lane and right into his face. It was bitterly cold. The snow was deep enough to cover his false foot and come halfway up his shin.

At the end of the lane he came into the field, the virgin blanket of white not even disturbed by foxes or badgers who thought better of it than exploring in the night; staying in their safe warm dens. He followed his instinct, around the hillside. Here the wind blowing more of a path as the snow drifted up against the hedgerow. He made slow progress. The snowstorm intensified, as if whipped up by unnatural forces, the wind blowing as much snow from the ground as was falling from the sky. A white sheet seemed to hang in front of him, blowing to one side only briefly to give him a view of the snowscape. The wind cut through his thick coat as if it didn't exist and chilled his bones. He shivered. There were two fields to cross and then the lane to Ashcombe. He kept moving forward, shuffling; he would have to keep going. There was nowhere to shelter. He wasn't going to be beaten. His teeth chattered. He rounded the wood on the lower side, down by the boundary wall. There were sheep cowering against the hedge line. If they were left alone, they would stand until buried alive. He would have to get them to safety.

Fighting the blizzard, limping and slow, it took him time; the ewes, unresponsive, wanted to stay out of the wind and the driving snow. He took his time. Snapping off a thin hazel branch, he used it to guide the sheep up into Piggots Field. The pens were where they had always been. After persisting for an hour, cold and with numb fingers, he had

In Fields of Gold and Red

them safely penned in. At last he would be able to get on and visit Connie. He had it all prepared: they could go back to France, buy a small house or a plot of land. He could go with Geordie, do some building work, perhaps even have their own farm, and start a family; she would love it there. They would be free to build their new life.

Red could feel the energy deserting him. He was going to see Connie. He staggered on, the snow deeper, reaching just below his knees. Where the lane should be was a mass of snow, compacted and frozen. It supported his weight. Walking on top of the hedgerow, he followed the line of oak, beech and horse chestnut trees up to Whites Farm.

* * *

He wanted to see her; he could hardly breathe. Back Lane out of the wind was clear and it was easier to walk. He struggled up School Hill, his wooden stump slipping on the ice. He supported himself in the hedgerow. He slipped up to the gates. He knew exactly what he wanted to say, it was all prepared in his mind. He felt his throat closing and his pulse rising at the thought of seeing her again. Would he feel the same when he saw her? His heart pounded. He passed the snowman in the schoolyard; two coals for eyes and a large carrot for his nose. There was no sign of children; they must have been sent home for the day. Would Connie even be here? Maybe she hadn't come in? He approached, up the sloping yard, looking in through the large arched window that looked down over the yard. And then he saw her face; he saw Connie. He smiled and waved and tried to catch his breath. Her face dropped. She waved back with a look of disbelief. He ran and skidded to the door.

23

13th February 1919

He waved. It couldn't be. It must be George. It couldn't be him. He was dead. Her face fell. How could this be? He was dead. How could he be standing in the schoolyard after all this time? The men who survived had been coming back to the village in dribs and drabs, the last surviving Smyth, David. He was the last back and that was last month. How could Red be in the yard? Theodore had been back. She felt the baby move. It must be a ghost. It was as if time stood still. She moved without realising, waving back. Was it him? She moved out of the classroom; she couldn't move so fast, her baby due.

He was in the porch when she reached him. He looked older, he looked cold. She hugged him, his coldness on her. He tried to speak but no words came out.

'Oh Red, Red, is it you?' She spoke into his ear. 'Where have you been? Where?' She pulled him with her; holding his hand she took him to the school kitchen. The only heat in the school coming from the range. There was a lingering smell of boiled cabbage. The school was deserted, only for Miss Appleworth who was in her office at the far end.

'You're freezing! Here, warm yourself. Give me your coat.'

She pulled the frozen coat from him. He stood in front of the open fire in his khaki tunic and trousers, his socks covered in snow and ice. The kettle hung over the flame. She took his hands and rubbed them. She saw his dirty khaki uniform. He looked older, his eyes tired. His face drawn, he looked hungry and thin, not as full in the face as she remembered. There were more lines on his forehead.

'Them ewes would have been buried alive; I had to stop and put them in.' He looked terrible as snow melted from his head.

'What? What are you talking about?' She noticed him stand lopsided, his weight on his left leg. 'Don't worry.' She found the teapot and filled it with tealeaves, she rinsed two mugs and set them ready. Her heart was beating fast, her pulse racing. He was here; he was standing here; how on earth could it be? He was dead.

'He had me paybook, didn't 'e. I was in bed sick on payday; Jimmy went, I forgot to get it back; that's what they found.' He looked at her. His face was long and drawn. His eyes looked from hers down to her large belly. 'My letter, my letter!'

'What paybook? What letter? You're not making sense, Red. I don't understand.' His paybook, that pink paper: it's what Captain Theodore had waved at her, what he put under her nose at Bovington. She didn't want to be sick, but her stomach was giving her the urge. It was boiling away, heating up. Slowly it was dawning on her. He wasn't dead; he was alive; Theodore and the others were wrong. 'If you weren't dead, what happened? And what do you mean, what letter?'

'I've been prisoner. They've only just let us back, 'cos there weren't enough boats. Then the train's been delayed because of the big landslide. I couldn't get the wagon through so I've walked from Wellbourne.' His face was sad;

he looked down at his foot. 'Cut me foot off they did, it got infected.'

She went to him. He was warming and she hugged him close and said, 'Don't worry, don't worry, it's over, it's over; you're home, you've made it home. I'm so glad to see you. I'm so glad you've made it back. I thought you were dead.' She felt his body tense and he pushed her shoulder back away from him.

'Who's the father, your husband?' She touched her wedding ring, turning it around on her finger. His face set calm.

'Yes. I'm so sorry. When I knew, I thought you were gone, we became friends; it happened. I'm sorry. I would have waited if I'd known you were coming back. I would have waited. It would have been different.' She could see the hurt in his eyes. 'It's Sampson.'

'Sampson, Sampson Fox?' Tears were forming in his eyes. Her stomach flipped and the baby kicked; she moved her hand to stroke her stomach. She leaned on the table. 'My letter, I sent you.'

'Can we sit down?' She pulled the chair and sat. 'I'm so sorry, I'm so sorry,' she said as she stretched her legs. She hoped Miss Appleworth wouldn't come in and find them together. She rotated her wedding ring. 'I never got any letter, not this year.'

'Oh, Connie, the thought of you is what's kept me going, through the fighting, through being captured, getting back; it was the thought of finally being with you, your promise to wait for me.' He took a chair and pulled it in front. Connie got up, took the rag to hold the kettle and poured the boiling water into the teapot.

'You know I was waiting; I was keeping my promise. I would have; you know that, don't you? It was you I wanted to spend the rest of my life with, Red. It was always you.'

She couldn't help it; she tried not to, but tears ran from her eyes.

'Oh, Connie, don't say that; it hurts.' He was crying; she'd never seen him cry before. He looked so sad she wanted it to stop.

'It's true, I would have waited, I would have. I went all the way to London, then to Bovington. I was told, Red; they said they knew for sure.' She could hardly dare look at him.

'I'm sorry. I should have got back sooner. I should have escaped.' He looked back to her eyes. She was so glad to be looking at his, but feeling so sick to her stomach, and so tired.

'It's not your fault. I'm glad you're alive! I'm so happy you've survived, Red.'

'We can still be together. There is a lovely village in France. They need builders. Me and Geordie, we can work together. I saved some money; we could buy some land, even have some animals, build our own cottage, our own farm. Whatever you want. You will learn the language in no time. No one will know; you know, we can bring up our family there together, be our own family. We can…' What was he saying? His face was alive, the calm broken.

'I can't, Red; I'm sorry; I can't break my vows; I've given them in church to Sampson. I can't break them, not now, not ever. It's my duty.' She knew she loved Red. Tears rolled down her cheeks. Red's face was coloured deep and his own tears fell. The sadness had returned; she could see no hope on his face, and it hurt.

'Please, Connie, please come back with me; don't say you won't. I need you.' His eyes looked deep at her. She felt them reach straight to her heart, which seemed to flutter, then fade.

'I'm sorry, Red, I've my family, I've my baby. It's my duty.' Tears stung her cheek.

24

4th March 1919

Connie looked up at the top of the four poster bed. The white patterned cloth showed a swirl of blue lines in a circular pattern. Her stomach was huge, the baby kicked and pressed against her. If only the baby would come. The midwife was certain that it was due last Wednesday; it was Tuesday now. Where was it? She was fed up.

The waiting, the tiredness, she didn't sleep well. She had had to tell Red to go; it was best for both of them. They only gave each other pain. She should have waited. If only she'd waited then she could have been with him. The letter, the letter! It turned up a week after Red; she kept it safe with the others. Sampson treated her well; she had everything she could possibly want and more. How on earth was she here? Having this baby she wasn't even sure she wanted. She moved to her side. There was a tap on the bedroom door.

'It's me, Violet. They said it was all right for me to come up.' Violet opened the door without waiting for a reply. Her hair was windswept, and she looked tired. William, now three years old, held his mother's hand. He had a shock of blonde hair, was dressed in small dark trousers and white shirt, holding a square of green blanket in his other hand.

'Oh, Violet, you didn't have to come; I'm all right.' She propped herself up on the two pillows behind her. 'I'm glad you did, I'm so fed up being up here. Dorothy has been so good to me; she keeps coming to check on me.'

William went to the window and looked out before sitting down square on the floor, and put the blanket in his mouth.

'I couldn't leave you all to yourself, you know that.' Violet sat on the edge of the bed and stroked her friend's fringe away from her face. 'How are you feeling?'

'I want it out. Why's it taking so long?' she said, letting out a long sigh and fidgeting her toes at the end of the bed.

'Sometimes it takes longer. William, he just popped out right on time; I was lucky, but well I know others who are waiting for ages, then labour begins and that takes forever. I was lucky like that.'

'Oh, don't say that, Violet! I hope it's not going to be forever.' She looked at her friend, she felt her face drop. It wouldn't last long, would it? 'It doesn't hurt, does it?'

'It can, Connie, you know it can be painful, it can hurt.' Connie remembered the look of pain on Red's face. She had said she couldn't go with him, that her duty was with Sampson; it wounded them both. That's why she couldn't see him anymore; it would be best for both of them if they didn't see each other. That way they could both forget and both move on. In time the memories would fade.

Connie could smell the rosewater on Violet, her sense of smell heightened. She could even smell the primrose in the vase of flowers that were on her dresser. She looked at Violet, at the deep bags under her once fresh face, and said: 'Why did my contractions start then stop like they did?'

'I don't know, Connie. What did the midwife say? Maybe it's like that; you know we are all different.'

'Oh, Violet, she didn't say much, the midwife, just seemed to be blunt, said that baby would come out when it was ready.'

'How's Sampson? How's he been, Connie?' Violet said, holding Connie's hand. She looked over at William who was content sitting on the floor, entertained by his blanket.

'He's fine; you know, busy out on the farm, watching over the ploughing. He's not happy, though, with his brother back. You know, he thought that because Admiral wanted him to shadow Mr Grey – you know, to look after the running of the farm when Mr Grey steps down. But now Theo is back, Theo thinks he has the right as the eldest to take charge. It's a nightmare; they can't seem to have two good words to say to each other.' Connie felt a twinge, not a full contraction but enough to notice.

'Well, that's brothers for you, I suppose.' Violet looked at Connie.

'I didn't think he would have the slightest interest in the farm; he never showed any before the war, Sampson says, and now he just wants to take over everything. Sampson says Mr Grey can't stand him interfering. How is William doing?' She breathed in.

'Oh, he's wonderful, he is really, and mother and father they can't get enough of him. They spoil him no end. That's why I have to get out, so I can get some time alone with him.' She laughed as she stroked Connie's hand.

The heat formed on Connie's forehead; Violet wiped the bead of sweat away for her.

'Are you all right? Do you want me to fetch the midwife?'

'Not yet, it's fine; I don't think it's ready yet. Keep talking; it takes my mind off it, please, Violet.'

'You know, Red came in to see me; said he'd been to see you,' said Violet.

'What else did he say?' Her heart pounded, her stomach contracted; it wasn't the baby.

'He just talked about Jimmy, about how brave he was,

how he was so sorry, he wanted to do more, how Jimmy always talked about me, how Jimmy kept their spirits up every day. He brought back the locket I gave to Jimmy.' Connie looked over at Violet and could see she was holding back her tears. 'He told me how Jimmy died. It was painful for both of us. The things they have seen, Connie; what they went through; it was terrible.' Connie could feel the anguish within her. She should have waited longer; there had been no hurry. Why hadn't she waited longer? Why had she believed them? Now to be in the same house as the man who had told her for sure, it reminded her every day.

'Where is Red, Violet, where did he go?' The contractions continued, stronger and more regular. 'Did he tell you where he was going?'

'He left on the train straight after seeing me; he walked straight on the train to Dorchester. He didn't say where he was going, just that he couldn't stay here any more. I told him I thought you should go with him.'

'I couldn't, Violet. You know that, don't you? I couldn't. I've given my word to Sampson. I couldn't leave him, not with his baby inside me.'

'Connie, I lost the man I love, but I've his baby; I've William to remind me to give my love to...' She held Connie's hand in the two of hers; with her top hand she stroked. 'You should've taken your chance. You love Red, don't you? I can tell you don't love Sampson, not like you do Red.'

'I'm having a baby, Violet. How could I leave and just go with him? He doesn't have a home, he doesn't have work. What would we do? We can't live on fresh air. I couldn't travel with him. Him saying we could live in France. I don't know anyone there. What if he couldn't get work; where would we get food? How could I bring a baby into that world? How could I have done that to Sampson? Taken his baby away with me.' Connie's urge to cry welled up.

'You could go after him after you've had the baby. I would look after the baby for you, if you wanted?' There was a knock on the door. Violet stood up.

'Connie, love, Connie.' It was Sampson; he called from outside the room.

'Come in, Sampson,' Connie said, clearing her throat and holding back the tears.

'Oh, Violet, you're here,' Sampson said as he walked into the bedroom. He was dressed plain in work clothes of brown cords and white striped shirt, black waistcoat and tweed jacket. He looked smart and tall, his shoulders back and an air of confidence.

'I was about to leave.' Violet made her way to get William.

'Don't worry; stay, stay. I just wanted to check on my wife. Isn't she magnificent? And already giving me a baby. At least that's something Theodore hasn't done.' He walked over to William. 'And how is this little soldier?' He patted him on the head.

'He's a good boy; I've been very lucky,' Violet replied.

'Well, he is going to have a wonderful new friend to play with soon. I think it will be a boy, a gorgeous little boy; then they can play and make camps like we all did, can't he?'

'Hmm, they can; I'm sure William will love that,' Violet said. She sat back down next to Connie.

'I've already made some enquiries for a nanny. 'Course, my old Nanny Hughes is long retired. I'm sure we can find someone just as good.' He walked over to the window and looked down across the green pasture to the railway line.

'I don't think we need a nanny, Sampson; I mean, I will do that myself,' Connie said, feeling her tummy.

'Oh, don't bother yourself with thinking about that, Connie, not now; you just concentrate on delivering that baby.'

'I'm fine; I haven't lost the use of my brain, just because I'm having a baby.' Sampson walked back to her bedside and touched her on her temple.

'Now, now, don't fret; it will all be fine. I know you've been worrying; I can tell by the look on your face these last couple of days. You don't realise how much it's been taking out of you.' She detested the way he was planning and making decisions without consulting her. She supposed that was the way it was to be.

'I don't think having a nanny… there isn't any need, Sampson. Look at Violet; she manages fine.'

'Well, yes, of course, Violet does; but we've always had a nanny, in my day and my father's and his father's; that's the way it's done in the Fox family, and I don't see any need to break with tradition.' Connie felt the baby move, the contractions tighter.

'It's coming, it's coming!' she screamed out.

'Oh, my God! What should we do? Where is that midwife?' Sampson exclaimed.

'Don't panic,' Violet said to Sampson. 'You take William downstairs; he'll be happy in the kitchen with Cook. Get her to boil up some water and get some clean rags; get Dorothy to bring them up.' Sampson stood straight and still, planted like a tall ash tree. 'Go, Sampson, go and get them now, and send Spencer for the midwife.' Violet looked Sampson in the eye. 'Go do it!' she shouted.

'Yes, of course, yes, Violet,' Sampson said as he moved from his spot. He ran out of the door. Connie could hear him shout for Dorothy as he ran down the corridor to the stairs.

'Oh Violet, it hurts so much!' Connie screamed as her face contorted. 'Why does it hurt so much, Violet, why? I'm going to die, aren't I, like my mother did? I am, I know I am!'

'Shoosh, Connie, shoosh. I'm here for you, Connie. I'm not going to let you die; don't worry about that. I've lost Jimmy; I wasn't there to look after him, but I'm here for you and you are not going anywhere, do you hear me?' Violet instructed her.

'Yes, Violet. Ahh…' She scrunched her face.

'You keep breathing, Constance, you darn well keep breathing there.' Connie gasped for air.

'Why didn't I wait? Why didn't I tell him how I felt about him? Why didn't I marry him like you married James? Why didn't I? Oh, Violet what am I going to do?' Connie felt so hot, so in pain. She could feel the baby move down.

'You did what you thought was right. It don't do any good to question yourself. Sampson will be a good father, I see that the way he was with William back there. He only wants the best for his child. If you did want to go after Red, I would look after baby, you know that.'

'Oh bloody hell, Violet, it hurts.' She gasped for air. 'Where is Dorothy? It's coming, Violet, the baby: it's coming.'

'Bloody hell, you awkward cuss, you would, wouldn't you? Have me deliver it for 'e?' Violet held her hand and mopped her brow.

'Oh Violet! Bloody hell, why don't they tell you it's so painful? Oh Vi, oh Vi!'

'It's all right, Connie, I'm here for you; don't worry.' She placed her hand on Connie's forehead.

Dorothy rushed into the room with a pail of boiling water and white rags under her arm.

'You're going be fine. Come on, Connie; look, we're both here for you,' Dorothy said, calm and organised. 'It's as natural as all the birds in the sky, and the fish in the sea.'

'It doesn't feel like that! It's coming! Oh, get out of me, for heaven's sake!'

'Come on, Connie; push, girl, push; breathe,' Violet said as Dorothy moved to the bottom of the bed. 'You can do it; come on, Connie, push.'

'I feel so tired, Violet.'

'I know, I know, but keep going. It's not long. Come on, you can do this; push!'

'Argh, argh, Violet, why didn't you tell me it was this painful?'

'Keep her talking, Vi,' Dorothy said. She was in her black maid's uniform and white apron, her hair tied in a bun.

'Its head is there,' Dorothy said.

'Relax, Connie, it's nearly over. Relax; come on.' Connie was drained, her energy gone, her back and head ached.

'Come on, Constance; you aren't done yet. Don't you let me down,' Violet said.

'Yes, Violet,' she said. Her breath short; she wanted a deep breath but it was painful.

'Hand me those rags, Violet,' Dorothy said. As she did so, Connie pushed, then relaxed as the baby emerged from her. Dorothy wiped the baby with the clean rags and pulled him up to her.

'It's a girl! It's a girl, Connie!' Dorothy shouted.

Connie breathed in; it was so hard. She felt dazed looking up at Violet and Dorothy.

'It's a girl! I've done it, Violet; I've done it, Violet,' she said, low in her breath. She felt her eyes shut. She wanted to sleep.

'Connie, don't you…' Violet was talking; she was quiet, her voice was faint. Connie wanted to close her eyes. She heard Violet and Dorothy talk, then other voices in the room. Then darkness.

25

March 1919

Red stirred. There was a flicker of light filtering through the wooden slats of the barn. He'd found it late last night, after a long day of walking. His feet ached but he only walked the pace that suited him. There was nowhere for him to be, no one for him to see, nothing for him to do.

His hopes were crushed. When he was in France the conditions had been awful, the threat of death was at every turn. Time and again they'd faced the enemy and he'd made it back; he made it back. Jimmy hadn't. He'd made it back only to lose the love of his life. But Jimmy: who had a wife and his child. Why hadn't he made it back instead?

He had carried his love for Connie all this time. It had got him through the war; and now for what? He had nothing and no one and no one to love.

Red pulled himself up from the bed of straw. He could hear the magpies chattering. The old chattermags, out there talking to one another. The blackbirds singing in the spring morning. He picked up his tan backpack and put it on his tired shoulders. The straw smelled damp and fusty and had kept him awake. The barn had wide holes in the roof. The farmer wasn't up yet. He headed back on the road. He didn't want to get spotted. The lane was deep under hedgerows and out of the breeze. He lost count of the number of showers that rained on him, blown in from the coast. He kept his head down. He walked through the villages of Puddletown and Tolpuddle. Village life continuing: the postman out delivering, all smart in his uniform. Horses and cart collecting the milk churns and taking them to the station. He limped as he walked, his peg leg tapping the road as he went. On his back he carried his blanket and a few old tins of supplies in his army bag. He didn't know where to go, or why he had chosen to walk. He tried to stop the thoughts coming into his head. He tried to stop the images but couldn't. He didn't want to forget how she had looked on the day of the fair.

He kept walking. Where should he go? What should he do? What was there for him? He'd had it all planned out, to see Connie, to be with her, to marry her and make a life in Dorset; after all, that's what she'd said in her letter. He didn't want to think of it, but it kept coming back into his mind. He breathed in deeply. He walked. He came around the bend, and towards the outskirts of Bovington Camp. He looked through the fence. He could hear the sound of tanks revving and pulling their mighty weight over the ramparts. He could go back, sign up. He could do something useful with the skills he'd picked up; make some use of them.

He walked past the fence and continued on.

Two days later he found himself on the outskirts of Southampton. He slept rough under the bridge of the railway line, the train waking him every hour. His beard irritating his skin. He could smell himself, stale sweat. He didn't care. He pulled his greatcoat over him and slept with the old soldiers. When the steam engine above didn't wake him with the clatter over the sleepers, shouts from nightmares did.

'Some of 'em would have been better off dead on the front, than coming back to this,' a bearded fellow tramp said from next to him. 'They'd be better being ten feet under than reliving those bloody nightmares every time they put their head down.' He scratched his beard and looked at Red. His beard was long and grey and unkempt, his breath smelled of stale beer, his old coat was ragged and torn. The hair on his head was thin, grey and patchy; his clothes, urine-soaked. Red noticed his hand on a green bottle. The tramp swigged on the bottle.

'I was a gunner, you know, and I keep hearing that pounding as if it was yesterday.' He sniffed. 'What did you do, lad?' He took a big swig.

'I was in a tank,' Red replied, scratching his beard and rubbing his chin.

'Well, you did a helluva thing; you must be proud what you did for your country.' He offered the bottle to Red.

'Ay, don't think of it. What's to be proud of if you've no one to do it for?' He put his hand up to decline the bottle.

'You've no one to come home to? No sweetheart? 'E should have a sweetheart, young fella like you.' He swigged down from the bottle. It smelled of gin.

'Nah, I've no one,' Red answered putting his arms across his chest and blowing out his cheeks.

'Me neither; but then I'm too old. The country has short memories; seem to remember those who are dead by putting up memorials and all, but don't seem to remember those of us who made it back, do them.' He ran his hand over his head.

'No, they don't.' Red coughed.

There were screams from one of the other half dozen tramps under the bridge. Screams of pain, screams of nightmares, screams of memories. Memories, open and raw; their bodies healed, their minds not.

'Shut up, shut up!' came shouts from an old soldier who could sleep, but was so disturbed by the screams he was awake. Why did they huddle together? Red wondered. Why not be alone? It was something they all missed: the bond they had been through together, that comradeship and shared experience. No one could take that away from them. They all carried wounds with them, whether on their bodies or in their minds; they all carried their wounds.

He lay out on his makeshift bed, an old rug he'd found discarded when he'd got there. He pulled his old blanket up under his chin and settled down to sleep.

* * *

He walked back into Albert. Rubble and masonry littered the streets. Wooden scaffolding lashed with ropes, tied haphazardly to buildings that stood half-built. Piles of slates stood on the street corners. Teams of building crews climbed up and down ladders, using pulleys to heave up baskets of stone to those above. Rubble lay piled in the town square. He looked over at the Hotel de Madeleine, its sign hanging straight and bright with fresh paint.

He had failed. He should have escaped the camp. Yes, he could walk; but not like he once had. Would he even be able to do a day's work, on one working leg? How could he have lost Constance? To see her… she looked so beautiful after all that time; how radiant she looked carrying her baby.

Albert was beginning to transform. There were buildings in different states: some complete with their slate roofs, some tiled. Built strongly from masonry. The sounds of chisels on stone, of shouting, of builders bantering. He felt crushed like fallen masonry, his world blown apart.

He stood and watched the frenzy of activity around him. He could smell the dust of chiselled stone as it hung in the air. Sampson was a good man. He would do his best to make Connie happy. He could tell she didn't love him. Not like she did him. That was life; at least he had his, not like Jimmy. In that one second, all his dreams and hopes flattened. He had only needed to see Connie and he knew that all was lost. He tried, but he believed it was in vain. He'd promised her a new life, but knew she would never break her duty. He stared at the Hotel De Madeleine and felt the tears forming in his eyes.

"Bout bloody time you got back!' Geordie shouted as he jumped down from the last rung of the ladder. 'I bloody spotted you soon as you walked in.' He went and hugged Red.

'Where's that lady you kept telling me about? She following on?' Red was so pleased to see his friend.

'No, she can't.' He tried to control the tears.

'Ay, why is that?' Geordie looked him in the eye.

'I can't explain it all. She can't; that's the end of it,' Red said, his stomach turning over at the thought of not being with her, not seeing her face again, not being able to hold her in his arms, never being able to kiss her. It was harder to take than death, knowing she was back home and he would never be there. He'd wanted to make her so proud, to achieve something to prove to her that he deserved her love. What did he have? Nothing. He couldn't even tell Geordie.

'It's all right, mate; you don't 'ave to talk about it. Come on indoors; you've not met the missus, and me sprogs, 'ave 'e.' Geordie put his arm over Red's shoulder. 'I'm glad you're here; we've got a helluva opportunity to make a few quid.'

* * *

There were thick layers of dust outside the hotel. He looked at the entrance. Did he want to go in? He could see the sign was fixed and painted. He looked at the door; would she want to see him? No, maybe tomorrow. He'd better get back; Eliza would have their supper ready. He could see Marie tomorrow. He turned to walk away.

He turned back, facing the hotel. He saw her as she came from the kitchen, her dark brown hair rolling over her shoulders, her face clear, her cheekbones shining. She was dressed in a green dress, which contoured her thin waist and her shapely hips. She dropped the tray of bread and ran to him.

'Rouge, Rouge! *Vous êtes de retour!* Back, you're back!' she said in French and broken English with a wide smile. Her face beamed.

'Yes; *oui, oui!*' She jumped up in his arms. Red blushed and staggered back, holding her up.

'Oh Rouge, I'm 'appy! *Vous êtes de retour!*' She held his arm.

'Who would have thought?' Red said. She looked at him as if she was going to question him, but didn't. He could tell she didn't fully understand. Marie's papa, Pierre, waved from behind the bar, his belly rounder and nose larger than Red remembered.

'With me, Rouge; *vous*; *je montre.*' She pulled Red impatiently by the hand. He didn't catch her meaning. Marie grabbed his hand, impatient to guide him. He followed.

She took him to the wide open stairs. They walked up together, Marie leading him to her bedroom. He held his breath; he could only think of Connie.

'Nicole.' She pointed at the baby asleep in the cot. '*Vous Papa!*' Red was dumbfounded. Was it his baby? Did she look like him? How could Marie be so sure? He didn't have feelings for her, not like those he felt for Connie. He didn't think he could love anyone like he loved Connie.

'She is pretty, just like her mother,' was all he could manage, his brain fuzzy. Much like when he was on morphine in the field hospital. Nicole looked so calm and snug. She smelt of warm milk and baby calves.

'She is… what you say? A beau, bonny baby. *Oui?*' She

laughed.

'We do.' Red didn't know what else to say.

* * *

The town glowed in the early morning sunshine of the spring day. Red heard the tree sparrows singing through the open kitchen door.

'Geordie, get your ass down here; it's time you got to work!' Eliza shouted up the stairs.

Red watched as Eliza in her light blue work pinny moved effortlessly from sink to range. She glided on her feet, placing the filled kettle down on the hob with one hand as she held the baby, Emma, with the other arm.

'You know, Red, I thought if the army could teach 'im one thing it would be to be able to get up in the bloody morning.' She stirred the large pan of porridge as it cooked.

'If he couldn't get up with Fritz pounding, I don't think he's goin' change now, is 'e,' Red said as he scoffed down a slice of bread and dripping. He watched Eliza with her short blonde hair as she glided over to the dresser and picked up two mugs in one hand. Emma was only a month old with a full covering of thin blonde hair like her mother. Eliza herself was thin and short, her legs sturdy.

Louise was the eldest of the four children with long black hair; the image of her father. Catherine and Edith, shorter with their mother's hair and eyes, played in the kitchen door. A thin breeze blew in the smell of honeysuckle. All were dressed in Eliza's handmade dresses.

'Thank you, Eliza; thank you for letting me stay with you. It won't be long, you know, once I get myself settled.'

'You're no trouble, Red. I mean, Geordie is pleased to have you work with him. He is; he tells me all the time. How it's so good to have you here with him. And to tell you the truth, I think you're a good influence on 'im; you keep his feet on the ground, at least more than usual.'

'I don't know about that; I don't think anyone can keep 'im out of mischief for long, do you?' Red laughed.

'I wish he would get a move on. 'Ain't you two meant to be starting over at the Mayor's house today?' She smiled.

'I think that's Geordie's plan,' Red said as Eliza dished him out a large serving of porridge. Red took some raspberry jam from the jar on the table and dolloped a spoonful in the middle of his bowl and stirred it in. 'He's struck up some kind of deal: we rebuild the Mayor's place, then Geordie can have permission to build that extension on here.'

'I hope so; we could do with the space,' Eliza said. ' I don't mean you have to go any time soon; you're no trouble. But I don't think it will be long before I'm with baby again.' Eliza took the boiling kettle from the hob and poured it over the tealeaves in the pot.

'Do I 'ear you too gossiping about me?' Geordie said as he wandered into the kitchen. Eliza went to him and kissed him on the cheek.

'It's about time you got up,' she said. Geordie pulled out a chair and sat down at the long table. He poured himself a mug of tea. Eliza filled his bowl with three large spoonfuls of porridge. 'You better get a move on. I don't want you letting the Mayor down; this is a chance for you to do a good job.'

'Don't fret, angel; me and the Mayor are like this.' He crossed his fingers over. 'If you know what I mean.' He winked at Red. Geordie grabbed Eliza as she went past and pulled her onto his lap.

'Don't! Get off! The kettle,' she laughed. Geordie puckered his lips and kissed her on the cheek.

'Get off, you lummock. I've too much to be getting on with. Not in front of your mate; you're embarrassing him,' Eliza giggled.

'Ah, don't worry about Red. He's family.' He released his grip on his wife. She got up and went to put the sheets in the wooden tub; she added hot water from the kettle. 'Anyway, Red, when you going to get out from under our feet? Ain't you going to make an honest woman of Marie?' Geordie looked at Red.

'Shut up, Geordie. In me own time.' Red looked down at the floor.

'I don't think you will do any better. She's a pretty young thing; and it ain't fair of you to leave her bringing up Nicole on her own, is it?'

'No, I don't know; I don't even know if she's mine, do I?'

'Look, even if she ain't, you can be the girl's father. Marie: she dotes on you,' Eliza said.

'How can you tell?' Red said, drinking from his mug.

'It's woman's intuition. I don't know what you're waiting for. If you leave it too long someone else will; she isn't short of admirers, you know. You only have to watch the boys flock to the hotel on Saturday night to see that.'

Red got up. They had a point; but he didn't want to admit it.

* * *

They walked out of Geordie's terraced house, carrying their tools in dusty old leather holdalls. Red looked across at the Hotel de Madeleine. He couldn't help but think back to when they first pulled up in David, the scene then of utter devastation.

Geordie employed six lads in his gang and there were two other building gangs working in the north of the town. It was a coup for Geordie, for him to talk the Mayor into letting him do the rebuilding work on his house. It was a calculated gamble of Geordie's: get it right for the Mayor and he would see to it that Geordie was busy for years reconstructing the civic buildings.

The Mayor was short with thin legs that didn't look strong enough to carry his portly belly. His wife stood a good foot and a half taller; she was eagle-eyed and had a long beak of a nose. If there were any pictures to be taken, Red noticed that the Mayor would insist on standing on an upturned crate; there always seemed one close at hand. The Mayor had a receding hairline but insisted on combing what he did have over the top of his head.

'Ah, Geordie, Geordie! *Bonjour, bonjour. Comment allez-vouz?*' the Mayor greeted Geordie; he patted them both on the back. He was a human bundle of energy; his English good, after all the negotiations with army commanders during the war.

'We would have been here earlier; but you know what it's like having a baby in the house.' Red could have laughed out loud, knowing full well that Geordie could sleep through an earthquake if he had to; it was poor Eliza who would wake up and see to Emma.

'You must call me Victor; you can't keep calling me Mayor. Only on official business you call me Mayor.' Victor winked at Red.

'Of course, Victor, of course,' Geordie said. 'We will get to work. We've the scaffolding up so we can make real progress, really get on with the second floor.'

'*Non, non, non*; I have something much more important for you two. Your men can stay here and continue, yes, *oui*; but you two, I have something else for you,' Victor said as he looked earnestly at the two of them. 'We must go; *allez, allez*, to see my friend Clement.'

* * *

Red drove Victor Joseph's horse and cart. Victor and Geordie sat on the back with Red up on the bench in front holding the reins and guiding the horses. Victor would tap him on his shoulder at the junctions in the lanes and point the way.

The cart rattled down the stony lane. Red looked out over the green rolling pasture on his left and fields of budding green wheat to his right, their buds not yet tall enough to be blown in the breeze. The ploughing that winter had been dangerous and macabre as shells and bodies of decomposing soldiers found their way to the surface. It was sheer necessity that meant it had been sown, the cratered landscape recovering from its pounding. Sparrows and crows searched for worms between the buds. Red saw two rabbits run back to their burrows, alerted by the sounds of stones pinging like gunshots from the cartwheels.

'It's not far,' Victor said, pointing at the farmhouse. It was at the end of the lane. Red took in a deep breath of fresh air.

Clement was in the farmyard forking dung from the cowshed into a heap ready to be loaded in his wagon and taken to be spread on his pasture. He greeted Victor first with a Gaelic hug, then Geordie, who Red thought hugged him like he was a long-lost brother. Red got his hug third, not sure he would ever get used to it.

Clement stood wide and stocky with a full moustache and flat cap, his skin darkly tanned. The cowshed had a patchy roof and a dozen stones missing from the wall.

Clement pointed over the brow. Red and Geordie looked at each other, puzzled. What was it Victor was getting them into?

Clement led the way, out of the opposite end of the farm. Red savoured the familiar smells of sweet hay and the pungent smell of animals. He couldn't resist patting the cows as he walked past.

'Cor, how could you work on a bloody farm? It's stinking!' Geordie said, holding his nose.

Clement and Victor walked in front. The lane was high-banked, roots of poplar and ash protruding high above them, snaking through the soil. A blanket of ivy covered the exposed roots. The sun moving high, they came out of the shadow of the lane and into the pasture. Red felt the warmth on his body. There were more fields of young wheat. Red felt his spine tingle. Clement strode on in front. Red felt he knew this landscape: similar but different.

The four of them rounded the small hillock, past a thicket of bramble. In front, a crater, grass springing to life, more brambles taking hold, inching their tentacles out over the lip. Red reached it and looked down and in. He looked at Geordie's face; neither could believe what they were looking down at. That old shape, inside a huge crater; a wreck, a wreck, but no less identifiable: it was a rusting tank. The six pounder barrels in position. It was a male, one track clean blown off, already the hull rusting orange, huge tears, metal sprayed inwards. Red and Geordie walked down to it; Red pulled back the bindweed.

'You know, yes.' Victor broke the silence.

'Ay, we know,' Geordie said, as he looked at it wide-eyed. Red walked around to his sponson door; he didn't want to open it.

'You can get it going, yes? I think it will be a good memorial, yes, for the town, for your comrades who lost their lives. We can put it in the square, for us all to remember our victory, to remember the sacrifice,' Victor said. 'You two, you can make it work.'

'Bloody hell, I don't know about that. Look at the bloody thing!' Red said. He walked around the side. 'It can't be, can it, Geordie?' He walked to the port side; he rubbed at the dirt and bird shit with his fingers. He could just remember where. As he rubbed he uncovered the letter D. It couldn't be! 'It's a D Company,' he continued to rub; then, A, V, I, D. 'Bloody hell, I'll be blown! It's only bloody David,' Red said to Geordie. He held back his tears as memories flooded him. He said a prayer for Jimmy.

* * *

Victor Joseph wanted them to work on it every day. He was eager to have it ready, so that the town could celebrate.

Red and Geordie worked on it first, digging it free from the shallow pit from where it had sunk. Then with borrowed horses from Clement's farming friends, six heavy horses, he used a thick leather harness to spread the load and six heavy three inch ropes. On Saturday, Geordie pulled his gang in to help. The gang of labourers laid down twelve round ash trunks between the back of the horses and the front of David. Red moved the horses on; two men ran from the back with an ash trunk and placed it in front of David. They crawled like this all the way to the town. By nightfall they had David in Victor Joseph's back yard.

Red was given dispensation to work on David, along with Victor's son Vincent who was the town's motorcycle mechanic; parts came in from far and wide. One Saturday Red went with Victor to Cambrai, where a cousin of Victor's was in possession of a caterpillar track, one he himself had taken from a wreck. Red didn't know what Victor paid, but by the look on his cousin's face, it was a worthwhile amount.

It went slowly, one part at a time. Red enjoyed the work, the satisfaction of putting David back together. He wasn't sure if it would ever work. Victor was very keen, eager to have something that no other Mayor would have for miles around.

Geordie would come and supervise from time to time, happy to stand back and offer encouragement rather than get his hands greasy. Red would work into the evening by acetylene lamp. Vincent would help, making up parts on his lathe.

Once finished, in the evening he would go to the hotel and Marie would cook for him. She would cook him egg and chips. He wouldn't dare eat snails even though he did admit they smelt good in all that garlic and butter.

On a Sunday he would walk out with Marie and Nicole down to the river and back. He got closer to Marie as spring warmed into summer. With the tank nearly finished and with harvest ready, Clement asked him to bring in the wheat. Red jumped at the chance. With the sun beating down and the wheat rippling in the breeze, he hitched up the reaper binder and went to the fields. He felt at peace.

Marie, Eliza and the children helped gather the stooks. Marie and Eliza set up the picnic on an old green blanket. They sat together with their babies, gossiping. When Red stopped with the field finished he sat with Marie, Eliza, Nicole and Emma as they lay out under the sun. Clement came and thanked Red: the first harvest since the war; he was grateful for such a huge crop. Nicole gurgled her first word: 'Mama.' Red felt his heart thaw.

* * *

Eliza took Emma in her arms and went off to gather her brood, as Catherine, Edith and Louise zig-zagged through the stooks. Louise was pretending to be the Sergeant ordering their marching.

Red lay back, feeling Marie next to him. Her skin soft and brown, darkening in the sun. He felt a great wave of pleasure move from his toe to his ear. He breathed in deeply, the smell of wheat surrounding him. He looked at Marie, her brown tendrils of hair running down her back, her young daughter nestled in her arms, and her feet stretched on the green blanket. Two poppies stood, dancing in the breeze in a patch of wheat uncut in the corner.

They looked at each other. Red put out his hand, took Marie's in his. She smiled back.

26

7th July 1919

It should be the most wonderful time. Connie thought of everything she now had: a husband, a beautiful baby girl. Her Lily, Lily Josephine. She was a bright young baby. She would cry to be fed, but her blue eyes were sharp and inquisitive.

They were seated around the large oak dining table for breakfast. Dorothy and Spencer served the smoked haddock. It was too rich for Constance; she stuck with a boiled egg and a slice of bread. She held Lily under her arm, and smiled at Dorothy, remembering her help. She'd wanted her for godmother; that had been overturned by the family, Admiral Fox insisting that Theo and Admiral's sister Agnes were godparents.

'You know, you shouldn't bring that baby down to breakfast,' Theo said from across the table. 'If anything, I don't think it hygienic; she'd be much better off with Nanny Thompson, now that she is here, or what point is there having her here?' He was dressed in tweed, the same as Admiral.

'Look here, Theo, it's not for you to say,' Sampson said.

'I'm disposed to agree with Theodore, Sampson; the baby

should be in the nursery with Nanny. I don't think we should have her at the table.' Admiral Fox looked down from the head of the table, squinting his eyes.

'Does anyone care what I think?' Connie said. She regretted saying it as soon as it was out of her mouth. Josephine sat quiet next to her husband, her fading hair piled on her head, her face narrow and drawn. Her dress was immaculate; her pearl necklace adorned her neck. Her eyes were dull.

'Don't you think you should control your wife, Sampson? It's not right for her to speak to Father like that, is it?' Theo looked at Sampson and ignored Connie. 'I think she is affected and weary from giving birth, and not thinking straight. I think that's common.' His lips pursed.

'Well, I am common, aren't I?' retorted Connie. 'I'm not gentry like you. But forgive me for thinking that a mother should be with her child; and I'm more than capable of thinking for myself. And forgive me for talking directly.'

'Now, now, child, you don't need to react like that,' Josephine said, barely audible. Dorothy came to clear plates and gave Connie a look as if to say: *bear up.*

'Look, it's best for the young baby that you let Nanny take over. I mean she is trained and comes with the highest recommendations in the county. That is the last word on the matter,' Admiral Fox declared. Connie looked over and saw a satisfied, barely disguised grin on Theo's face. She looked at Sampson who was quiet as he ploughed on eating his smoked fish.

'If you will excuse me.' Connie pushed out her chair and got up to leave. She headed for the door, walking past Admiral and Josephine.

'Where are you going? You haven't had any toast,' Sampson said. 'I'll come with you.' He went to get up.

'No, you stay. I need fresh air! I'm going for a walk! Don't worry; I won't be long.' She looked back from the door, shouting to Sampson. She heard Admiral and Josephine tut under their breath.

* * *

Connie walked down Farm Lane. She noticed the cows in the pasture happily grazing. She heard the tree sparrows, singing out as if calling to her. Lily was wrapped in her blanket in the old family Victorian perambulator. How could she defy the family? She didn't want Lily being looked after by the nanny. She wanted to look after her own baby. If the vicar blocked her teaching, the least she could do was be a mother to her child.

She came to the station, which was a hive of activity. There were sheep and cattle penned waiting to be loaded for market. Milk churns stood in the back of the wagon waiting for attention. She waved up at Oscar who was busy organising the goods and instructing his porter, happy to have his station back under his sole command.

She walked into the café and saw Violet, with William being entertained by old Miss Crabb.

'Connie, what are you doing here?' Violet said from behind the counter. Connie manoeuvred the pram into the corner and took out Lily, to rock her in her arms.

'I just had to get out! That Manor house is so large, yet it suffocates me more than the old cottage does; the walls seem to press down on me.' She rocked the crying Lily to sleep. Connie looked around the little café, with its five small tables and chairs. Miss Crabb returned William to Violet.

'I'm glad I can give 'em back; I've to get on to market,' she said. She picked up her bags and left to catch the train to Dorchester. The café emptied except for the two friends. Violet came out and wiped down the vacated table.

'He doesn't much stand up for me, Violet. Does he not realise I've given everything up for him? I give him a child, and then they take everything away from me.' She rocked Lily in her arms. 'They've got this flipping nanny; a nanny of all things! Why?'

'I guess it's the way they do things in that family.'

'They think it's so normal, Vi. Well, it doesn't feel like that to me; it feels like they want to take away the only thing I have left, my Lily. It wouldn't be so bad if Theodore wasn't back, sticking into our lives. Oh, Violet, what am I going to do?'

'There doesn't seem like an awful lot that you can do. You've got your life now, and you have to live it, the same as I'm too with William. I think if I had a chance of a nanny I would jump at it, letting me off with some of the burdens. Don't get me wrong: I love William and I wouldn't be without him. But some days, it would be nice to have that help. I know I have Mother but she is no spring chicken, not no more; and it's not fair me hoisting William on her all the time.' She went back behind the counter and wrung out the dishcloth.

'I know I should be grateful, but I can't stand this not being listened to, being instructed on how to bring up my own child. Oh Violet, what a mess of things I've made.' Lily let out a cry, and Connie rocked her. 'It's like I don't have any control over my life. Most things are done for me, most decisions are taken for me. I didn't realise this is what married life was going to be like. I imagined we would discuss and agree together. Sampson's a good man, but he doesn't seem able to keep the promises he made to me. He promised me so much, Violet, and foolishly I believed them all. How naïve was I?'

'You're not naïve, Connie. It's just life, isn't it? It has a way of disappointing. Be grateful for what you have; you have a man who loves you, a wonderful healthy baby.'

'I'm sorry, Violet. Talking to you I must seem so ungrateful. After all you've been through and lost. It isn't fair for me to come and talk to you like this.' She put Lily down inside the pram. 'Thank you for listening.' She navigated her way through the tables and chairs and pushed the pram towards the door.

'Don't go, Connie; I didn't mean for it to sound like that. It's that you... well, you do have so much to be happy about.' Violet busied herself brewing tea for the next rush, which was due in ten minutes.

'That's all right, Violet, thank you.' Connie took the pram and wheeled it through the café doors and into the station yard. She walked up the lane, not sure where she was heading, her head a blur.

* * *

She found herself walking up School Hill with the pram, the thin wheels sketching on the road. Clouds were sweeping in, blocking out the sun. The temperature was falling. She wished she'd worn something more than her thin old work dress. She looked in at the school gates and she remembered Red's visit, and all the happy days teaching.

It would be time for morning break. The children would run and scream, let loose into the schoolyard. The first drops of rain fell. Then there was a crack of thunder. She should get under cover. She walked; Lily let out a cry at the sound of more thunder in the air. Connie increased her pace to the top of the hill, then turned right into the churchyard. The door to the church was open. She walked inside. It was cold as the thunder cracked. The sky opened to let its deluge fall.

She picked Lily up out of the pram and sat on the wooden pew at the back of the church. She looked around at the emptiness. Raindrops hitting the roof more frequently

In Fields of Gold and Red

played like heavy drums.

'Ah, young Mrs Fox. How are you?' Startled, she looked around. It was the vicar.

'Reverend.' It was the last person she wanted to see. 'I'm fine.' She tried to hide the contempt from her face.

'And how is Lily? Let me see.' He moved close to her and pulled back Lily's blanket from her face. 'She is so wonderful, such a lovely baby. She is a credit to you and Sampson; you must be so happy. And you, are you well?' He peered at Lily through his spectacles.

'She's fine; I'm fine. Thank you, Vicar. I'm only in out of the storm.'

'Yes, yes, of course.' He made himself comfortable as he sat down next to Connie. 'It will put a stop to any haymaking today, and for the rest of the week, I'm sure.'

'I suppose.' Connie brushed Lily's head, moving her hair back. 'I'll go as soon as it stops.' She brushed her own hair with her hand and sighed.

'Oh, I don't mind, dear; it's good to have a chance to talk to you.' He smoothed down his gown, brushing away rainwater. 'I was so sad I missed young Master Kingson. I would have like to have talked to him. What a rum business! Mistakenly taken for dead and then making it back only to leave. I wanted to thank him for doing his duty. I can't understand why he left so soon. He should have stayed with his family, where folk care about him. Have you heard where he's gone?' He looked at Connie.

'No, not really. He talked about France.' She looked up and then away.

'France? What does he think he can achieve there? His family and friends are all here.' He shook his head from side to side.

'I know, but I guess he wants to start fresh; a new beginning.' Connie wanted to change the subject.

'Hmm, well, I suppose he has his reasons. And you, you must be so happy you have your Lily to look after and bring up.' He smiled.

'Yes, well, it's difficult, with having a nanny and getting used to my family.' Connie held her breath and sighed.

'I'm sure it is, dear, but you have to persevere to make things work. You're in a marriage now and you have your duty to your husband.' She didn't want another sermon, not from him. The rain continued to fall on the church roof.

'Miss Appleworth's only had good things to say about you, Mrs Fox, and she doesn't impress easily. I'm sure I wouldn't want to be one of her naughty pupils on the end of a telling-off!' He smiled at Connie.

'No, but she is always fair, and is only stern if they deserve it.' Connie breathed out, more confident.

'I'm sure. We are so lucky to have her. I'm sorry that there was no way I could let you continue. I hope you see sense in my decision after all, now that we have the arrangements made. The new schoolmaster – he's an old officer, Mr Trevell – is to start in September.'

'I'm glad for the children. I'm sure he will work well with Miss Appleworth.' Connie bit the inside of her cheek.

'I'm sure he will. And you: what will you do with your time?' He repositioned his spectacles and placed one hand on each knee.

'I've no idea; it's something I'm going to have a lot of.' She sighed.

'I was thinking about this. An old friend's been in touch, and I think you would be well-suited, being educated. He's bought the local paper, the *Bridport Gazette*. He is looking for help writing up articles, news stories; you know the sort of thing. It would only be a trial but I think you would be good at it, and it would give you a chance to get out of the Manor. What do you think?' She didn't know what to say!

What would Sampson and the Admiral have to say? Could she leave Lily with the nanny? How could they argue? It's what they wanted.

'I'd love it, I think; say yes to your friend. When could I start?' She smiled.

'Mr Foster would want help straight away. He's an old friend from my college days. He's taking over from Mr Galpin. He made his money in the city, so he will need a lot of help, but – well, I couldn't think of anyone better when he asked me, said he was having terrible trouble getting anyone who was educated.'

'Yes; oh, please say I will, of course if Sampson agrees!' She felt her energy return.

* * *

She went into the library, so excited to be starting at the paper on Monday. She picked up *Pride and Prejudice* and went and sat in the window seat. Lily was upstairs with Nanny Thompson. Sampson strode in, his face sour.

'It's this darn rain; we should be getting the sun now. It could ruin the hay if we don't get it in, and Theodore is no help, pushing everyone to get on with it. You can't rush it after all.'

'Yes, well, there is no stopping your brother, not once he gets a bee in his bonnet, is there,' she said.

'No, I don't suppose so. I would have thought even he would know by now that there is no way you can rush nature.' He came and sat opposite. She could smell wet grass on him. His hair was damp from the showers.

'What've you been doing today, darling?' She did so hate it when he called her that; it felt so demeaning. She put her book down, sure to put her marker in the centre.

'I wanted to talk to you. Well, last week I was talking to the vicar; and his old friend has taken over the running of the newspaper in town. He's short-staffed; he can't find anyone to help him. Well, Vicar suggested me; he thinks it would be such a good idea. Of course I told him I would have to talk it over with you, but if you give me permission… now that Nanny Thompson is looking out to Lily; well, it would be good for me to get out of here, only a couple of days a week, and it's nothing permanent.' She looked Sampson in the eye. She wanted this but she would have to be careful; she didn't want him to stop it. She put her hand on his knee and moved it up his thigh. 'It would make me happy, and you did promise to make me as happy as I could be. It would only be temporary.'

'I don't know, Connie; it's a lot to ask. I know we have Nanny, but Mother does like your company during the day.' He scratched his neck.

'Does she? I wouldn't have known. Please, Sampson, let me try. I might not like it. Let me help. You know, it sounds interesting; I'll only be writing up small pieces of news.' She looked him in the eye.

'I'm not sure Father will approve.' He sighed and rubbed his cheek.

'He never approves of nothing that makes progress or has women doing anything, does he?' She smiled.

'Well, he's from a different time.' He squirmed in his seat.

Connie moved her hand back down to his knee. She looked at him, smiled and said: 'Women are doing so much more nowadays, and you won't even miss me.'

'Go on then, Connie, you have my approval. God knows what Father will think.' He sighed.

She got up and gave Sampson a kiss on the cheek and said: 'Thank you. I'm going up to check on Lily.'

27

8th August 1919

Marie had given Nicole to Eliza to babysit and said: 'Come; *viens avec moi, s'il te plaît.*' She pulled him to the stairs. She held his hand and led him up. He noticed her green and white flowered skirt flow; she swayed up the stairs, putting him in a daze. He noticed her slender petite legs, so perfectly true. Her scent a mixture of roses and freshly baked bread. He was growing excited at the anticipation of touching her silky smooth young body and holding it close to his.

Marie reached the landing. Red was still on the last step but she was eager. She, equal in height, put her hands on the back of his head and clasped him to her face; she kissed, parting his lips with her tongue, and nibbled on his lower lip, kissing with her tongue. He could feel her delicate fingers move around his head onto his cheeks. Her kissing was intense; he could feel her eagerness. He ran his fingers up and down her shoulders and arms, stroking her; she gasped for air. He moved his fingers to her face, caressing her cheeks and moving her hair behind her shoulders and away from her face. He could feel Marie pushing her aching body against his; she was feeling so warm. She went to pull away to head for the bedroom. He pulled her back, not wanting the kissing to end. She willingly complied; he could tell she wanted him. He kissed her neck; her hair smelt so light and rose-fragrant. He nibbled on her ear; she pushed herself harder against him. She turned to the door; he bunched her hair up and kissed the base of her neck. She turned again and ran her fingers through his hair. He ran his hands through hers; it felt so soft. He touched her cheeks and ran his fingers down to her neck, down entering her shirt, running his fingers down and around her soft full breasts, teasing her by running his finger around her right breast, before using his whole hand to cup her, it feeling so wondrous. She groaned as she took him by the hand and moved him into the bedroom. Red closed the door behind him.

Sunlight was flooding the room in the early afternoon and the bed looked so inviting.

'Oh, Marie, I want you.' He touched his hand to his cheek.

Marie said as she looked at Red: 'You would be a good papa to Nicole.' She paused, looking at him. He went to talk. 'Shh, *non*.' She moved her finger over his lip.

She kissed Red on the mouth, on his cheek and on his neck. She ran her fingers through his hair and unbuttoned his shirt. She ran her hand to his chest. He felt his nipples harden with the touch of her fingers and his desire strengthened. She pulled at his shirt impatiently, and then more carefully pulled it over his head and off. She kissed his chest and bit his nipples. He felt carried on a wave. He drew her shirt up and over her flowing hair; it made her look even more alluring. He moved his mouth down to her breasts, licking and biting on her large nipple. He moved his mouth up to hers and moved his hand to her breast, tenderly caressing. She kissed him harder, then pulled away. They both undressed. She stood with the sun cascading through the window behind her: a natural picture of beauty with her narrow waist and shapely hips, her hair rolling down in front of her shoulders to contour her figure. She glided over to the dresser and leaned over. Supporting herself on her hands, she looked back over her shoulder at Red, sweeping her hair from her face, and she smiled. Red thought she knew exactly what she was doing. Red moved behind her and she guided him with her hand. He could feel her hot body. He moved slowly at first, before quickening. He could feel her excitement. Wanting to kiss her again, he turned her around and held her hand; he led her to the bed and gently positioned her on her back. She smiled up at him; he looked into her eyes and smiled. Her eyes sparkled and he felt happier than for a long time, for longer than he could remember. He knew it was lust. They kissed and continued to make love in the heat of the afternoon.

'Oh, *oui*, Rouge, Rouge!' she screamed out.

They lay there together, falling asleep in each other's arms, both physically satisfied. When he woke, Marie gave him a kiss on the cheek.

'Nicole, *elle aura besoin d'un papa*. You papa,' Marie whispered in his ear.

Red was confused.

Marie rolled over onto her back, looking up at Red, and said: 'You think?' She looked him in the eye.

'*Belle Nicole and belle Marie.*' She looked back, her hazel eyes glowing. He looked at her skin, which seemed to radiate light.

'*Oui, oui*, Rouge.' Marie kissed him on his cheek.

Red didn't want to lie; he felt for her. It just wasn't the same as for Connie. It made him feel guilty sleeping with Marie and it felt like he was cheating on his own feelings.

'I do mean it, I do. You're so lovely.' Her head tilted to

one side.

Marie pushed herself up on her elbows, and then inched her way up on to Red. She was light; she held herself above him, letting only the very tips of her nipples touch his body. She ignited his desire. Red lay still on his back, watching her as she used her whole body to run up and down his, her long mane of brown hair looking golden in the dimming sunlight. She continued to run her body up and down against his. She moved back up to his mouth, her hair falling down lightly onto his chest, soft like feathers. She kissed him full on the mouth, then on his neck. He used his hands to cup her face and her hair, gently stroking her. He looked her in the eye and she looked back, deep with desire. He was hungry for her.

He felt so content; she was so passionate and sensual. They made love. They drifted off. He fell into the deepest most satisfying sleep he could remember.

They woke and it was dark; early morning. They made love again, Marie seeming to be insatiable. When finished she fetched Nicole from Eliza and they all sat together, wrapped in a blanket on the end of the bed. Red could smell the warm cosiness of Nicole. It was early but the hotel would have to open soon.

'*Oui*, I'll stay, I'll stay. *Je reste, toi*, with you and Nicole.' He smiled.

'Oh, Rouge, *oui*, Rouge.' She kissed him passionately and he could see there was a small tear in the corner of her eye. His own tears followed.

* * *

Red walked out from the hotel into the town square. People were already about their business. The Saturday morning was clear and bright. He looked at the buildings as he walked: most of the works finished, the town hall's new facade clean stone. He looked to his left and saw the neat terrace of houses. The last one nearest the hotel was Geordie and Eliza's. He would walk around the town before calling on Geordie; no point being there too early.

The smell of freshly baked croissants escaped from the baker's on his right. The sun rose slowly over the eastern edge of the town, rising above Victor Joseph's imposing town house, which was next door to the town hall fully rebuilt by Geordie and his gang; Geordie having sourced stones from the local quarries. People chased chickens, racing to put them in baskets for market.

His own wedding would be the first ceremony in the finished town hall. It wasn't until two o'clock; there was plenty of time for whatever Geordie had planned. He looked around, taking in the town. It was the right thing for him to do, to marry Marie. He knew he could be a good father and learn the language. Still, he felt nervous. He came around again to Geordie's front door and walked in.

'Me head is bloody hanging.' Geordie was slumped over his tea. 'How come you don't have a head like a mashed-up turnip?' He rubbed his forehead.

''Cos I wasn't drinking like there was no tomorrow last night,' Red said as he pulled up a chair.

'Oh, Red, what we going to do with him? I told him not to drink so much to keep a clear head. Does he listen to me?' Eliza said, coming through with two large sheets and Emma under her free arm. 'And 'im being your best man and all. Can you get 'im out from under my feet?' She pursed her lips.

'Red, that's code for get out of here; you'll have to learn women's code now you're to be married,' he said, scratching his head, then taking a slurp of tea. 'It's more complicated than anything the army could cook up; it's all secret meaning and looks.' He winked.

'Don't listen to 'im, Red; it's nothing so complicated. I'm

sure you'll be much better than Geordie, as you will listen to your wife; I'm sure that is all she will really want.'

'Come on, Red, I can't win here! Let's get out of 'ere; I've a lot to get done.' They walked outside and to the Renault car that Geordie had done another deal on, this time with Vincent, Victor Joseph's son. Red didn't dare ask what he'd given for it or what he said he would do. It was four cylinders and ten horsepower with a top speed of forty miles per hour. Red thought it looked large and slow, with a gaudy bright green body and a black pull-over canvas roof.

'Crank it over for me, will 'e,' Geordie said.

'Yes, sir, captain.' He cranked over the Renault. 'Where are we headed?'

'That's a secret! I've got a couple of errands to run, ain't I.' The petrol engine started and turned over. Red got up in the passenger seat and Geordie drove out of the village, clipping the corner of the forge.

Geordie drove out of the town on the road to Cambrai. He pushed hard down on the accelerator. Red felt the wind press on his face and chest with such force, he struggled to breathe. Geordie threw the car into the tight bends, two wheels coming off the ground. Red knelt on the seat and leaned out over his door, pushing all his weight down; he grinned from ear to ear. He looked at Geordie; he was grinning, too.

'This is the life, ain't it!' Geordie yelled. Red nodded his head, beaming with a smile.

They got to Cambrai and parked up on a side street. They walked out and onto the wide bridge over the canal. Cars and trucks passed but the traffic was mainly horses and wagons. Red looked down at the many barges waiting to pass through the lock. They walked along the streets, busy with market day. Chickens squawked in their cages. There was all sorts of livestock: ducks, cockerels strutting, rabbits, pigs and cows, goats tethered; everything was alive and for sale.

'Here, this is the one,' Geordie said, standing outside the men's outfitters. The huge window display was impressive: men's suits, shirts, all types of hats, blazers, slacks, shoes. Red looked in the window at the price tickets.

'Don't you worry about the price; this is my and Eliza's wedding gift. We can't have that pretty Marie marrying some old tramp, can we? Anyway, Eliza has insisted.' He patted Red on the back.

'I won't let you. You can't go getting me that; it's too much money.' Red tried to walk on, but Geordie caught his arm and dragged him to the door of the shop.

'Aw, shut up. 'Course you can. It's what friends are for, ain't it? And I happen to agree with Eliza on this one.' He pushed open the door and dragged Red in.

'I'll pay you back; I don't know how, not this minute.' He relaxed and followed Geordie in.

'Don't worry about that. Let's get in and get that suit on. I want time to take you for a drink before I have to have you back; you can't be late for your own wedding! Eliza would never forgive me for that!' he joked.

* * *

'Are you sure you should be driving?' Red said. He looked at Geordie, who having downed two whiskeys in quick succession seemed pretty near drunk.

'Ay, lad, ain't no problem for me.' Red cranked over the Renault GS and then hopped in the passenger seat. Geordie navigated the streets slowly, passing horses and wagons before getting the car out onto the straight Roman road which cut through the large plains of wheat.

Geordie accelerated, the Renault GS bouncing over ruts as he speeded along the straight. Red could see the S-bends coming up. He felt Geordie should start applying the brakes and he pushed his foot down; still Geordie didn't brake. He threw the car into the tight bends, the poplar trees tall each side. Red's heart came into the back of his throat. He could smell hot rubber. He leant over. He felt the car out of control. Geordie wrestled with the steering; they came out of the bend. Red was relieved. Geordie regained control, only to see the horse and wagon too late. Geordie swerved to avoid them. The car left the road and launched over the ditch. In the air with no means of steering, it sailed. Red felt weightless and useless. The car ploughed down into the wheat, nose first. Red was thrown forward, then back. The motor car headed for the ash tree. Soil and earth stopped the car feet from the tall thick trunk.

'Bloody hell, Geordie, you could have killed us!' Shocked and relieved, Red began to laugh.

'We're in one piece,' Geordie said, as he got out of his side. Red jumped out and went and flagged down the next passing horse and wagon. They pulled the car out backwards; luckily, it still drove.

'This time, try not to kill me before my wedding day, will 'ee,' Red said.

Back in the town, Red got ready in Geordie's house. He'd never had a new suit. He looked in the mirror; he looked smart. He, Geordie, Eliza and the children walked across the square to the town hall. Marie, Eliza and the girls had decorated it with bunting the day before. The whole of the town squeezed in. Red and Geordie went to the right side at the front, and Eliza stood with the bridesmaids on the left. Victor Joseph came to the front and stood behind the large table with the register, ready to perform the ceremony. Red waited. Marie entered, arm-in-arm with Pierre. She was dressed all in white with a train flowing behind her, held by Eliza and Louise. Pierre beamed a wide smile, looking so proud in a navy suit and tie. They approached and stood with Red. Victor looked at them. Red looked Marie in the eye; he handed the rings to Victor, who pronounced them husband and wife. Red saw that Pierre was crying.

The ceremony finished, they all retreated to the hotel where Pierre threw open the doors and they enjoyed the biggest party since the end of the war. Geordie didn't make it home. He fell asleep in the old rocking chair. Eliza left him, coming back in the morning to collect him.

28

16th September 1919

The strong south-westerly wind blew up West Street. The wide open pavements stretched either side of the main street. As wagons pulled by, horses cantered to and fro. Connie looked back up at the sign, W G Foster & Co, the newly painted sign in white lettering over a black background. She crossed the street in front of the large windows of West End Dairies who were busy with queues of women. Connie walked as quickly as she could. Why was it she got to run all the errands? Couldn't young Frank Herbert do them? She wanted to write more articles and impress Mr Foster. So far she'd been sent to watch the football, write up the weather report and write up who'd been in court.

Connie entered the town post office through the imposing stone doorway, with the package she'd been sent by Mr Foster to post. It would need to be weighed. There was a long queue. She would show Mr Foster; she would show him how good she could be, if he would only give her a chance.

She shuffled forward with the heavy package in both hands. Standing up straight, she began to wonder: was she doing the right thing? The Admiral and Josephine didn't understand. What a furore she'd had to put up with when she told them all she would be going out to work. They couldn't believe her attitude. Sampson tried to be on her side, giving her support and standing up for her, but little by little his support wavered, as his brother and father dominated him. He'd pleaded for her to reconsider. She'd even had thoughts of turning the opportunity down, going back on her word. She wanted to do it, and they could hardly argue that she was needed at home, not with them employing Nanny against her wishes.

'Thought it was you.' A voice from behind addressed her.

Connie looked round. She already knew by the tone of the voice that it was Edna Palmer. Of all people she would meet at the post office. She still had the big old conker of a nose and her sour look.

'You're not too posh yet, then,' Edna sneered.

'No, I've always wanted to work.' Connie tried to keep her face a picture of calm.

'Thought you'd be putting your feet up, looking down on the likes of me now you're married into gentry.' Connie took a deep breath and hoped Edna didn't realise she was winding her up. She hoped the queue would move on.

'I'm surprised you had a baby so soon and all. You didn't wait around, did you?' Edna sniffled, her nose running. She took out an old rag and wiped it. 'You know I've heard all about Redver; have you?' She grinned.

'No, I haven't heard. Where is he? How is he?' She hated asking. Edna always so glad to rub it in.

'I'm not sure he'd want me telling you, would he? You not waiting for him to come back from the war before marrying and having Sampson's baby.'

'I was told he was dead, wasn't I? I went to find out; I was told. I never got his letter, not until weeks after he'd come back.' She was about to lose it; why did Edna have to be like this?

'Oh, there's no need to get all uppity, is there! I thought you might like to know, that was all. To hear where he is and what he's doing.'

'Is he well? Is he all right?' Connie looked down at the floor. She didn't want to look Edna in the eye, she didn't want to give her the satisfaction of seeing her upset. The package in her arms wore heavy. She tried to shift the weight, holding it in her arms, moving from foot to foot.

'He got married, didn't 'e, and got a baby when he was back in France. Must have slept with the girl even before he returned, I reckon!' Edna laughed, failing to hide her joy.

'What… what, he's in France?' Connie stammered.

'Yes; went back to where he was stationed by all accounts. He's written to his brother; so he's not written to you, then, Connie? I'm surprised, the way you two were carrying on before the war; thought you were set to be married like Violet and Jimmy did, I really thought you would.' She smiled, taking great pleasure in her knowledge.

They shuffled forward in line. Connie hoped she would be at the counter soon and out of the post office.

'Serves you right if you ask me, running to Sampson soon as Red was gone and out of the way. Anyway, looks like he didn't love you that much, not if 'e was carrying on in France, was 'e, and not writing to you now. Well, seems like he's forgotten all about you.' She scratched the side of her nose.

'Look, Edna, it's none of your business.' Connie turned and faced the front.

'I was just saying. There's no need to get all snooty, Mrs Fox,' Edna finished.

* * *

Connie sat at her desk. Mr Foster came in and said: 'Mrs

Fox, come with me! There's a story breaking.' He was forthright and to the point. He was taller than her, she would imagine five feet ten inches; his jaw was square, covered in a long beard. You would never have guessed he was sixty. Connie got up and grabbed her raincoat from the coat stand in the corner. Her desk was small in comparison to Mr Foster's; his large, made from mahogany, with a desk light. She'd never seen an electric light before. 'Come on, Mrs Fox; I've heard there's been an accident, on the railway line.'

'What... what's happened?' she said, shocked.

'Something at the tunnel.' He looked at her, scratching his beard.

'Another landslide?' she asked.

They rushed out to Mr Foster's large Morris motor car. It was dark green, nothing as bright as Sampson's.

'You crank it over for me, Mrs Fox.' Connie walked to the front of the car, the wind blowing her hair from her bonnet. The metal handle was cold to the touch. She turned the crank with all her strength.

'Come on there, girl; we don't have all day!' he shouted.

She tried harder, using all her strength. This wasn't what she'd had in mind when she joined the paper.

'Come on, come on!' At last, she turned the crank and Mr Foster was able to start the engine. The motor car spluttered into life. He drove the car up West Street, taking the left turn onto Barrack Street before racing along St Andrew's road.

'It's at the tunnel, that was what Fred Dunn said. Something about a train not reaching Toller, and the tunnel collapsed.'

* * *

'Connie, Connie, you're here!' Violet ran out from the railway café to meet her friend. She looked distraught. 'My god, it's horrendous; the tunnel's collapsed. They're trying to dig them out. There was a whole carriage full. It's not far up the line. Come on.'

'I'm not sure it's a place for you ladies. Mrs Fox, Mrs Crabb, you should stay in the café,' Mr Foster declared.

'Not on your Nelly. Come on, we can be of help,' Connie said, pulling Violet with her. Mr Foster followed.

'If you insist; on your heads be it,' he said.

The three of them went through to the platform. Connie and Violet jumped down onto the line. Connie put her hand back and helped Mr Foster down. It was strange to be walking on the sleepers. Connie was glad of her stout shoes. They walked up the line towards Toller.

'We didn't realise anything was wrong, not for an hour or so. The train left on time from here, but never got to Toller. It wasn't till Mr Grey came in, told us there had been a landslide; seen it happen from the field, he did, said the noise was horrendous, and the train to be caught in it!' Violet said, wiping sweat from her brow.

The tunnel was one mile from the station. The wind blew from behind, pushing them faster along the track. They increased their pace.

'How many got on, Violet?' Connie asked.

'It must have been seven or eight. Oh my god: old Miss Crabb, Mrs Wrixon the vicar's wife, Mrs Smyth; I'm not sure of the others; they were in the café, all of them. Connie, oh I hope they're all all right.' She gasped for breath.

'Don't you think the railway should have done more after the last landslip? You know, to make sure that old tunnel was safe?' Connie said.

'It's easy to say now, but who would have thought it would happen again; and now it's closer,' Violet said, breathing hard as they walked.

'Come on, Mr Foster,' Connie said. 'We have to get there.'

They called back as he struggled to keep up.

'You two can walk quicker than me; you go on ahead.' He bent over to take a breath.

Connie and Violet walked down the straight track. The incline grew. Through the cutting, the high banks on either side with tall ash trees. The tunnel was further on, round the bend another half a mile.

'Men from the farm have gone first. We sent Fredrick Dunn around the village to raise the alarm. He's not fast on his feet at the best of times, but Father lent him his old bicycle; you should have seen him move,' Violet said, catching her breath.

'Oh, I pray they're all all right, Violet.'

They rounded the bend, seeing the scene of mass carnage. George Kingson and his uncles were labouring with shovels and their hands, loading the mud, dirt and branches onto the farm wagons. As fast as they dug, more sand-coloured mud rippled down to replace what they had removed.

'Whatever can we do?' Violet gasped. There were branches, tree trunks, and upended shrubs blocking the tunnel entrance, so high the brickwork couldn't be seen.

'Why did you come? You two should go back,' Oscar said. 'It's no place to find yourself. We don't know how safe that bank is up there. I'm sorry, Connie, but Sampson got on that train, right at the last minute; said he had to get to Dorchester this morning. I even held the train for him. I'm sorry,' he said, looking down.

Connie's face dropped; it couldn't be true.

After conferring, Oscar and Mr Grey started to point and organise more men who turned up. Connie could see they were all working together as one; but it seemed a useless task. There was so much earth, so much to clear.

'Come on, give me a shovel; I can help, and my husband

is in there.' She didn't wait to be stopped; she grabbed a shovel from Oscar. 'Give that to me. I can take a turn as good as the rest of you.' Violet joined her, and gave a look to her father.

Connie started to dig in the line of men. She prayed in her mind for all of them to be safe. She shovelled, moving the earth as quickly as she could. With the wooden handle in her hands, her soft skin began to blister at the base of her fingers. She took her handkerchief, tore it in two and wrapped it around her hands. The rain began to fall; she was so engrossed she didn't feel it on her back. She kept working. Thinking of the time she had wandered the streets of London looking for Red; thinking back to when she had hope for him. She thought of Sampson. She didn't love him, but she didn't want him dead. She cared for him even if he couldn't stand up to his father or brother. He was Lily's father, after all.

Oscar pulled her back: 'Connie, it's been an hour, love; take a break. Come on, you need a break.' Violet took her hand and walked her to the wagon, set with the old tea urn. Dorothy handed her a mug of tea and a rag to clean her face.

'Violet, I don't want to lose Sampson, not after all the loss we've had to endure,' she said, with tears in her eyes.

'I know, Connie. They may be safe; don't think like that,' Violet said, supporting her friend's arm.

Connie and Violet finished their tea and returned to the line. Men and women worked together. All the village were encamped. When evening fell, they continued with acetylene lamps brought down. A train and carriage were backed up the line from Bridport, so there was a dry place to rest.

Theodore Fox and Admiral came; they appeared on a wagon. Theodore stood on the wagon barking instructions, taking over from Oscar and Mr Grey. They worked on through the night. Connie's hopes began to fade.

'Keep your spirits up, young lady,' Mr Foster said. His clothes were smeared in mud, his beard wet and unkempt, his hair a tangled mess. 'We'll get 'em out. Word is that most of the tunnel is intact; otherwise the hill above would be so much lower. There is hope; keep thinking that, my dear,' he stressed.

'I want to, but we are only scratching the surface. How long is it going to take?' Connie asked.

'We just have to keep going, one shovel at a time. If we all work together you will be surprised how quick we can get to them.' He touched her on the shoulder. Violet held her hand.

They went back to the mound of mud, trees and vegetation. They filled baskets with shovel load after shovel load. Baskets were handed down the chain line and emptied; women and children returned the empty baskets.

Connie could feel her eyes closing as she worked. It was dark, not yet morning. She'd never been so tired. She had to keep going, for the sake of Lily's father. She forced her eyes open; her body ached all over. There was silence; at the early hour before dawn, people didn't want to talk; there was nothing left to be said, and they were so accustomed to the routine, they didn't need to take instruction. They took shifts, taking a turn to sleep in the carriages. Small food parcels got brought.

Then she heard it. A tap, tap, tap, metal on metal. They all heard it and increased their efforts.

As the sun came up, with a clear sky they broke through. First a small gap, then larger. The brickwork visible. A hand poked through. It was Miss Crabb, followed by Mrs Wrixon. They were pushed through, dishevelled but uninjured. All seven; then at last, to Connie's amazement and joy, Sampson. He clambered through the cleared gap, his clothes dirty, his face smeared in mud. She went to him and hugged him as hard as she ever had.

* * *

'Connie, come into my office, will you?' Mr Forster called from the back. The only light came flickering in from West Street through the large rectangular window. Connie got up from her desk, her shoes clicking on the wooden floorboards. The smell of ink wafted in from the printing press further back in the building.

'Yes, Mr Forster,' Connie complied. She wondered what he wanted to speak to her about. He'd been quiet since the big landslide, somewhat subdued by the whole experience. She came into his office and sat down on one of the chairs in front of his desk. The room held the deep aroma of tobacco.

'It's been a month now, hasn't it, since you came to work here as a junior.' His brown eyes peered at her from above his bushy beard. 'I want to say, you've made a good start; better than good. The landslide showed me another side of you: something I have to admit I didn't expect, but I should have seen coming.' His hand went to the back of his neck, and he took a deep breath.

'You, Violet, the other women there that day, you were all a credit. Much more help than I was able to be. You've shown that you are more than capable. You are more than equal to most men I know.' He let out the breath.

Connie was taken aback. To hear a man speak like this! She said: 'Thank you, Mr Foster. I wasn't thinking, I was just acting, to save my husband. I expect anyone else would have done the same.' Her spine tingled as she stood straight.

'I doubt it, Mrs Fox, I doubt it very much. You're a very special woman, and don't forget that. You showed bravery and determination out there, and you've proved to me that you have the intelligence necessary. So, from now on, I will promise you that you can have more writing duties, and young Frank Herbert, he can do more of the office junior's running the errands and the like.' He brought his hand back to his face and scratched the beard on his chin.

'I don't want to take anything away from Frank.' She tried to keep a smile from crossing her entire face.

'I don't think he will mind, Mrs Fox; he's got no appetite for reporting and writing as you have.' He smiled. 'You can make a start by getting over to Gundrys and finding out what the hell is going on and why they're calling for that strike.' He stood up and ushered her out.

29

18th October 1924

It didn't suit him, the work in the hotel; he didn't like serving customers and Pierre irritated him with his orders.

'Rouge, *nettoyer cette bière renversée,*' Pierre would say. 'Red, *évacuer ce drain bloqué dans la cour.*' 'Rouge, *laver les pots.*' 'Rouge, *obtenir un nouveau tonneau de la cave*; Rouge, *apportez-moi une bouteille de vin.*' Red didn't understand most of what he said, and when he did try and guess and got it wrong, Pierre would call him '*imbécile.*' Red understood that all right.

He could live with the long hours; he knew how to do the jobs – it hadn't taken him long to pick them up – it was just routine, day after day. Did Pierre have to go on so much, nagging and nagging at him? Chipping away hour by hour at him. He bit down on his lip to stop himself speaking back; he did it for Marie and Nicole's sake.

Mealtimes were the worst, when they sat down together, Pierre noisy as he ate, roughly chomping down. His use of cutlery clanging and banging his plate, it was needless; why did he have to tap, tap, tap with his knife life that? It was so noisy and irritating. Red would try talking to Pierre but he couldn't understand talking so fast; it was a blur of words. He would learn a few words and phrases but Pierre made it hard for him. The trouble as far as Red could see was that Pierre was drinking more and more, his cheeks and face ballooning up, his nose growing larger with all the wine he was drinking every day.

He gave away more wine than he sold. He grew more hateful and vindictive towards Red. Red knew Pierre called him names and insulted him behind his back. He knew the look he gave him.

Marie was a good mother, tender and patient. She tried to teach him more words but he was slow to pick them up. She doted on Nicole as they all did, even Pierre when he was sober, which was less and less.

* * *

He came out to the stables; the hotel was busy. There were four horses newly housed that afternoon; the familiar musky scent of the animals wafted out. Nicole loved the horses and Red held her hand as she watched. He took out three carrots and gave one to Nicole.

'Daddy, do horses like carrots?' Dressed in her green dress, Nicole looked up at her father. Her dark hair curled to her shoulders.

''Course they do, honey.' Red smiled at his daughter.

'I like carrots too, Daddy.' She giggled. She was pretty with dark hair like her mother.

'Go on, feed it to him; break a chunk off and hold it on the flat of your hand. That way he won't try and eat your little fingers.' Red placed his hand on Nicole's head and reassured her.

'Will he bite me, Daddy?' she asked.

'Of course not, Nicole, not if you give it to him right. Look, watch me.' He smiled.

Red broke a bit of carrot off and put it on the flat of his hand before holding it out; the big stallion took it and chomped. Nicole let out a squeal of delight.

'He likes it! He likes it, doesn't he?'

'Go on; he will want some more; he has the taste for it.' Red broke a bit more carrot off and handed it to his daughter.

She took the carrot in her small hands, her fingers a smaller version of her mother's. The big horse which towered above her snorted and licked his lips. Then he bent down over the stable door, stretching his neck to reach the carrot. Nicole laughed as the horse's tongue tickled her hand. He swept it up in his mouth before chewing on the tasty treat.

Red smelt the smoke in the air, dark and pungent; the smell of timber and masonry. It got stronger and he could see trails of black smoke; it was coming from across the square. It reminded him of war. He picked Nicole up and ran quickly into the kitchen, where Marie was working.

Red said: 'Here, take Nicole. I see smoke; something is on fire. Stay indoors!' He ran back out across the courtyard and under the arch, sprinting as fast as he could, his peg leg slipping on the cobbles. He saw men running to gather children and their wives. He looked up. The fire was taking hold on the terraced houses, the first closest to the blacksmith's forge already destroyed. A spark must have caught the timber. The adjoining roofs were ablaze, fanned by the strong wind.

The fire was moving fast from house to house. It engulfed Geordie's house. Red looked up; he could see Emma at the bedroom window. She seemed frozen.

'Help me, help me, please!' Emma screamed from the upstairs window. Eliza came running out of the front door pulling Louise, Catherine and Edith with her.

Eliza said: 'Please, Red, please help us; Emma, she's stuck upstairs. I tried but I couldn't; it's so hot in there.' Her face was flushed and her hair covered in ash.

Embers, ash and smoke filled the sky; wind fanning the flames increased the intensity. Red ran through the front door of the cottage. The smoke, blinding and acrid, made his eyes water. Adrenaline filled his veins. The fumes were reminiscent of battle; it was suffocating. He took his hanky and tied it around his face. He raced up the stairs, two at a time. He saw Emma standing at the window. The fire crashed through the ceiling; a roof truss came burning down, missing him by feet. He ran through the bedroom door, the landing now blocked by burning timbers. There would only be one way out, from the window.

Emma stood looking down, rooted to the spot. With burning timbers falling to the floor of the bedroom, Red ran for Emma. Holding his breath, he picked her up under his arm, looked out of the window and without hesitation made a leap for the cart. They tumbled head over heels, time standing still. Red, feeling as if time had stopped, felt the wind, smelt the smoke and felt the heart of the raging inferno. Then they were landing in soft blankets and straw on the cart positioned by Victor. Eliza ran to Emma and picked her up in her arms, kissing her and touching her hair.

Red went to help six men who were desperately trying to douse the flames with water from an old wagon tank and pump. If the fire continued to spread it could take the whole town. Buckets of water were thrown, no more use than a thimble to the flames. The men struggled and struggled, fire against men and the fire was winning, now taking all of Geordie's house. The hotel would be next. Red could see it was a battle they were not going to win. There was no way they could fetch enough water to douse the flames.

* * *

There was only one thing Red could think of: he ran across the town square. He saw Geordie running towards him.

Geordie shouted: 'How are Eliza and the sprogs?'

'They're fine, all safe! Quick, come with me!' He indicated for Geordie to follow him.

The fire continued to rage, spitting sparks, the beast tearing through the masonry and wood of the house, the noise loud as timbers cracked and masonry fell, the smoke thick and acrid.

David moved slowly into the village square; the engine roared as Red pressed the accelerator forward. Red was driving, with Geordie and Vincent on the gears. Together they positioned David in front of Geordie's house. Red knew that if he failed now, the hotel would be the next to be ablaze. He couldn't let that happen. Red engaged the clutch, and indicated to Geordie and Vincent; they selected low gear. It was easier without enemy fire.

He drove David head on at the remaining cottage. The thundering noise of David was inaudible above the cacophony of sound coming from the fire which was causing massive destruction. Red bit down on his lip, the sense of nausea sweeping over him; it wasn't long before a familiar headache and the taste of metal in his mouth returned. David crashed through the front wall; bricks, stone and wood fell below its massive tracks. Inside, Red, Geordie and Vincent were thrown from side to side. Red kept the power down; David, still moving, slowly rocked and rolled over the stone. It inched into the house, coming up against the interior wall. David pushed, Red revved more; but the wall only moved and didn't collapse. Red indicated for Geordie and Vincent to engage reverse, which they did after a time. He reversed David, and then engaged first then second quickly to gain momentum. The fire was still raging above them in the upper floor. He needed to get David to demolish the wall and create a fire break. If it wasn't done quickly, the fire would soon spread to the hotel.

He powered ahead towards the wall again. This time, David crashed through, bringing the upper floor down with a huge burst of dust, ash and embers, all cascading down on top of David. The remaining ceiling and roof all came down with a tremendous weight. Luckily there wasn't too much left and David was able to continue to rumble forward. Red drove it at the remaining back wall and with no other support, the wall crumbled easily. Where the house had stood less than half an hour ago, there was now just a slowly smouldering heap of rubble. Red moved David slowly back over the pile of bricks, timber, and masonry and stopped it on the village green. David gave a last gasp from its huge engine.

'Thanks a bloody lot, mate; now looks like I'm flippin' homeless,' Geordie said as they crawled out and surveyed the destruction. He smiled at his friend and patted Red on his back.

* * *

The hotel was full, the town happy to celebrate the avoidance of loss of life. It was a good excuse for a party and a celebration. Red insisted that Geordie, Eliza and the children stay as long as was necessary.

Eliza was good on the piano and she started to play and to sing and led them all in a rendition of *La Marseillaise* amongst other things. It was a passionate outpouring. All the men of the town came and slapped Red on his back and put money in the pot for drinks.

'Rouge, Rouge, Rouge!' they sang. Red could see Pierre drinking heavily. He was drinking brandy, very quickly with no pause in between each shot, a bigger and bigger shot each time. He soon slumped in his old chair in the corner.

Victor Joseph came over, putting his arms around Red's shoulders: 'The town owes you; we might have lost four houses but it could have been so much worse. You can have the freedom; it was your quick thinking that saved the rest. We thank you.'

Marie flitted from one group of friends to the next, being the perfect host, filling the glasses before the dancing started. She came and grabbed Red by the hand and pulled him from behind the bar.

'Rouge, I love you. *Merci beaucoup,*' she whispered in his ear.

'You don't have to thank me; I would have done anything to protect you and Nicole. I think any father would have done the same,' he said.

'*Chanceux, chanceux, chanceux!*' Pierre slurred.

'*Oh, Papa, vas au lit; tu ne sais pas ce que tu dis,*' Marie said, going to her father and pulling him up from the chair. He staggered to his feet. He pushed Marie hard away as he stumbled out of the bar.

Red moved to follow Pierre but Marie stood in his way.

'What are we going to do about him? He is getting worse and worse,' Red said.

'I don't know; he's my papa; I love him,' Marie said.

'Can't he see he's got a beautiful grandchild and loving daughter? Perhaps even a chance of a grandson one day?'

'Oh, do you mean it, Rouge?' She smiled at him.

'I do, Marie; would you like that?' He took her hand and put it to his lips.

She didn't answer him; instead, she leant in and kissed him on the mouth. She took him by the hand and they walked up the stairs, the party continuing without them. They walked into Nicole's room, and stood for an age watching her sleep; they held hands, looking down at her, looking so peaceful and content. They then walked together into their room. Marie pushed him down onto his back on the bed. He looked up at her and watched as she undid the buttons to her dress; it fell to the floor and she stepped out of it. She turned around so her back was facing him; she looked over her shoulder and smiled. She likes to tease me, Red thought. Looking at her naked shape, Red was aroused. She turned to face him, covering her breasts with her hands; she slowly crawled up the bed towards him; she pulled his trousers off. They made love frantically, fuelled by a mixture of alcohol and adrenaline. Afterwards, they got changed quickly and returned downstairs to clear up.

30

20th October 1924

Connie ran in from the rain. She stopped to throw her coat over the banister. She was soaked but so happy with the day. Her piece about the strike in Gundry's was good and Mr Foster had promised to put it on this week's front page. To see her name on the article gave her a feeling of satisfaction even greater than that which she had got when she was teaching.

She skipped up the stairs two at a time, then walked down the long corridor to the bedroom, to the second set of stairs. She couldn't wait to see what Lily had been doing.

'What do you want?' Nanny Thompson exclaimed as Connie opened the door to the nursery. 'Lily is having a nap after her tea; she is not to be disturbed. You should know that!' Nanny Thompson stared at Connie, daring her to answer. Nanny stood in her brown uniform, her hair up, her face solemn. She was slender, tall and thin with a pudgy chin.

'She's my daughter and you and no one else can tell me what I can and can't do with her.' Connie tried to push her shoulders back and to stand tall.

'Mrs Fox, you are out of order. My word, I have never

known such insolence! You wait until I tell the Admiral how you are speaking to me.' Nanny Thompson's face reddened and she gasped for air.

'Go on then, go and tell him now,' Connie dared her, not knowing where she'd found the strength to challenge her. Nanny stormed out past her.

Connie lay down next to her daughter and stroked her blonde hair, watching her sleep. Lily rolled over and opened her eyes and said: 'Oh Mummy, here you are.' She smiled.

'I am, dear; I'm better than all right. How was your day?' she asked, smiling at her daughter's wide eyes.

'It was all right. Nanny taught me more words but I wanted to go play outside and she wouldn't let me.' Lily looked at her mother and held her hand. 'Will you play outside with me tomorrow, Mummy?'

'I can't tomorrow, Lily, but I promise you I will on Sunday.' She felt a pang of regret.

'When is Sunday?' Lily looked up from under her blonde hair.

'It's soon, Lily, it's soon.' She smoothed Lily's hair. 'Now I'm sorry for waking you, but you should go back to sleep to keep Nanny happy.' She got up from the bed and tucked Lily back in.

Connie went down the narrow staircase from the nursery to the main bedroom corridor. She walked along to her bedroom and entered.

'Sampson, are you all right? What are you doing?' Connie said, concerned to see her husband in bed.

'I think it's flu; my head's a thumping headache, and all my body aches; I've no energy, Connie, I just feel tired all the time. Don't come close.' He shifted up onto his elbows to look at her. 'I'll be fresh and up and about tomorrow, I'm sure.' He winced and attempted a forced smile.

'Let me get the doctor; he can check you over, make sure

you're all right.' She walked to the window and looked back.

'I'm fine; don't worry, Connie, I'm sure it will pass.'

'If you're sure you know, Sampson. If we do have to have a Nanny, do you think we could look for someone else? Nanny Thompson doesn't like me; we've been arguing up in the nursery. If we are to have someone look after Lily, I would prefer to have someone I know.'

'Don't fret, Connie.' He sighed. Connie could see his strength had deserted him. His colour was pale, more yellow.

'I think you need the doctor. You look so gaunt, and you have no strength.'

'It's not necessary. I'm not that bad; I must look worse. I'm sorry, Connie.' He sighed, his breath weak, his brow sweating.

'You look really bad, Sampson. Has anyone been in to see you? How long have you been in bed?'

'I came up, I don't know, this morning sometime. I get so warm, then suddenly I'm cold again.'

'Has anyone been to check on you?'

'No; yes, I think Mother popped in, and of course Dorothy. She brought me some soup earlier, but I couldn't manage it. I had no appetite.' He murmured, 'I'm tired, Connie; I think I need to sleep.' He lapsed from his elbows and groaned, his face colourless yet sweating.

'I'm getting the doctor.' Connie rushed out downstairs to the dining room.

'We should get the doctor; Sampson is very sick,' Connie said as she burst in.

'Look, girl, it's just a cold; no one ever died of a cold, did they? It will make him tougher,' Theodore said. He was seated at the dining table.

'How can we all eat as if nothing is wrong? He needs the doctor and needs him now.' Connie stood in the doorway.

'Connie, don't be so dramatic. If you want the doctor, I

will send Spencer after he's served dinner. Now let that be the last word on it.' Admiral looked over from the head of the table and declared, 'He was always a sickly boy as a child. He would make his mother worry for no account, then next minute he would be up and about without a care in the world.'

Josephine looked at her husband, daring to challenge him. 'Dear, if Connie insists, then perhaps we should delay dinner, and let Spencer go now. He could be in town and back within half an hour. He could even take the motor car.' She cowered, waiting for his response.

'All right, all right! If you two won't keep quiet, I can see I won't get any peace till I give in,' Admiral said, holding his spoon still. 'Spencer, leave Dorothy, would you, and go fetch Doctor Moore?' Spencer put down his serving spoon and dish and went out, leaving Dorothy to ladle out the soup.

'Bloody hell, you'd think he was on his death bed, the way you women are carrying on!' Theo barked out through his pursed lips. 'Any man should be able to chuck off that small cold. My god, I've seen men carry on with much worse in the war.'

'All right, Theodore, let's hear the end of that,' Admiral said. Connie, relieved they had seen sense, returned to Sampson in the bedroom.

* * *

Doctor Moore came out of the bedroom. Connie and Josephine stood waiting for him. Connie could see his face, drawn and tired. He was dressed in a black suit and white shirt. He looked old, tired and worn out, much like his leather bag.

'You're to keep him isolated, Mrs Fox,' he said as he put his stethoscope away in his leather bag.

'Yes.' They both replied in unison.

'Constance, you are not to sleep with him in the bed

tonight. You are to keep him isolated. No visitors. If you do have to enter, then keep your mouths covered. I'm sorry; there is a lot of this flu. If he makes it through the night he should be fine. But it's touch and go. We've already lost Miss Crabb, and Mrs Wrixon is ill too. I'm sorry.'

'What, you mean he might die?' Connie wasn't sure what she was hearing. 'No! I mean, Sampson's not old or weak, not like those older ladies.' She felt her stomach drop and she shivered to her core.

'I've seen fit and healthy men go down with it and not make it back from their beds; I've never seen anything quite like this flu. Sorry; it can be as harsh as that. Keep an eye on him tonight. If he makes it through, he will be fine.'

'Thank you, Doctor, thank you,' Josephine said, ushering him down the stairs.

* * *

Connie sat at his bedside watching, mopping his brow. She tried to cover her mouth but she would forget and drop the handkerchief in her lap. She dozed off and on in the chair. Sampson would wake, sleep, wake. His fever raged across his face. He would push the sheets back soon after pulling them over. Connie helped him drink.

'I'm sorry, Constance, I'm sorry I didn't keep my promise to make you happy,' Sampson uttered under his breath. 'I wanted to; I was too weak. I'm not a strong enough man. I'm sorry.'

'Shut up, Sampson, don't talk like that. You did your best and we have a daughter. You gave me Lily. Don't go making yourself feel bad. You can still make me happy. Don't go. Stay; you stay and make me happy.' She stroked his forehead.

'I can't, Connie, I'm too weak. I can feel it. I can feel myself giving in to it. I'm sorry I couldn't stand up to my family. I only ever wanted to make you happy.' His eyelids came down.

'I know, Sampson; I know.' She began to cry as she saw his life ebb away.

31

21st October 1924

Pierre was drunk, seated in his chair by the hearth in the bar.

'*Putain de bâtard!*' Pierre swore. '*Anglais imbécile!*'

Red knew it was the alcohol talking. But it still felt personal and he resented being talked to in such a way.

'Shut up, old man,' Red said.

Pierre got up from the chair and staggered back to the bar. The restaurant was full, with villagers looking for breakfast. Red hoped they wouldn't hear. He didn't want Geordie or Eliza hearing his father-in-law like this.

Pierre stumbled as helped himself to a brandy, the bulk of his frame colliding with the wooden counter, his belly so wide he could hardly fit behind the bar any more.

Pierre drank from the glass. He swayed and Red watched, hoping Nicole wouldn't come near him. Pierre shouted: '*Soldats d'Allemagne s'en vont!*' He gulped. '*Soldats d'Allemagne s'en vont.*'

'*Fini, Pierre, fini, Pierre,*' Red said. Pierre's face looked startled, as if he was seeing German soldiers again. He cowered in the corner of the bar and went down on his knees.

'*Laisse la tranquille,*' Pierre said, kneeling in the corner. Red went to him and knelt down; he touched Pierre on his shoulder. Pierre waved his hand in the air.

'My wife,' Pierre said, looking Red in the face. 'She was my wife. Les soldats. The soldiers, Rouge, they took her life.' Pierre cried and moved his head into Red's shoulder.

'*Je suis desolé*. I'm sorry, Pierre.' Red cradled Pierre's head in his hands.

'*Allez-vous en. Allez-vous en.*' Pierre stood up and shoved Red out of the way as he stumbled out of the door. Red knew he would be heading for the stables to drink, to dull the pain.

* * *

The hotel was busy. Marie was doing as much as she could but Red could see she was getting tired much more easily; their baby was growing large inside her. They employed Louise Tucker, Geordie's eldest, to help. She was more like her father than her mother in attitude but she was pretty, with blonde hair and a trim figure. She was more keen to smile and talk to the young men of the village. Having four houses to rebuild meant Geordie was as busy as ever. The working gang flooded in at lunchtime, attracted by the savoury aroma of Marie's home-cooked chicken casserole and a smile from Louise.

Pierre was less than useless, drinking more and more. Red picked up the slack; he would look after the bar. He still got to be close to horses when travellers came through, although this was becoming rarer, as there were more motor cars than ever.

'Oi, oi, oi.' Pierre staggered back into the bar and lurched onto Victor.

'Get off me, old man,' Victor said.

'Come on, Pierre, come on with me,' Red said.

'Oh, fuck off, you bastard English boy,' Pierre slurred.

Red tried to get hold of Pierre and lead him out. Marie

came running in from the pantry to see what all the commotion was. Red could see her face contort in distress at seeing her Papa like this.

'You've been drinking too much; come on, Papa.'

'Let's put him to bed,' Red said.

'Get off me! Let me be!' Pierre pushed him away.

Red managed to get hold of his arms. Pierre was heavy and big and Red needed all his strength to control the man, as he was awkward and unpredictable. As they went up the stairs, Marie went in front and Red came up behind, with Pierre in the middle. As they walked up step by step, the same steps creaking as they always did, Pierre was lunging. Marie was pulling him by the hand and Red pushed from the lower steps. Pierre lurched back, pulling Marie with him. They toppled towards Red; he stood firm, pushing all his weight back against Pierre and Marie. Their combined weight was heavy against him. He jammed his wooden stump into the gap between the wall and the floorboard; it began to slip, before becoming wedged. Even though pregnant, Marie was still strong on her legs and managed to hold her ground. They managed to push and pull the old man up the final few steps and into his bedroom.

* * *

They were curled up together under the duvet, feeling nice and cosy. Red was lying behind Marie; he pulled her closer so he could kiss the back of her neck softly. He ran his hands over her bump, his baby. He was so proud of Nicole: a bright flame. She was so interested in everything and loved to climb. Yesterday he had caught her climbing up the kitchen dresser. She had made it all the way up to the middle shelf. He told her to get down but secretly he was very impressed. It triggered a memory deep within him; hadn't he been good at climbing trees all those years ago back in Ashcombe? Could it be possible that he was her father? He would never know for sure. It felt to him that he was. This time he would know. Marie stirred; she clasped Red's hands to hers and they felt the baby kick together.

'Mmm, nice; he's going to want to play football when he's grown up,' Red said.

'You know it's a *garçon*?' Marie smiled and ran her finger through her hair.

'Oh, I just have that feeling. See how he kicks so well! My Granfer always said that if the mother has a big old bump it will be a boy!'

'Your Grandpapa had a saying for a lot.'

He moved his hands up to her full breasts and caressed them with his fingers. They were growing fuller in anticipation of the baby.

Marie groaned lightly in pleasure and pushed herself back against Red. Red moved his foot gently up and down her calf and toes. He felt her pushing against him and he pushed forward. They made love.

'My Granfer was a character all right; some said he could see what was in the future!'

'I think it might be *une fille*, a sister for Nicole.' She smiled.

* * *

Red picked Nicole up; she was tired and worn out from running down in the meadow in the summer afternoon. He carried her up the stairs and into her bedroom, put her in the bed and tucked her in.

'Papa, please can I have a story?' Nicole said.

'Yes, of course, honey pot,' Red said tucking her in. 'Nicole, Mummy is going to have a baby, a baby brother or sister for you to play with.'

'Really, Daddy? I like that. Can I tell them what to do?'

'Yes, of course, Nicole, you can tell them what to do,' Red said, smiling.

'Can I have my story? Can you tell me about Bumble? I want to hear about Bumble's adventures in Ashcombe. Tell me the one about him and Ragamuffin and the fawn. Please, Daddy, please, Papa!'

'Okay, Nicole, okay,' Red said, laughing to himself.

'Well, Nicole, there were two mischievous calves, Bumble and Ragamuffin. Bumble was a boy and Ragamuffin a girl. They lived in a big warm barn with their Mommies. One day, bored by being cooped up, Bumble pushed through the broken door. Ragamuffin, not wanting to be left out, followed Bumble out, their mothers still sound asleep. It was winter and the farmyard was four feet deep in pure white snow. In the lane, the snow was piled up to the top of the hedgerow, which was half the height of the big oak.' Red paused and stroked his daughter's hair.

'Bumble and Ragamuffin were so excited! You see, they didn't know what snow was, they were not born the last time it was like this.' He paused.

'Daddy, do they get cold?' Nicole whispered, lying with only her head above the blanket.

'Not so much; they have very woolly calf coats, they were warm from the barn and the excitement kept them moving. So they ran into the field and they did feel a bit cold, Nicole, especially on their hoofs which were under the snow. But it was all new and they loved it; they ran around kicking up their back legs; they liked to see their footprints. They were having so much fun they didn't see the doe and her fawn until they nearly bumped into them. "How do, young'en?" the mother deer said.' Red spoke in a high-pitched woman's voice. Nicole giggled, moving her face under the blanket and then back.

'"Hello, deer," Bumble said. The fawn just squealed a hello as it couldn't talk yet. "This is my baby fawn; she likes to play, too," the mother deer said. All three of them played chase in the snow, taking it in turns to run after each other. The fawn, even though young, was too fast for Bumble and Ragamuffin. The fawn was so light she could leap and leap; her energy was limitless. They were having such fun, running, leaping and jumping in the snow, that they forgot where they were. The mummy deer was nowhere in sight; and soon they found themselves lost in the hedge, looking into a garden of the biggest house you ever did see.'

Marie came into the bedroom and sat down next to Red on the side of Nicole's bed. She smiled to Red and stroked her tummy.

'What happens next, Daddy? Don't stop,' Nicole said.

'Yes, come on Rouge. *Qu'est-ce qui se passe ensuite* to Bumble and Ragamuffin?'

'Maybe Mummy should carry on,' Red laughed.

'*Oh, non, non*, Rouge! *Tu es un très bon contour d'histoire*! You continue.'

'Please, Daddy, what happened next?'

'Well, Nicole, just as he said this, a little girl, a boy, and a Mommy come out with a big orange carrot for the snowman they were building in the garden. The girl and boy stuck the big orange carrot in the middle of his face. Of course Bumble and Ragamuffin love carrots as they only get them at Christmas, so this made them feel all happy and hungry inside.

'Mommy said to the boy and girl that it was time for tea and they were to go in and get changed and wash their hands as good children would. So the boy and girl ran in with Mommy following and they took their boots and coats off not to make a mess for Mommy to clear up. They were good and thoughtful children. So as soon as the boy, girl and Mommy went in, Bumble, Ragamuffin and fawn made a run for it. They ran as fast as they could and came skidding to a stop in front of the snowman. Bumble bit on the snowman's nose and pulled back; pulling the carrot straight out, he fell down on his back legs.

"'Zee, I got zee carrot!" Bumble couldn't speak properly with the carrot lodged in the corner of his mouth.' Nicole giggled and Red looked at Marie who was smiling back.

"'You look funny, Bumble," Ragamuffin said.

"'I don't have a carrot! We need two! What are we going to do? I don't have one," Ragamuffin said with a sad look in her eyes.

'Unknown to Bumble and Ragamuffin, the little girl was up at her bedroom window watching them down below; and being a smart, caring little girl she could see that the calves wanted another carrot. So with her Mum busy in the kitchen, she quietly tiptoed back down the stairs carefully; and to skip the fourth step from the bottom which creaked, she jumped from the third step down to the floor. She stopped at the larder door and opened it slowly; she found the supply of carrots in a sack near the potatoes. She took one of the biggest she could find. She put her boots and coat back on and skipped outside.

'Bumble and Ragamuffin saw the little girl and were going to run, but they saw her holding the big orange carrot. They stood brave, rooted to the spot. The little girl walked slowly over and held out the carrot. The fawn was scared and ran back to the cover of the hedge.

'The little girl held out the carrot, and Bumble, being brave, went over and took it gently in his mouth from the little girl's hand. She said, "Well done, Bumble, good boy." Bumble was surprised she knew his name, so in cow language, he said thank you.

"'That's all right, Bumble; you're welcome." She was still young enough to speak 'cow'.'

Marie laughed at Red and play-poked him on the arm. Red smiled and giggled, finding it hard to continue.

'Bumble and Ragamuffin turned to run back to the fawn in the hedge. As they did, the little girl waved at them before running back in the house to get ready for tea before Mommy missed her. Bumble and Ragamuffin followed their hoof marks all the way back to the farm.

"'Oh, where have been all this time? I've been looking everywhere for you,' Deer said as she bounded over and licked her fawn.'

'Oh, Daddy, is it true? Is it true? Can we go and see Bumble and Ragamuffin?' Nicole said.

'It's a very long, long way away. Perhaps one day, honey; one day. Well, of course, Bumble and Ragamuffin are grown up now; Bumble is a big bull and Ragamuffin is a mother cow.'

'Can I take out some hay for them both, Daddy? Can I?'

'Maybe one day,' Red said.

Marie leaned over and kissed Nicole good night. Red did the same and said: 'Night night, Nicole; don't let the bedbugs bite.'

'Night night, Mommy. Night night, Daddy,' she said.

32

6th July 1925

Connie held Lily's hand. The small girl had dark hair inherited from her father; her small legs thin as twigs. Connie breathed in the sweet grass pollen from the mowed field. It was already warm, the sun glowing down on Ten-acre Field.

'Mummy, why do they cut the grass?' Lily asked, looking up at her mother.

'It's so that in the winter all the horses and cows have something to eat.'

'Why don't they eat cake like we do?' She looked up.

'Cake isn't good for them; not all that sugar and fruit,' Connie answered.

'Why not, Mummy? I don't like grass to eat; they won't like it, will they?'

'Well, to them, Lily, they really like grass. They like it more than you like Violet's fruitcake.'

'No, they can't, can they? I like that the best.' Connie looked out over the field. Violet would be here somewhere.

'Mummy, look! There's William! Can I go and play, please?'

'Go on then, but don't get your dress mucky.' Connie

knew it was useless telling her. Lily would be running and rolling around in the drying hay in no time. Connie watched as she ran and met William. It was hard to believe he was eight years old. Violet walked over as William escaped her hand.

The field was busy with workers tedding the lines of cut grass. Connie watched as further over towards the copse, Theodore Fox and Mr Grey discussed the strategy for the rest of haymaking.

'Oh, Violet, I'm glad to see you!' She smiled at her friend, relieved.

'Connie, what on earth is it?'

'I don't think I can stay in the big house, not without Sampson. It's unbearable. What am I going to do?'

'What, what? Slow down; what's the matter?' Connie's face contorted. Her blonde hair rolled down over her shoulders. Tree sparrows flew from the hedgerows as swifts darted and bobbed, hunting for flies and midges.

'I can't put up with it any more! It's suffocating me in there. Their ways of doing things, having to share Lily with Nanny Thompson, who I swear is getting worse and worse; and then there is Theodore, bloody Theodore, trying to poke his nose in where it's not wanted. Violet, whatever am I to do? It's like I can hardly breathe in there.'

They walked the hedgerow, watching as William and Lily played chase, jumping the drying grass.

'It can't be that bad! You're so lucky; you don't go without anything.'

'It is, Violet, it's awful. Not having my freedom. Having to kowtow to Admiral is bad enough; but Theodore and his wife Elizabeth… She especially looks down on me. If it wasn't for the sanctuary of the kitchen and good old Dorothy, I don't know what I would have done; walked out years ago. I think it would be better for me and Lily if I did.'

'Yes, but how would you live? You have a nanny, and all your cooking and washing is done for you. I tell you it's not easy. I've my mother and father to help me, and it's not like the café keeps me so busy all the time, is it?' Violet brushed her hand across her face, clearing hair from her eyes. She walked slowly, her stocky frame slow.

'I know; I know I have everything I could wish for. But oh, I don't know why I feel like this, but it's a prison. I have to live by their rules and conform to their ways. I don't know if I want to bring my daughter up in that way. I know Elizabeth resents me; I don't know why.' Connie sighed. 'I've tried to make her feel welcome. You know, to be nice to her, talk to her. We could be friends, but she doesn't want any of that.' Connie paused and looked at Violet.

'Well, some women are jealous, especially when they are as attractive as you, Connie.'

'Oh, I'm not attractive, Violet. Years ago, maybe. Look at us: we're two old widows already, aren't we!' She laughed.

'Ha-ha! You may be but I'm clinging on to me youth, I am. Least William makes me feel younger.'

'Oh, Violet. I'm sorry, I must sound like an ungrateful brat. Going on about my problems like this. I don't know what to do for the best. I know that my neighbour's corn isn't always more plentiful than mine. But... Oh, I don't know.'

'Where would you go, Connie? How would you bring up Lily on your own?'

'I don't know. I don't know, Violet. What am I going to do?'

* * *

Connie walked around the big house. She went and sat in the library window, looking down over the railway line. She breathed in the smell of the old leather-bound books. She relaxed. What on earth could she do? She picked up *Sense and Sensibility* and examined the worn cover.

Spencer walked in and announced: 'It's dinner, Ma'am.' He was dressed in his black tailcoat and white shirt and looked formal, his gaze steady.

'You don't have to call me Ma'am, Spencer, not after all these years. Call me Constance, Connie,' she requested.

'Yes, Connie,' he replied, his face sombre and motionless.

'How do you ever do it? Day in, day out, serving them like you do?'

'Oh, I enjoy it; it's a privilege for me to do my best every day, to give the best service I can.' A small smile appeared.

'Don't you ever want more, Spencer?'

'No, Ma'am. I'm happy that if I've done my job to the best of my ability, then… well, that is what gives me satisfaction. That I've done as well as I possibly can. Come on, you'd better come through before you annoy Admiral.'

Connie followed the butler through into the large oak-panelled dining room. She was last in; Admiral and Josephine sat in their seats, Admiral at the head of the table, Josephine to his left. Seated opposite, in front of the window, was Theodore; and next to him his wife, Elizabeth. She had a slim face and fair complexion, and her ginger hair spiralled to her shoulders. Connie sat down on her side; there was space to her left where Sampson had once sat. She wished Lily was allowed at the big table.

'The hay is going well, Father; we should have a very good cut this year,' Theo said.

Dorothy busied herself under the eye of Spencer and smiled to Connie as she brought her soup.

'Good, good. Glad to hear it. How many acres left to get in?' the Admiral asked, pausing with his spoon.

'Can't be no more than twenty; only Ten-acre and Meadow Field to do.'

'You know,' said the Admiral, 'I was thinking that this

year we should hold a memorial tea in the gardens. A celebration for the village, for their hard work; and to remember those we've all lost. Make it special for the younger ones. After all, we've been lucky with the harvests these last few years.'

'Oh, that's so lovely, dear; what a lovely idea,' Josephine said.

'Good; that's decided then. Theodore, can you get Mr Grey to start the arrangements?'

'Yes, Father; and Elizabeth can help organise.' Theodore looked over at Constance. 'I expect you will be too busy to help, won't you, Constance.' He stared at her above his bowl. They all stared at her; she felt the intimidating eyes of the family on her. 'Well, would you?'

'If you like, me and Violet could run a cake stall.'

'Oh, would you, Constance? That would be so kind,' Josephine said. She smiled weakly over at her daughter-in-law. 'Of course, Lily and William will lend a hand.'

'Oh, that's a bit common, isn't it? Running a stall?' Elizabeth snapped, and screwed her nose up as she looked at Theo.

'Well, we did it in the war; the soldiers welcomed it,' Connie replied.

'No, no,' said Josephine to Elizabeth. 'I think it shows we care, that we are giving something back to the village for all their hard work and sacrifice.' And to Connie she added, 'I think I will even give you a hand, dear.'

'Mmm, well, I will think about letting you out there, Josephine; I don't know you should be out there. Not on your legs; that's a bit too much.' Admiral looked at his wife. Connie thought she looked disappointed.

'Isn't it about time that we got a governess for Lily?' Theodore declared.

'That's none of your business. I thought she could go to

In Fields of Gold and Red

the village school.' Connie looked at Theodore. How dare he tell her how her daughter should be educated?

'It's one thing laying on afternoon tea and cake for the village, but it's something altogether different, letting the girl go to the village school. I think Theodore might be right about this,' Admiral said.

'She's my daughter. I taught at the school, I went to the school and I was good enough for Sampson to marry.'

'I think we should let Constance decide on this one, dear.' Josephine touched her husband on his hand. He moved it back as they waited for the salmon to be served.

'No, I think we should get a governess for our granddaughter. I don't think it would be wise to send her down to the village.'

'I agree, Father; we can't be seen sending her down there with all the riff-raff.'

'It's none of your business, Theodore! She's my daughter! You got in a nanny, and I went along with that. But there is no way I'm letting a governess in for her! She goes to the school or I will educate her myself.' Connie stared at Theo.

'Now, now, Constance, keep your voice down. The servants will hear. We will discuss this further.' Admiral looked down at her.

Connie held her breath and let out a large sigh. Why couldn't they see it from her point of view for a change? Why did Theodore have to put his tuppence worth in all the time?

'Why don't you shut up, Theodore? When you have your own children you can decide how you want to bring them up, but when it's my daughter I'd prefer it if you didn't interfere.' She looked across at him, her shoulders pushed hard against the back of the chair.

'I really don't think you should speak to Theo like that, Constance. Remember where you've come from; after all, you're only a shepherd's daughter.' Elizabeth looked over, squinting her blue eyes.

* * *

Connie walked down the steps to the Manor's kitchen. She undid her bonnet, glad to remove it and let some air to her head. She felt hot after being out in the heat of the sun. Happy to be handing out tea and cake to the village; and having Violet by her side at least made up for putting up with Elizabeth all afternoon.

'We need some more hot water, Dorothy. I'll take it back; you've your own work to do. It's my turn today.'

'Don't be silly,' Dorothy replied.

'No, it's all right; it's good to be doing something different.' Connie made her way to the range.

'Yes, of course. How are you bearing up out there, with Elizabeth and Josephine?'

'Well, Elizabeth only wants to stand around looking important; Josephine has had to sit down. She's not used to standing on her feet. It's me and Violet doing all the running around as usual.'

'It won't be long now, Connie, then it will be all over,' Dorothy said.

'I know, I know.' Connie walked back out of the kitchen with the large copper kettle full of boiled water, a rag wound around the handle. It was heavy and cumbersome and she had to walk with her back bent to keep the liquid from spilling.

'Ah, Constance, glad to see you've been keeping busy!' Theodore shouted as he bounded down the stairs dressed in his Oxford Blue blazer and tan slacks. 'How is it all?' He smiled.

Why was he trying to make conversation? Connie tried to hurry out but was slowed by the large kettle.

'It's fine.'

'I'm glad. Isn't Elizabeth doing well, meeting all the villagers like that? She's very impressive, isn't she? So refined.'

'I suppose. Look, this is really heavy, and I don't have time to be chatting.'

'I don't suppose you do.' He descended behind her.

'Your dress looks very nice; I like the blue and white. Your hair looks so pretty today.' He was behind her and she couldn't move away. 'I see why Sampson married you: blonde hair, green eyes and slim waist. You must have made him very happy.'

'That's not appropriate, Theodore.' He must have been drinking.

'Look, Elizabeth is outside. Why don't we go up to the bedroom? You know, if you do, then I can persuade Father not to get that governess in. You would be happy about that, wouldn't you, Constance?' She sensed him move closer behind. The strong smell of whisky permeated from him.

'Have you been drinking?' Connie asked. He came past her and blocked the corridor.

'It's the only way I can get through this bloody awful do.' His speech was slow and deliberate.

'No, Theodore, you have Elizabeth and I wouldn't anyway; I hate you.' She tried to move to the door. Constance hoped Dorothy would follow her out.

'Oh, come on, Constance! Hate's a strong word. How much do you want Lily to go to the school and not have a governess? Look, it would be good for both of us. I know you want to.' He sneered.

'You don't know anything. Keep away from me.' With all her strength, Connie flipped the kettle forward. Hot water spilled from the spout, towards Theo. A sprinkle of hot water fell on his trouser leg. He brushed it off before it could burn him. 'You stupid bitch! You'll regret that. You know, we could have had a good arrangement that made each of us happy.'

'I wouldn't want any arrangement with you, Theodore. You may have been decorated in the war, but you are a weak man, a weak and stupid man, and not half as good as your brother was.' Her cheeks blushed red.

'I tell you now, Constance, there is no way on earth you're going to get your way on this. No way at all.'

* * *

Connie got up as quietly as she could from her bed. Her clothes were laid out ready. She'd packed up as many clothes as she could for her and Lily into the big case. Was she doing the right thing?

She crept up the stairs to the nursery at the back of the house. She could hear sparrows singing from the roof. She would have to try and not wake Nanny Thompson. She walked up the creaking staircase. Would she go through with this? Wasn't it completely stupid, to leave all this behind? Where she had so much?

'Lily darling, wake up.' She rocked her daughter gently from her sleep.

'Mummy, Mummy, what is it?' Lily was bleary-eyed.

'We're leaving, dear, we have to go. We're going. It's for the best; we can't stay here any more,' Connie pleaded.

'Where are we going? It's early. What about Nanny?' Lily rubbed her eye with her finger.

'No, Nanny is staying here. We're going now.' Connie knelt down and whispered.

'But where, Mummy? I want to sleep.' She tugged on Connie's arm.

'Don't worry; we'll be safe. It will be just you and me.' Connie got Lily out of bed and helped her into her little green and white dress, a smaller version of her own. The room was full of toys handed down from Sampson, and from his father's time. There was an old rocking horse in the corner, faded and worn, with a leather saddle. Lily's favourite. How could she take her daughter from this, from all this wealth, where she would never want for a thing? Was she mad, or stupid, or both? How would she look after them both?

She knelt down: 'Lily, we have to be very quiet. It's like a game of hide and seek. We have to be so quiet, going down the stairs.'

Connie held Lily by the hand and tiptoed out onto the stairs. They crept down the stairs and passed Nanny Thompson's room. Connie could hear loud snores. They walked on down the corridor past Admiral and Josephine's room. Further down, past her own room's door. There was only Theodore and Elizabeth's room to pass. She heard the creak of a floorboard; someone was up and walking around in the room. It was a heavier footstep; it must be Theodore. Her throat caught as she swallowed and she put her hand over her mouth to subdue a cough. Should she go on, or go back? She looked at Lily, whose eyes were green like hers. Her innocence... What was she doing, taking her daughter from this life to something unknown? She had seconds, seconds before Theodore would open the door. Should she turn back?

She thought back, to how her father had brought her up. He'd managed it on his own, with help from friends; from Redver's mother and father. She'd missed her father. She missed Redver. She missed Sampson. She must be cursed. Could she manage it, keep working and bring Lily up? Why was it so hard to decide? She heard the footsteps heavy across the creaking floorboards getting closer to the door. Stay or go, it was as simple as that. If she didn't do it now she never would. Stay or go? A life of privilege for her daughter, or one of struggle and want? She took Lily by the hand.

'I'm sorry, Lily, I'm sorry.' She squeezed her daughter's small hand and moved to the stairs, holding the case in her other hand. She walked as fast as she could, making as little noise as possible. The door opened behind her. She turned the corner of the stairs, increased her pace and made for the kitchen.

Dorothy and Cook were up preparing breakfast. 'Quick, Connie! George is outside; he will help you with the case,' Dot said.

* * *

Lily was fast asleep next to her, in her old bedroom in the shepherd's cottage of George and Dorothy. They were so kind to let her stay with them. She couldn't do it for long. For now, it was enough to be out of the big house. To be with friends. Albeit back to the cottage where she had lived and been brought up. How had it come to this? She was back at the beginning, back starting over. This time with her daughter to bring up.

She got out of bed. Remembering which floorboards creaked and which didn't, she made her way to the dresser and washed her face. The water was cold. She pulled the hessian curtain back and looked out. Weak sunlight shone on the farm. She had to get to work and Lily would have to go to Violet's.

She would have to find somewhere to live. Could she leave the village, maybe to live and work in Bridport? She couldn't let Theodore bully George and Dorothy, not on her account. She couldn't live with Violet; there was no room. She couldn't go back to Miss Appleworth's. She would have to find somewhere to rent. Somewhere which was out from under the control of Admiral and Theodore. Somewhere she could bring Lily up, safe, secure and free.

33

12th July 1925

The kitchen was exactly as she remembered it: the grange in the fireplace, the smoke-covered mantel above; the Kingsons' wooden clock in the centre. The fire permanently lit. It was early, and she'd had to wake Lily. She'd drop Lily into Violet's on her way through the station and be at her desk for eight o'clock.

She sat down at the kitchen table, as she had done with her father many years before, and she couldn't help but think of him. How kind and generous he was and how he'd managed to bring her up; giving everything and more than she needed. Connie wished he was alive.

Dorothy busied herself bringing the hot water and porridge to the table. Connie felt free, free at last from the suffocating Manor House, free from their opinions and free from their control. George sat opposite, wearing his father's old wide-brimmed hat, his black waistcoat and white striped shirt, his face weathered and furrowed. Lily sat next to her, waiting patiently.

'Thank you so much for having me and Lily stay; it's more than I can possibly expect. Let me help,' Connie said. She was wearing her long pale yellow dress. She fiddled with her bonnet in her lap.

'Oh, shut up, Connie; you will always be part of this family,' George said as he leaned down and tied up his hobnailed boots.

'Yes, 'course; you stay as long as you like. You are more than welcome, both of you,' Dorothy added, finishing George's thoughts. 'I'm glad to see you've a smile on your face this morning. It made me feel terrible seeing you round the table at the Manor, them ganging up on you. I can tell you, I wanted to thump that bloody Theodore so many times, the way he talks to you. And all the times us women have to keep away from his roaming hands.' She sucked in through her lips.

'I hope he doesn't make things hard for you now. You know, I will have to find my own place soon. I won't be here long. Violet's going to look after Lily when I go to work. I don't know what I will do when I move. I can't take her to work; Mr Foster won't stand for that. And if I live in Bridport, it will be difficult to get back to Violet's and back to work in time.'

'Don't worry about that. You stay here for as long as you need,' Dorothy said as she poured out the tea.

George got up, his boots on. Wearing his green cords and white shirt, with his sleeves rolled to his elbows, he said: 'That's me. These sheep ain't goin' trim their own toes.' He walked out of the house.

'I can't thank you enough for helping me get out of there, Dorothy. You know, if it wasn't for you and George, I don't know what I would have done.' She cut the bread.

'Oh, Connie, will 'e bide quiet, girl! It's nice to get one over on them up at the big house. It's only what you and Lily deserve, ain't it. I mean, they have been making your life miserable. I don't know why. I think they don't realise they are doing it to you. It's because their lives are so different to the likes of you and me.' Connie took a sip of tea from her mug and buttered a slice of bread for Lily, who for once was sitting quiet on the chair, not awake enough to make a noise.

'Look, I don't mind you staying, Connie. You take your time and get yourself sorted.'

Connie knew she meant it.

The sound of footsteps filled the kitchen; more than one pair, approaching the back door.

'Who's that this time of the day?' Dorothy exclaimed. The back door flung open. Theodore Fox stood tall, filling the frame, dressed in his tweed suit and flat cap, and he said: 'Thought I would find you here; you were too damn obvious.' His eyes were blazing. 'You're to come back with me. You and Lily. Father has decided.' He put his hand on the door frame. Spencer was standing behind him.

'You can't dictate to me. I've left for good. I'm afraid I can't live up there any more.' Connie put her hands around Lily.

'You don't have a choice, Constance. You're to come back, because if you don't ... Well. I will find myself a new shepherd and a new maid.' He smiled back and looked at Dorothy. He walked in and stood in front of the kitchen table.

'You wouldn't. You can't do that; they haven't done anything wrong, have they? You know they are good workers, reliable; you couldn't replace them.' The words came out but Connie knew he wouldn't see reason.

'Oh, please! I could replace them today, the number of people looking for work. You know I would do it without hesitation, don't you? Do you want to be responsible for making their lives a misery? And is it so bad with us? You can't prefer this!' he said as he pointed around the small bare kitchen.

'You don't get it, do you? It's who you're with, not what

you have, that matters.' She picked Lily from the chair and held her close.

'If you don't come back with me now, then George and Dorothy will be out on the streets, homeless, tonight. Do you really want to be guilty of that?' His face contorted to a satisfied smile. He seemed to be enjoying every moment of this. She had no option. She got up, took Lily by the hand and went and fetched the case. She'd had so much hope, the thought of getting away; and it had only lasted a day. How pathetic. She couldn't win. There was no way she could live with seeing George and Dorothy homeless and out of work.

'I'm glad you've seen sense. Don't just stand there, Spencer; help Constance with her suitcase.'

34

12th July 1925

Red was overjoyed to have a son. His hair was dark brown like Marie's and they called him Thomas. Marie couldn't take much time away from work; the very next day after the birth she was back cooking and serving meals.

Nicole doted on her brother. Red liked nothing better than holding his Thomas close to him; he loved his fresh smell. He couldn't wait for him to be older so he could play football with him. He was a good baby, but he would scream out in the night, meaning none of them got much sleep.

Pierre seemed happier for a while, coming out of his drunkenness to enjoy holding his grandson. Red felt a little sad that none of his family would see his children; it was so many years since he had been with his brother. Town life continued at the same pace, the buildings that had been destroyed in the fire more or less habitable, Geordie having rebuilt them, and rebuilt his own house even bigger.

David sat out as a memorial in the town square. Red didn't have the energy or time to devote to a second restoration; its engine was blown. He bolted down the hatches so the children couldn't get inside; they loved to play all over David, using it as a climbing frame.

In Fields of Gold and Red

The children were out with Louise, who was taking them for a walk. Red was in the hotel kitchen, helping prepare for the lunch service. Marie was behind him, stirring the pot on the large range.

Pierre stumbled in. His belly was large, his back hunched over.

'*Je veux une casserole de poulet!*' he shouted. His face was bloated, his nose large, his skin blotchy.

'*Non, non! Sortir de la cuisine,*' Marie replied without turning to face him, keeping her eye on the pot.

Red spun around to see what was happening. Pierre went to grab Marie by the arm, but missed and stumbled; he pushed Marie on to the range. She yelped, her hand burned.

'*Papa, non, zut alors!*' She spun back, pushing her father. Red grabbed Pierre by the arm and marched him outside.

'What, Pierre, what in hell do you think you are doing?' Red said. He pushed Pierre.

'*Tu as pris ma fille loin de moi, tu as emmené ma maison, tu as même emmené mes amis,*' Pierre said as he slouched towards the door.

'Don't be stupid; you've pushed them all away. It's you! Can't you see it's you who has done all that?' Red shouted. It was no good; Pierre didn't listen to him or to reason, he didn't want to understand. They couldn't get through to him.

* * *

Nicole beamed down at him from the third step of the stairs. Red noticed this was her favourite game. She would jump from the step, landing at the bottom with a big smile and a giggle. She was a very mischievous little girl.

'Daddy, Daddy! Can we go see the horseys?' She giggled.

'We can, honey, if we have time later and your Mommy says so.' Red smiled down at his daughter, looking pretty in her small yellow frock.

'And can I bring Thomas? He will like the horseys, I'm sure.' She skipped down the last step and into the hall. Red followed her down, bringing dirty sheets.

'Yes, of course we can; but you will have to look after your brother. Can you do that?'

'Yes, Daddy, 'course I will. I like Thomas. When will he talk?' Nicole skipped towards the kitchen.

'Soon, dear. It will be when he is older; when he is two, like you were.' Red followed. 'First, you can help me get these washed. We can race and see who is fastest; it will help Mama and mean we can see the horseys later!' Red laughed.

* * *

Pierre hardly moved from his corner of the bar. Red could see he was already drunk, slumped in his chair with a brandy next to him on the small wooden side table that was old and worn. It was very damp and grey, as it had been for the last two weeks. Red much preferred crisp, clear blue skies, even if it meant it was colder.

Pierre lurched up from his drunken slumber; he only ever got up to go and pee or to get another drink. He smelt so, of a mixture of dried body odour and urine. He wouldn't listen to Red; he would feign not to understand him. He kept seeing things, hallucinating, seeing people and things that weren't there. Marie would try and get him in the bath regularly but he was so large and argumentative it was easier to let him stew in his own mess. It was becoming a problem; even Pierre's old friends stayed away from him, one too many sarcastic comments made. His drunkenness was no longer funny or humorous or entertaining as some had once found it.

Red would have to try and say something. It was no good putting it off any longer; takings were well down, and with Thomas to feed and clothe they needed all the money they could make.

In Fields of Gold and Red

Red went out into the yard to find Pierre. He found him with his old Winchester shotgun scuttling across to the empty stables. He was loading it as he went, not looking where he was going. He knocked into the wall of the stables before righting himself and going in through the stable door. Red followed behind at a distance. Pierre staggered into an empty cubicle and then fell into a corner. When Red reached him he was sitting with the shotgun between his legs, pointing upwards to the bottom of his large double chin. Red thought he should have picked up his service pistol. Of course, Red knew of men who had shot themselves in the war if it was too much, or they went a little mad; they just sloped off and did themselves in. Pierre looked like this to him, all hope gone.

'Daddy, what's Grandpa doing?' Nicole said from behind him.

'Go back, darling, and find your Mommy; tell her it's Grandpapa.' He guided his hand on Nicole's back. Nicole ran off back indoors.

'Pierre, don't do this; you have so much, can't you see?' Red knelt down. He could smell the alcohol through the stench of Pierre.

'Je ne me le dis pas, garçon; j'ai perdu tout, j'ai perdu ma belle épouse, et mon fils; tu as pris ma seule fille; qu'est-ce que j'ai? Tu as pris ma maison, ma fille et mes affaires; je n'ai rien; tu as pris ma vie!'

Red didn't understand, he was talking too fast. Red only caught *garçon*; taking his daughter, taking his wife? Pierre wasn't making any sense.

'*Non, non, non! Tu as assassiné ma femme.* You... you murdered my wife,' Pierre slurred. He ran his hands over the old Winchester shotgun.

'Don't be so stupid! I did not!' Red looked at the gun.

Marie came into the stables, followed by Nicole.

'He won't listen to me, Marie; he won't talk sense.'

'Red, leave. *Je vais lui parler.*' She knelt down on the other side of Pierre. She put her hand on his shoulder.

'I can't leave you…' Red said, standing up.

'*Il a tué Camille!* Murderer!' Pierre cried out, pointing at Red.

'*Allez, partez. Laisse Papa avec moi.* You better leave. Take Nicole inside,' Marie said. She brushed Pierre on the shoulder. 'Before he attack you. *Allez.*'

'Are you sure?' Red said. Lingering at the cubicle door, he held Nicole's hand. 'I don't want to leave you on your own with him; he's not right in the head.'

'Go on, go, I'll be fine. *Je peux lui parler.*' Red could see that Marie was crying.

'Don't do anything without me,' he said as he walked out of the stables with Nicole.

Red left Marie with her Papa and went outside. It was still damp and miserable and the temperature was dropping. He should go and get the fire lit in the bar and tidy up for opening. The building work in the village was more or less all done so they were getting quieter. He would open up and hope for some passing trade. He didn't want to be too far away in case Marie called out for him.

'Daddy, look what I can do! I can jump backwards as well!' She smiled and hopped.

'You can, can't you, dear.' Red tried to force a smile.

'See how high I can do it!' She jumped.

Red heard shouting: Pierre first, then Marie. The sound of a shot. He ran for the door. There was a second shot as he ran across the yard. He skidded on his wooden stump and fell against the stable door. He pulled himself up. He got in through the door. He couldn't believe what he saw. There on the ground was Marie; she was bleeding heavily. He went to her, knelt down and held her tight. Pierre looked dead in the corner, with his brains splattered on the wall behind. It was as gruesome as in the war.

He went to Marie and sat down with his back against the wall. His spine shivered from the cold.

'Rouge, do you love me?' Marie murmured.

'I do, pumpkin, I do love you. 'Course I do. Don't go now; come on, fight, Marie! We need you.'

'*Je suis désolée, je suis désolée. Promis-moi, Rouge, s'il te plaît: je veux que tu sois heureux;* be happy; look after Nicole and Thomas, please, Rouge.' Her eyes blinked shut, then opened weakly.

Red could see Marie's breath was escaping, her life retreating; her lively bright eyes becoming extinguished in front of him. He felt sick to his stomach. How could her father have done this? Why didn't he stay?

He did love her; why didn't he tell her? Why was he so stupid? Nicole and Thomas were losing their mother. His tears streamed down his face as he sobbed. Pulling Marie's head to his he buried his face in her hair. Marie's blood was on his hands and on his face. He held her and brushed her hair.

'Oh, Marie, I love you, I love you, I promise. Oh, please don't go; don't leave me. Please, my pumpkin.' She looked up and the smile left her face. He looked around; Nicole was standing in the doorway, watching.

* * *

He was sitting with Eliza and Geordie in their small kitchen. Tears streamed down his face. He didn't care who saw him like this. The children were all outside playing. Nicole was looking after Thomas, as they played hopscotch with Catherine, Edith and Emma.

'What am I going to do? I can't run the hotel and bring up two children, not on my own,' Red said. Eliza busied herself as she washed a huge bedsheet. Geordie and Red sat at the table, drinking from their mugs of tea. Red held his close, trying to gain comfort from the warm mug.

'Ay, lad, I don't suppose 'e can. You could always sell it; it must be worth a good old price. You could always work with me, or out on Clement's. He's always been happy with your work when you've helped 'im out in the summer,' Geordie said as he took another huge slurp.

'I don't understand why he did it. Why would 'e? Why would 'e shoot his own daughter like that?' Red sobbed.

'He was mad, wasn't 'e. You know; we've seen it, seen it in the war; and that 'e was completely crazy, wasn't 'e, Eliza?'

She joined in. 'It's true; we'd seen 'im out in town talking to himself, seeing faces from the past,' Eliza said as she took the sheet through to the back.

'Why didn't I do more to stop him? I should never have left him out there with Marie. I should have stopped him. I should have shot him. I knew he was bad. Oh god, if I had done something, anything. I could have saved her, Geordie. I could have her with me. It's on my conscience. All we've been through in the war; I should have seen it coming. Oh, why didn't I do more?' Red wiped a tear from his cheek. His stomach turned over and he felt sick.

'Stop it, Red. You can't bring her back and you can't go on blaming yourself. It was her father who pulled the damn trigger and it was him alone who killed his daughter. You are to stop blaming yourself. That will only lead to you going mad. You've two beautiful children. You are to make the best life possible for them, do you hear me?' Geordie put his hand on Red's shoulder as Eliza came back with a second dirty sheet and began to wash it in the large sink.

'He's right, you know, Red. Marie, she loved you and she would want you to be a good father to those two children. You can't sit moping around; you've got to pull yourself out of it and think of them, to put them first. You can't undo what's been done, thinking about the ifs and maybes. You've to pull out of it and get on with life, for Nicole and Thomas. I know it's what Marie would have wanted; you've to do it for her,' Eliza said, looking back over her shoulder at Red and Geordie.

'I've been thinking…' Geordie said.

'Oh, here we go, Red! This sounds dangerous, my husband thinking! Why does that always lead to trouble?' Eliza said, with a half-smile on her face. 'What are you cooking up inside that 'ead of yours?'

'Look, I've been doing well with the building work and we've saved up a fair bit. That building work, it's slowing down, ain't it.' Eliza and Red nodded. 'If Eliza was thinking… Well, we need work for them children of ours, don't we, and I could pay 'e a good deposit and the rest from the earnings of the place. That would give 'e an income and a bit upfront like.'

'Are you saying we buy the hotel then, Geordie?' Eliza said.

'Well, if you agree and Red wants to sell, it could work out well for all of us. 'Course, you can take as long as you want to think things over.' He paused. 'There ain't no hurry.'

'It's a great idea, with the girls to help us with it all,' Eliza said, coming to her husband's shoulder and caressing his neck. 'That's if Red agrees.' She looked over at him.

'I do! I can't live there, not with those memories and not with everything that has to be done. Thank you,' Red said, looking at his friends, holding back the tears from rolling down his face. 'Thank you.'

'Don't be so silly; don't give us thanks. You make sure whatever 'e do you get that smile back on your face and look after them two children of yours.'

'I will, Eliza, I will.'

35

11th August 1925

The sun was shining over Ashcombe Beacon. It was a cold, cloudless late summer morning. Red had bought two large shire horses and a cart in Dorchester market, a seventeen hand stallion and a fifteen hand mare. It cheered Nicole up, feeding them oats in the morning. She also held some apple out for them which they ate softly off her palm. She liked it when their mouths touched her small fingers. Nicole named them Topsy and Turvy. The air was so still and clear; it wasn't hot enough for a heat haze. From their vantage point on the ridge track, Red could see all the way to Golden Cap and Comer's Hill, the hills in the distance undulating away, neat hedgerows boxing in rectangular and square fields. He noticed the gang ploughing in the lower field near Marsh Farm, hearing the sound of steam engines straining.

He could see over to his old home at Kingcombe Cottages.

'Nicole, love, you see that house there in the distance straight ahead? That's where Daddy was born.' He pointed.

'Was it? When was that?' she asked.

'That was a long, long time ago before the war started; before I even came to France. I'll show you the old oak tree in the garden one day.'

'Will you show me how to climb the yoke tree?'

'Yes, honey, I will show you how to climb the oak tree. It has a special way, you know. If I teach you how to climb it it will then be your job to teach Thomas. Will you do that?' Red said.

'Yes, Daddy; I'm good at teaching. I will, promise.'

'Thank you, Nicole, you're a good girl.' He touched her on her head.

Red wanted to cry for the loss of Marie. He could see her in Nicole's face.

Red set the horses moving and they moved from the old Roman road onto the stony farm track down from Ashcombe Beacon. It was the shortest route from Dorchester to Ashcombe. The track meandered around and down past Marsh Farm. The cart jumped and wiggled underneath them. Nicole was so light she was bouncing up and down on the wooden seat next to Red; she was holding on tight to Thomas. Red could see it was tough for her but she clung on to him with her free hand.

The day was warming up in the summer sun. He could smell the scent of wild parsley and buttercups. Red purposefully drove the horses into the stubble field to get a closer look at the two steam engines. He came across the field and saw it was Titan. The gang was made up of six men. They were trying to get things started, hauling out the long steel cable to pull the plough.

'Hey there! How's it all going?' Red said.

The rotund gaffer from the top of the first engine looked down; a flicker of recognition showed on his face. His white teeth shone from his sooty face.

'I'd be damned if it ain't young 'en!' John said.

'Bloody hell! Is that you, John? Thought you'd be retired.'

'Not far from it. If truth be told, my missus has wanted

me to for a while. It's not like I've any family to pass these onto, and I'd want a good home for them. Don't suppose you'd be interested, would 'e, boy?'

'I'm looking for summink; I've got two young'ens of me own and I want a business. You know, not having someone to tell me what to do and all!'

'I was like you back in my day. So what do you say? Shall we shake on it? We will agree a fair price.' He stuck out his soot-covered hand.

'Go on then, John; why not? I've always wanted my own steam engines, and you can stay on to get me into the swing of it,' Red said, shaking John's hand.

'Yeah, it's best I don't land meself on the missus full time for a bit!'

Red couldn't believe his luck. On his way home, and already he was in business.

* * *

She had to get out of the Manor House; it was stuffy and hot. There was no one around. Left on her own she had been reading to Lily. Now they walked out to the meadow. The grass was green and lush. She held Lily's hand as they went and looked for daisies, buttercups and cowslips in the grass.

They walked through Piggots Field, the sun hot on their backs, glad to be out in the fresh air. She watched as the sheep grazed, with their bright eyes and short coats. She looked up and saw a horse and cart navigate the narrow track down from Ashcombe Beacon.

It looked like a man and two children, the older child holding a younger one. She didn't want to believe her own eyes; she couldn't; but the way he was stroking the horses and talking in their ears… She'd only ever seen one man do that. The man got back on the cart with the girl and the baby and continued down the track. If she could get up the hill she could cut the cart off at the lane. She ran through the long grass as fast as she could, holding Lily's hand.

'What is it, Mummy?' Lily called, laughing and running, happy to be playing.

'Run, Lily, run as fast as you can!' Connie called out, with a smile on her face.

She felt like a child again. The cart was moving slowly; but still, she needed to run faster. She could see clearly it was him: it was Redver.

'Wait, wait, Red!' She shouted as loud as she could but she was too far away; her voice was carried away by the wind.

'Redver! Redver!' She shouted louder; but he didn't turn.

She saw the girl, her pretty young face with the same nose as Red. The girl tugged at Red's jacket sleeve and pointed at Connie. He looked around; and his face broke into a broad smile which went from ear to ear. He pulled the cart to a stop and hopped down.

She ran to him and jumped into his arms; she kissed him hard on the lips.

'Daddy, Daddy! Who is this?' The girl jumped up and down excitedly.

'This is Connie. Connie, this is Nicole; and this is Thomas,' Red said.

Dear Reader,

You got to the end of my book. I hope that means you enjoyed it. Whether or not you did, I would like to thank you for giving me your valuable time to try and entertain you. I am truly blessed to have such a fulfilling job, but I only have that job because of people like you; people kind enough to give my books a chance and spend their hard-earned money buying them. For that I am eternally grateful.

If you would like to find out more about my other books then please visit my website for full details. You can find it at https://www.christopher-legg.com. Also feel free to contact me on Facebook, Twitter or email (all details on the website) as I would love to hear from you.

For the latest news, offers, and freebies sign up to the official Christopher B Legg Newsletter.

If you enjoyed this book and would like to help, then you could think about leaving a review. On Goodreads or anywhere else that readers visit. The most important part of how well a book sells is how many positive reviews it has, so if you leave me one, then you are directly helping me to continue on this journey as a full-time writer. Thank you in advance to anyone who does.